PRAISE FOR
THE FRESH-BAKED MYSTERIES

"Engaging . . . a cozy distinguished by its appealing characters and mouthwatering recipes."

—Publishers Weekly

"This is a great cozy to get you into the holiday spirit— because even though there's a murderer on the loose, there's lots of holiday cheer (and some yummy-sounding recipes at the end of this book)."

—AnnArbor.com

"[A] fun and captivating read . . . full of holiday cheer, mystery, murder, delicious treats, endearing characters, and evil villains . . . a cute and grippingly good read."

—Examiner.com

"[Livia J. Washburn] has cooked up another fine mystery with plenty of suspects . . . a fun read . . . great characters with snappy dialogue, a prime location, a wonderful whodunit. Mix together and you have another fantastic cozy from Livia Washburn. Her books always leave me smiling and anxiously waiting for another   ends."

a Good Book

"This mystery is n   ending. The camaraderie of the Fresh-Baked Mystery series cast of retired schoolteachers who share a home is endearing. Phyllis is an intelligent and keen sleuth who can bake a mean funnel cake. Delicious recipes are included!"

—RT Book Reviews

"The whodunit is fun and the recipes [are] mouthwatering."

—The Best Reviews

"Washburn has a refreshing way with words and knows how to tell an exciting story."

—Midwest Book Review

"Delightful, [with a] realistic small-town vibe [and a] vibrant narrative . . . A Peach of a Murder runs the full range of emotions, so be prepared to laugh and cry with this one!"

—The Romance Readers Connection

"Christmas and murder. It's a combination that doesn't seem to go together, yet Washburn pulls it off in a delightfully entertaining manner."

—Armchair Interviews

"A clever, intriguing contemporary cozy."

—Romance Junkies

"I loved it! . . . Definitely for people who just love a good mystery."

—Once Upon a Twilight

Other Fresh-Baked Mysteries

A Peach of a Murder
Murder by the Slice
The Christmas Cookie Killer
Killer Crab Cakes
The Pumpkin Muffin Murder
The Gingerbread Bump-off
Wedding Cake Killer
The Fatal Funnel Cake
Trick or Deadly Treat
The Candy Cane Cupcake Killer
Black and Blueberry Die
The Great Chili Kill-Off

Baker's Deadly Dozen

A Fresh Baked Mystery

Livia J. Washburn

Fire Star Press

Baker's Deadly Dozen
Copyright© 2017 Livia J. Washburn
Published by Fire Star Press
www.firestarpress.com

Fire Star Press

This book is an original publication of Fire Star Press.
First Printing, October 2017
All rights reserved.
ISBN-13: 978-0692353233
ISBN-10: 0692353232

Dedicated to my husband, James, and my daughters, Joanna and Shayna, for always being willing to read a passage or taste a cookie.

Chapter 1

"You know the old saying," Phyllis Newsom told her friend Sam Fletcher. "The more things change, the more they stay the same."

"Yeah, maybe so," Sam said, "but I never quite expected 'em to stay this much the same." He lifted his right hand and knocked on the door of one of the second-floor bedrooms in Phyllis's house in Weatherford, Texas. "Six-thirty, Ronnie. Time to get up for school."

Phyllis stifled a yawn and said, "I'm not sure *I'll* ever get used to getting up and going to school again."

"Well, it's for a good cause."

Phyllis's expression grew more solemn as she nodded. "Yes, at least Molly and Frank don't have to worry about their classes while they're down in Houston. And it's not like these jobs are permanent."

"Long-term sub jobs sometimes turn into permanent ones," Sam pointed out.

"Yes, but not for us. We're retired, remember?"

"And it's not like the school board would hire a couple of geezers like us on a full-time basis, anyway."

"Speak for yourself," Phyllis said with a smile. "I may be a senior citizen, but that doesn't make me a geezer."

"Yeah, it takes certain qualities to aspire to geezerhood." Sam returned the smile. "And I've mastered all of 'em."

So far, no response had come from behind the door. Sam knocked again. This time a girl's voice called, "I'm up, I'm up!"

"You think we can believe her?" Sam asked.

"Probably. But it wouldn't hurt to check back in five minutes."

"That's long enough to get a cup of coffee."

They turned to walk toward the stairs. Both wore robes over their pajamas and were still tousle-headed from sleep. Phyllis yawned again, and it proved infectious. Sam yawned so big it seemed like the hinge of his jaw would creak.

For decades as educators, they had gotten up and gone to school at least nine months out of the year. But having been retired for quite a while, they had gotten out of the habit of rising early, although neither of them could be considered a late sleeper.

Sam sniffed the air as they started down the stairs. "Coffee's on. Carolyn must be up."

"It wouldn't be Eve," Phyllis said. "I'm sure she's still asleep."

Carolyn Wilbarger and Eve Turner were also retired teachers who rented rooms in Phyllis's big old house, as did Sam. It was an arrangement that had worked well over the years. Phyllis had come to think of the others as family, not boarders as people used to call them. And like family, they had been through a lot together, triumphs and tragedies alike, and had grown closer because of it.

When Phyllis and Sam walked into the kitchen, Carolyn looked over her shoulder from where she was standing at the stove, mixing a bowl of gluten-free banana nut pancake batter. "Is Ronnie up?" she asked.

"She claims she is," Sam said. "The truth remains to be seen."

Phyllis poured coffee for both of them. "We've been at this for weeks now," she said. "I ought be more used to it than I am." She sipped the coffee and sighed. The world might be inhabitable for another day after all.

Sam took his cup and sat down at the table. He was just taking a sip when he jumped a little and sloshed out a few drops of the hot liquid.

"Dang it, speakin' of gettin' used to things, you'd think Raven wouldn't startle me so much. Been a long time since I had a cat rub up against my bare ankle, though."

Phyllis looked under the table where a large, short-haired black cat continued to rub against Sam's ankles. Raven was something else they were taking care of for their friends Molly and Frank Dobson. Molly and Frank were in Houston at the moment, where Frank was in the hospital being treated for cancer.

His diagnosis and the seriousness of his condition had come as a shock to all of them. About ten years younger than Phyllis and Sam, the Dobsons had seemed like a healthy, vital couple, teaching high school and being heavily involved in extracurricular activities there, and they had spent their summers exploring all over the country in the travel trailer Sam had dubbed the War Wagon when he, Phyllis, Carolyn, and Eve had borrowed it to make a trip to far West Texas a few months earlier. Frank had been feeling under the weather, and that was why they hadn't been using the trailer. Since then, after a battery of medical tests, it was discovered he had cancer.

When Frank had to go to Houston for what might be months of treatment, though, there was no longer any keeping it a secret. And after their families, Phyllis and Sam were some of the first people they told.

"It would be such a tremendous help to us, knowing that our classes were in good hands," Molly said as they sat in Phyllis's living room. A sense of surprise and sadness at learning the news still hung in the air. "I mean, you taught American History for so long, Phyllis, it wouldn't be any problem for you."

"Yes, but in junior high, not high school," Phyllis pointed out.

"History is still history, though."

"Well, that's true . . ."

"I never taught math," Sam said as he looked at Frank Dobson, who still appeared fairly hale and hearty except for a certain gauntness in his face. "I was a history teacher, too, but mostly I just coached."

"But you're certified to teach math," Frank said, "and most of my duties were coaching, too. I just had a couple of classes of freshman level algebra."

"Well, I remember how to solve for X. I think."

"There you go. I have confidence in you, Sam. You can handle it."

Phyllis said, "We've both been retired for years. The principal will never go along with hiring us as long-term substitutes."

"Oh, I don't know about that," Molly said with a smile. "Tom Shula is going to be the principal at Courtland."

Phyllis raised an eyebrow. Sam asked, "Who's Tom Shula?"

"He used to be vice-principal at the junior high when I taught there," Phyllis explained. "I didn't know he was going to be the principal at the new high school."

Weatherford's booming population had finally caught up to the school system. Although the move was fiercely opposed by some, a bond election had passed to add a second high school to the district, which was named after J.C. Courtland, the long-time superintendent who had retired a year earlier. Weatherford Courtland High, built northeast of town to balance out the existing high school on the southwest side, was finished and ready to launch its first year.

Molly and Frank Dobson were supposed to be there when the school opened, but fate had intervened and now long-term substitutes would have to be hired in their place. The Dobsons wanted those substitute teachers to be Phyllis and Sam.

Molly said, "You know good and well that Tom will go along with the idea. He'll be thrilled to have two top-notch, experienced teachers holding down the fort while Frank and I are gone."

"And it probably won't be for that long," Frank added. "I'll have this licked in no time."

"Of course you will," Phyllis said. "There's never been any doubt about that." She looked at Sam. "What do you think?"

"Well . . . I never figured I'd set foot in a classroom again, at least serious-like. But since all the lesson plannin' is done already—It is, isn't it?"

Frank nodded. "Everything will be ready for you."

"I suppose I could give it a try. But only if you want to, Phyllis."

"I feel the same way," she said. "It'll be a challenge, but sometimes that's a good thing."

Frank grinned and said, "I'd think that solving murders all the time is a challenge, too, so I'm sure you're used to it."

Phyllis waved a hand. "It's not all the time."

"Yeah," Sam said, "sometimes months go by without anybody gettin' killed."

She was sitting close enough to him on the sofa to reach over and swat him on the shoulder.

"It's settled, then," Molly said. "We'll talk to Tom and he'll get in touch with you. I can't tell you how much we appreciate this."

"You just concentrate on getting Frank well and don't worry about *anything else,"* Phyllis said.

"Well, speaking of that . . . There is one more thing you could help us out on."

"Name it," Sam said. *He hadn't known the Dobsons before, but Phyllis's high opinion of them was more than enough for him.*

"We're going to have to do something with Raven—" Molly began.

"Our cat," Frank added.

"You want us to come over and feed your cat?" Phyllis asked.

"Actually, we were hoping that she could stay here. She's used to having people around, you know, and I'm not sure she'd be happy being stuck alone in the house all the time."

"We've, uh, got a dog," Sam said.

"Who lives outside for the most part," Phyllis said.

"Yeah, except for durin' thunderstorms." Sam grunted. *"Never saw a dog more scared of a little thunder and lightnin' than ol' Buck, even though he's got a mighty fine doghouse on the porch he could get into."*

"Raven gets along with dogs," Molly said. *"Actually, she's very friendly with everybody. And she's perfectly house-trained. Never an accident."*

"That's good," Phyllis said, wavering. *She'd had cats before in her life and sometimes missed having one around. In most ways, they were less trouble than dogs, although she'd never liked having to clean out litter boxes. From what she had read, though, they had fancy litter boxes these days that practically cleaned themselves. So that might not be too bad. She looked over at Sam.* *"Buck's your dog. What do you think?"*

She knew it was his nature to be agreeable, so she wasn't surprised when he said, *"We can give it a try, as long as Carolyn and Eve don't mind."* *He chuckled.* *"They were here first, even before me and Buck."*

Phyllis was sure Carolyn and Eve wouldn't object too much, although Carolyn might have a few caustic things to say. That was her *nature.*

"It's all settled, then," she said, *and the gratitude on the faces of*

Frank and Molly were more than payment enough for whatever trouble this new arrangement might be.

Sam reached under the table to scratch Raven's ears. Phyllis could hear the loud purring coming from down there.

That was still going on when the blue-haired teenage girl came into the kitchen, sighed dramatically, and said, "It's the middle of the night. I need coffee!"

Chapter 2

"It's not the middle of the night," Sam told his granddaughter. "It's light outside. The sun'll be up in a few more minutes."

"Well, it *feels* like the middle of the night," Veronica Ericson said as she got a cup from the cabinet and headed for the coffeemaker. Her natural hair color was blond, and some streaks of it were still visible among the bright blue strands.

It had taken some time for Phyllis to get used to hair that color, especially on someone in her own house. Goodness knows, she saw all sorts of odd-looking people out in public, but not in her kitchen.

Now, however, after more than three months, that was just Ronnie. Phyllis would have had trouble thinking of her any other way.

She had never met Sam's granddaughter until they got back from that trip to West Texas back in July. Ronnie had been sitting there waiting for them when they got home, having taken the bus from Pennsylvania to Texas and gotten the neighbor who was taking care of Buck to let her into the house. She was petite enough that she didn't look like any sort of threat, even with blue hair.

Sam's first thought was that she had run away from home, because he knew there had been a lot of friction over the past year between Ronnie and her parents—Sam's daughter Vanessa and her husband Phil. In truth, Ronnie had run away, sort of. Less than twenty-four hours after leaving home, she had called her mother and let Vanessa know where she was and that she was on her way to her grandfather's place in Texas.

Short of having the police pick her up, the only other thing to do was to let her continue on to Weatherford and then deal with the situation once she was safely with Sam. All that had been established fairly rapidly.

Then there was the matter of deciding what to do with her.

"I won't go back," Ronnie declared. "I can't stand living there anymore. It's a suburban hell."

"I think maybe you're overstatin' the case a mite," Sam said as he sat on the sofa, leaning forward with his hands clasped between his knees. Ronnie was across the living room from him, fidgeting in an armchair. She wore fashionably torn jeans and a t-shirt.

Sam went on, "I've been in your hometown, remember—"

"Home!" Ronnie said. "I can't breathe there. I can't even think there."

"I know you've been arguin' with your folks a lot. That's what teenagers and parents do."

"Is that what you and my mother did?"

"Some, sure, but she was mostly . . ."

"Go ahead and say it. She was a good girl, wasn't she? Played bas-

ketball for you, made the honor roll, top ten in her class, never did anything wrong."

"I wouldn't go that far," Sam said.

"But she never dyed her hair blue, did she?"

"No. She did cut it like Farrah Fawcett's once, though."

"Who?"

"Never mind. Let's just figure out what we're gonna do here."

Ronnie sat back, crossed her arms, and looked determined. "I'm going to live here in Weatherford with you and go to my last two years of high school here."

"I think you're forgettin' . . . This isn't my house."

"Mrs. Newsom isn't going to care. She's your girlfriend, isn't she?"

"I wouldn't go so far as to say . . . Now, never mind about that. The point is, it's not up to me who stays here and who doesn't."

"I can get an apartment," Ronnie said. "I can go to court to get emancipated. Everybody knows that. I just need a lawyer. Maybe I can hire that guy you and Mrs. Newsom work for sometimes when you're investigating murders."

Sam had to close his eyes for a moment and rub his forehead. He had no doubt that Jimmy D'Angelo could manage to get Vanessa and Phil's parental rights set aside. Jimmy was a good lawyer. But that wasn't what Sam wanted, at all.

"Look, you can stay here for now," he told Ronnie. "I don't think that'll be a problem. Shoot, you came all the way down here, I'm not gonna turn you away. You're my granddaughter."

The smile she gave him was dazzling. "I knew you wouldn't let me down, Gramps."

"But I'm gonna call your mom and we're gonna have a long talk about this. There's nothin' wrong with a vacation, but I don't think it's a good idea for you to plan on stayin' here permanent and goin' to school here."

◀ ◆ ▶

And yet here Ronnie was, months later, living in what had been an extra room upstairs and attending Courtland High School. Phyllis knew that Sam had been surprised and even a little flustered by his daughter and son-in-law's decision that maybe it would be a good idea for Ronnie to stay in Texas for a while. That would give things a chance to cool off. Evidently Ronnie had changed drastically during the past year, and her parents were at a loss how to explain it—or deal with it.

"You know what it usually means when a kid changes overnight like that," Sam had said worriedly to Phyllis when they were discussing the circumstances. "Drugs."

"Not always," she'd told him. "Ronnie comes from a good family, a good background."

"That doesn't always make a difference," he had said with a doleful shake of his head. That attitude was far out of character for Sam and told Phyllis just how concerned he really was.

"I don't have any problem with her staying here, and neither do Carolyn and Eve. We've talked about it. Sometimes a change of scenery will make all the difference in the world. And it might be fun having a young person in the house again."

"It'll be different, that's for sure."

Phyllis wasn't sure it would be all *that* different, since part of the time Sam was pretty much a big kid himself . . .

That had been in July. In August, the Dobsons had come to see Phyllis and Sam with their news—and their request for help. Once Phyllis and Sam had agreed to take over as long-term subs for Molly and Frank and the principal at Courtland had agreed to it, it hadn't been difficult to make arrangements for Ronnie to attend the same school. On the first day of classes, all three of them had walked into a new school.

New not only to them, but to everyone else there. It was actually kind of exciting.

Things had settled down into a routine, of course. Even though the students had changed in some ways since Phyllis and Sam last taught, kids were still kids, and teaching was still teaching—although Phyllis didn't remember the teachers having *quite* as much paperwork to do when she was at the junior high. She had taught eighth grade there, only one year younger than freshmen, but there seemed to be a world of difference between those eighth graders and the juniors and seniors she saw walking the halls at Courtland. Most of her students were sophomores, with a few juniors mixed in, sort of halfway between her former students and the near-adults who would be graduating in another year.

Sam had had it a little easier, since he had taught and coached at the high school level for many years, although most of his career had been spent at Poolville, a much smaller school. The sheer size of Courtland had been an adjustment for him.

"It's like bein' in a shoppin' mall," he had told Phyllis. "Wings goin' off here and there and different floors and people everywhere."

"That's what schools are like these days, I guess," she had said.

"Big schools. I don't mind doin' this to help out your old friends, but I sure wouldn't want to come back to it full-time."

Phyllis thought about everything she enjoyed about retirement and said fervently, "Me, either."

Now, on this morning in early October, they were all fortifying themselves with coffee while Raven wandered around under the table, rubbing against everyone's legs in turn. The cat was affectionate and well-behaved—as long as Buck wasn't around. Raven wasn't quite as friendly to dogs as Molly and Frank had claimed. All it had taken was one barking, growling, hissing, spitting encounter between the Dalmatian and the black cat to prove that. The confrontation had ended with Buck retreating and howling in pain from the scratches on his nose, and since then the humans had been careful to keep the animals apart.

"You know it's Friday the Thirteenth next week, don't you?" Ronnie said.

Carolyn turned from the stove where she was moving pancakes from the pan to a stack on a plate and said, "It is? I hate to hear that."

"Are you superstitious, Mrs. Wilbarger? I'm a little surprised. You don't seem like the type."

"Superstitious? Not at all! But everyone else in the world seems to be, and I get tired of hearing about it."

Sam said, "There's gonna be a dance at school, right? I saw posters about it, sayin' how you can buy tickets from student council members."

"Are you going, Ronnie?" Phyllis asked.

"To a school dance?" Ronnie made the question sound like it was the most ridiculous idea she had ever heard.

"Yeah, I suppose that wouldn't be a very cool thing to do, would it?" Sam said.

Ronnie shrugged. "It's all moot. Nobody's asked me, and nobody will."

"You don't know that," Phyllis said.

"Yeah, I pretty much do."

"No reason you can't go anyway," Sam said. "You'll have plenty of friends there. You don't have to have a date."

Ronnie arched an eyebrow eloquently and said, "Plenty of friends? Not exactly."

"You've made friends. I see you sittin' at a table in the

cafeteria with the same bunch of kids every day."

"Yeah, they're all right. But they're not really the type to go to school dances, either."

"Ah. Outsiders. Like the book."

"What book?"

Phyllis said, "You don't read *The Outsiders* in English class?"

"Yeah, no, I never heard of it."

Phyllis and Sam looked at each other. Earlier, Phyllis had said that the more things change, the more they stay the same, prompted by the fact that not only were she and Sam getting up and going to school every morning, they also had to make sure Ronnie got up and made it to class, too. That brought back memories for both of them, reminding Phyllis of her son Mike and Sam of his daughter Vanessa.

But some things *did* change, like blue hair and assigned reading in English classes . . . and friends with cancer.

Phyllis was solemn the rest of the morning as she got ready to go. The odd circumstances of the past few years, when she had found herself mixed up in a number of murder cases, meant that she had seen more than her share of death and tragedy.

But in the end, she thought, everyone's share was the same, wasn't it?

Chapter 3

Thankfully, she had put those dark thoughts aside by the time she got to school.

Most of the time, Phyllis drove her Lincoln and Sam took his pickup, because they might have different things scheduled after school and it was just easier to have two vehicles, even though they lived in the same house. Ronnie usually rode to school with Sam, although sometimes she went with Phyllis, and she rode home with whichever one of them was more convenient for her. Sam had learned to coordinate this with text messages, which was new for him. He was pretty computer-savvy but had never done much texting until now.

Phyllis parked in the faculty lot behind the school and enjoyed the cool autumn breeze as she walked inside. Huge, fluffy white clouds tumbled through the sky. Fall was one of her favorite times of year. As she had gotten older, she'd come to enjoy the extremes of winter and summer less and preferred the more moderate climates of spring and fall.

The walk into the school was the last time she would be

outside until she went home that afternoon, unless she left the campus during her conference period, which was rare. The rest of the time would be spent in the climate-controlled building, where there wasn't much to see except brick, concrete, tile, and steel. There were very few windows in the school, and those were tall and narrow and didn't provide much of a view. Phyllis missed being able to see the outside world, even though she knew from experience that if there were windows, some students would spend all day staring out through them.

Ray Brooks, the school's full-time security guard, was standing beside the entrance closest to the faculty lot. A stocky man in his thirties with already thinning brown hair, he nodded to Phyllis as she came up to the double glass doors.

"Good morning, Mr. Brooks," she said.

"Mornin'." The curt response was all she ever got from him. Brooks wasn't unfriendly, he just wasn't friendly and never seemed to be glad to see any of the teachers or other school staff. Phyllis didn't feel slighted since he was that way with everybody.

Or maybe not *everybody*, she thought as she went inside. From what she had heard, Brooks had dated at least one of the single female teachers in the past, although there didn't seem to be any scandal attached to the rumors.

"Good morning, Phyllis," a voice called through the open doorway of one of the classrooms she passed. It was next door to Phyllis's room, although she supposed that technically it was Molly Dobson's room. Molly had never taught there, however, and Phyllis had, so for now, at least, it was her room.

She paused and looked in at the woman who had greeted her. "Hello, Frances," she said. "How are you this morning?"

Frances Macmillan laughed and blew back a strand of graying blond hair that had fallen over her glasses. "Overwhelmed," she said. She'd been standing beside her desk, but she came over to the open door as she went on, "But why should today be any different?"

Frances taught AP World History, as well as a couple of classes of regular World History. She was also the student council sponsor. During the week of staff development before school started, which Phyllis had attended even though strictly speaking she didn't have to, being a substitute, she and Frances had met and hit it off immediately. Frances was twenty years younger, which still made her old enough to be a well-seasoned veteran of the educational wars. Phyllis had come to her for advice about dealing with high school students on more than one occasion, and Frances had been quite helpful.

"Anything in particular have you frazzled today?" Phyllis asked now.

Frances pushed her glasses up. "It's this Friday the Thirteenth dance. You know, the one that the student council is putting on next week."

"Of course. In fact, we were just talking about it at home this morning."

"Oh?" Frances smiled.

Phyllis suddenly realized she might have stepped into a trap. But it was too late to retreat now, and anyway, she wasn't sure she wanted to.

"I could really use some more volunteers," Frances went on. "It's the one Friday during football season when we don't have a game, and people are taking advantage of that to do other things."

"Like have a dance," Phyllis pointed out.

"Well, yes, but that's not the only activity going on. So I

don't have as many chaperones as I really need, and I'd really love to have someone provide some snacks, maybe a bowl of punch . . . I was hoping I'd see you this morning, since with your background . . . I mean, you must have dozens of wonderful recipes for cookies and other goodies. Maybe hundreds."

Frances was talking fast, probably trying to get her whole pitch out before Phyllis could say no. Phyllis wanted to tell her to slow down. She'd been halfway expecting Frances to approach her about this.

"I can probably do that," she said.

Frances looked surprised. "You mean bake something for the dance? Or chaperone? Or . . . dare I hope it? . . . Both?"

Phyllis had to laugh at her friend's dramatic phrasing. "I think I can manage both," she said. "I can probably get Carolyn to help me with the baking, too, and I believe Sam would be glad to chaperone with me."

"I'm sure he'd do anything you asked him to, but I wouldn't want to inconvenience either of you . . ."

"It's no trouble," Phyllis assured her. "When we were talking about the dance this morning at breakfast, I thought then that it might be fun to go. I haven't been to a school dance in, well, ages and ages."

"This is just wonderful. I can't tell you how much I appreciate it."

"I should probably check with Sam to make certain he's all right with it, though. Although I'm pretty sure he will be. I just don't want to speak for him . . . too much."

"Of course."

"I'll let you know later."

Frances nodded, put a hand on Phyllis's arm, and squeezed. "Thank you. I'm thrilled to have someone with your reputation involved."

For a second, Phyllis thought the other teacher was talking about the notoriety that had begun to follow her around during the past few years when she had found herself involved in those sensational murders.

But then she realized Frances must mean her reputation as a baker. It was true that Phyllis had either won or finished high in various recipe contests, often in heated but friendly competition with Carolyn. Also, she had been writing a column for the magazine *A Taste of Texas*, although recently she had begun to think that it might be time to retire from that. It was nice to be known for something other than ferreting out killers, though.

"I'll talk to Sam at lunch and then check back with you later," Phyllis promised.

"That would be great. Ready for today's classes?"

"Always." If there was anything Phyllis had learned from her many years of experience as both a teacher and a baker, it was how quickly everything could fall apart without proper preparation.

Phyllis and Sam had the same lunch period. It had just worked out that way; they hadn't asked for the arrangement, and they wouldn't have. Lunch schedules, like everything else, needed to be set up in the best interests of the students. That wasn't always how things were done, of course, but at least it was a reasonable goal.

Neither of them had cafeteria duty this week, so when Phyllis had gotten her food, she carried the tray toward the table where Sam always sat. His classroom was closer to the cafeteria than hers was—by the length of a whole wing, in fact—so he was nearly always there first.

That was true today, too. She spotted him near the end of

the table, sitting next to a dark-haired, very attractive young woman who was smiling and laughing at something Sam was saying. Amber Trahearne was one of the other math teachers, and she had befriended Sam and helped him out during the first few weeks of school, just as Frances Macmillan had given Phyllis a hand.

Phyllis wasn't jealous, exactly, but it was impossible not to notice how young and pretty and, well, downright perky Amber was, even though she knew that neither Sam nor Amber would ever have any sort of romantic interest in the other.

"Hi, Phyllis," Amber greeted her before Sam could say anything. "Sam, scoot over and make room for Phyllis."

"Yeah, that's just what I was doin'," Sam said as he moved his tray. Phyllis sat down on his right. Amber was on his left. Sam looked back and forth between them and grinned. "Mighty good company."

The noise level in the cafeteria was high, as usual in a school cafeteria, but Phyllis heard the self-satisfaction in Sam's voice. Despite his overall level-headedness, he wasn't immune to the appeal of an attractive young woman's attention.

Amber leaned forward and said across Sam to Phyllis, "Sam was just telling me he's forgotten all of his advanced math, but I'll bet he hasn't. It would all come back to him if he started using it again."

"You're wrong there," Sam said, shaking his head. "I barely understood calculus and trigonometry when I was studyin' 'em. Shoot, I even called it triggernometry startin' out. I figured out enough to pass, but that's about all. Today, I don't have even the foggiest notion of what a cosine is, unless it's one sine sittin' next to another sine."

Amber laughed again. Phyllis wanted to tell her it wasn't

that funny, but what would be the point? Let her pretend-flirt with Sam. At this late date, it wasn't really going to matter.

Anyway, it didn't have anything to do with Sam. That was just Amber's personality. She was bubbly and outgoing, and with men that came across as flirtatious. With her looks, it couldn't really do anything else. Her attractiveness was enhanced by the expensive designer clothes she wore, the fancy bags and matching shoes, like the outfit she had on today. Jacket, bag, and shoes were all decorated—although not ostentatiously—with gemstones.

"I've been trying to talk Sam into giving me a hand with the math team," Amber went on. "I think he's got a natural talent for general mathematics and number sense."

"I couldn't ever do the calculator," Sam said. "These ol' fingers of mine won't move that fast. When those kids on the calculator team get to goin' on those things, I can't even see what they're doin'."

"It's just a matter of practice. But with number sense, it's all up here." Amber tapped a finger on the side of her head.

"I do that and I just get a hollow sound."

That drew another laugh from the young teacher, and despite herself, Phyllis began to feel a little annoyed. She said to Sam, "Frances Macmillan talked to me this morning about the dance next week. She was hoping I could make some snacks for it . . . and that you and I would be chaperones."

"What did you tell her?"

"I said I'd be happy to do both of those things. I didn't promise that you'd do it, though."

"Would've been all right if you had," Sam said. "That's sounds like fun."

"So you're going to be at the dance?" Amber said. "Now I'm glad I agreed to volunteer, too."

That didn't work out exactly as she had planned, Phyllis

thought . . . but it would be all right. And Amber had just as much right as any of the other teachers to help out at the dance.

Still, they *were* talking about Friday the Thirteenth. Maybe she was a little superstitious after all, Phyllis realized as a vague sense of unease stirred inside her.

Chapter 4

She didn't get a chance to talk again with Frances Macmillan until after school, but she went next door to Frances's classroom then and told her that she and Sam would definitely volunteer to be chaperones at the dance.

"That's fantastic," Frances said. "What about the snacks? Do you have any ideas?"

"Well, since the dance is going to be on Friday the Thirteenth, the first thing that popped into my head was chocolate mint brownies decorated with black cats." The whole concept of the day being bad luck had led her to think about Raven and how black cats carried that same association. "I also thought about something we could call Killer Sugar Cookies. Those would be sugar cookies with white icing and spots of red icing sprinkled over them . . . like . . . blood . . ."

Phyllis's voice trailed off as she saw the look on Frances's face.

"Too much?" she said, then put her fingertips to her forehead and closed her eyes for a second as something else occurred to her. "So many people know that I've been mixed up in all those murder cases. And some of them have been pretty bloody. I guess . . . that wouldn't be in the best taste, would it?"

"It's not just that, Phyllis. You know how school administrations are these days about *anything* controversial."

"Yes, there's nothing you can do that somebody, somewhere, won't complain about."

"I'm afraid somebody might see cookies like that as promoting violence," Frances said. "I know, it's crazy to think that somebody could believe that about any kind of cookie . . ."

"But it could certainly happen," Phyllis agreed, nodding. "And what's the point of taking the chance, when I could make plain sugar cookies instead." She smiled. "I'll bet the kids would have liked the 'bloody' ones, though."

"Oh, I don't doubt that!"

"What about the black cat brownies? Too controversial? Will basing something on a superstition be considered, I don't know, promoting Satanism or something?"

"I hope not. But you'd better let me check with Mr. Shula."

"Of course. I'm a little surprised they let you advertise it as a Friday the Thirteenth dance."

"Well, if you look at the posters we put up," Frances said, "they don't have any pictures or graphics on them, just text. I figured that would be safe."

Phyllis hadn't noticed that, but she was sure she would the next time she saw one of the posters.

They chatted for a few more minutes, then Phyllis went back to her room to finish getting ready for the next day's classes. While she was doing that, her cell phone chimed its text message tone. She picked it up from the desk and read:

Going home w/u K? She would have known the message was from Ronnie even if the phone hadn't shown her name on the display.

Okay, Phyllis responded, typing out the whole word. *I'll be done here in about 20 more minutes.*

K

Phyllis wondered idly if everyone in her generation who texted took the time and trouble to spell out words and punctuate correctly. That slowed down the process, but she had realized very quickly that she would never master the technique of using her thumbs and composing messages with blinding speed, the way most of the kids could. It was like those math team kids punching keys on the calculator, as Sam had mentioned. Some skills were just beyond people her age, and there was no point in feeling guilty about it.

She could still do a lot of things most of these youngsters couldn't, she thought, then grinned wryly. Maybe she was closer to being a geezer than she had claimed to Sam.

When she was finished getting ready for the next day, Phyllis locked up the classroom and walked along the hall toward the doors closest to the faculty parking lot. At this time of day, with a lot of after-school activities going on, all the entrances were unlocked, of course. All the kids involved with band and athletics and other extracurriculars were still here, as were many of the teachers. The school wouldn't really clear out until six or seven o'clock, and even after that there were liable to be a few people around other than the custodians.

When Phyllis stepped outside, a flash of something blue caught her eye off to the right. The attached gymnasium loomed in that direction, up a slight, grassy hill. Where the gym met the main building, there was a small alcove where a service entrance was located. A concrete walk along the back of the gym led to that area. Supplies on dollies could be wheeled in that way.

At the edge of that alcove was where Phyllis had seen the flash of blue. She wouldn't have thought anything about it, if the color hadn't been an exact match for Ronnie's hair.

Of course, there could be other things that same color—a shirt, a jacket, a backpack. Ronnie wouldn't have any reason to be around that service entrance.

As Phyllis paused, though, she realized she had finished with her preparations for the next day's classes a little sooner than she'd expected, and sooner than she had told Ronnie. Ronnie might believe she still had a few minutes before she needed to meet Phyllis at the parking lot.

Which still didn't explain what she was doing up there . . . if, indeed, that was her Phyllis had seen.

The simplest thing would be to go on to the car, Phyllis told herself. She could ask Ronnie about it, if she decided to be that nosy. But she wasn't the girl's grandmother, so maybe it would be best for her to just mind her own business.

She might have actually done that if Ray Brooks hadn't come around the corner where he could see along the walkway into the alcove at that moment. Brooks stopped for a second, then strode quickly toward the service entrance that Phyllis couldn't see from where she was. His attitude clearly indicated that something was wrong.

If there was even the slightest possibility Ronnie was involved in whatever it was, Phyllis knew she couldn't ignore that.

She started up the little incline toward the gym.

By the time she reached a point where she could see, Brooks was already at the alcove. She heard him say in a loud, angry voice, "All right, that's enough."

Brooks was confronting two students who stood in the alcove. One was a dark-haired, medium-sized boy who looked vaguely familiar to Phyllis, as if she had seen him in the halls but didn't have him in any of her classes.

The other student was Ronnie.

The boy said, "We weren't doing anything—"

"I saw what you were doin'," Brooks interrupted. "I don't care what you horny little bas—" He must have caught sight of Phyllis approaching from the corner of his eye, because he stopped short for a second and then went on, "I don't care what you do other places, but you're not gonna do that on school property."

Phyllis's first thought was that Brooks must have seen Ronnie and the boy smoking. But there were no cigarette butts on the concrete floor inside the alcove, she noticed, and no smell of tobacco—or anything else that could be smoked—in the air.

That just left one reasonable possibility.

Ronnie looked surprised and upset to see Phyllis, but there was a note of determination in her voice as she began, "This isn't Chase's fault—"

"Don't give me that," Brooks said. "I know what kind of kid he is."

"You might not know as much as you think you do," the boy said tightly.

Although *young man* would probably be a better way to describe him than *boy*, Phyllis decided. He had to be a senior, but something about his eyes, the way he carried himself, spoke to a maturity greater than that. She saw that in rare students. She had seen it in her own son Mike, who was now a Parker County deputy sheriff.

"What's going on here?" Phyllis asked.

Brooks glanced at her, looking annoyed that she had interjected herself into the situation. He jerked his head toward Ronnie and said, "Isn't this your granddaughter?"

"No, she's my friend Sam Fletcher's granddaughter."

"I knew there was some connection. If you're Coach Fletcher's friend, you'd better warn him that his granddaughter doesn't have any more sense than to be slutting around with a punk."

"Hey!" Ronnie said. "You can't say things like that!"

"You were makin' out with Hamilton here, weren't you?" Brooks demanded.

"You don't know what you saw," said the young man, whose name, evidently, was Chase Hamilton.

Brooks shook his head and sneered. "I've worked around schools long enough to have seen it all, kid. Don't waste your breath denying it." He pointed with a thumb. "Get outta here."

Ronnie said, "This is public property. You can't—"

"It's school district property, and I sure can. In fact, I'm pretty sure one of the resource officers is still here, and I can call him if you want." Brooks reached for a walkie-talkie clipped to his belt.

The resource officers were actual police officers assigned to the school, and Phyllis didn't particularly want one of them called in to handle a problem that involved Ronnie. She knew Sam wouldn't want that, either.

Chase Hamilton appeared to feel the same way. Before Phyllis could say anything, he told Brooks, "All right. I'm sorry. I'm going, Mr. Brooks. No need to make this any worse."

"I won't be the one makin' it worse. You did that already."

"Okay." Chase glanced at Ronnie but didn't say anything

or make a move to touch her. He walked away quickly.

"This isn't fair!" Ronnie said.

Brooks grinned, but it wasn't a pleasant expression. "Whoever told you life was fair was full of it, kid."

Ronnie looked at Phyllis and said, "Aren't you going to do anything?"

"There's really nothing I can do," Phyllis said. She didn't like Ray Brooks, but she didn't know anything about Chase Hamilton except that he was older than Ronnie and shouldn't have been in the alcove making out with her. "Why don't you go on to the car? I'll be there in a minute."

Ronnie managed to look worried and defiant at the same time. "Are you going to tell Gramps about this?"

"We'll see."

Ronnie blew out a disgusted, angry breath and stalked off toward the parking lot. Even though there were still quite a few cars there, she wouldn't have any trouble finding Phyllis's Lincoln. There was a good reason Sam sometimes called it a gunboat. It was a large, distinctive vehicle.

Phyllis started to follow the girl, but Brooks stopped her by saying, "I meant what I said. If Fletcher's your friend, you'd better warn him. He doesn't want his granddaughter hanging around with Chase Hamilton."

"I agree, they shouldn't have been doing what they were doing, but . . . they're teenagers. Like it or not, Mr. Brooks, we knew there's going to be a certain amount of that going on around a school. There always has been, and I suspect there always will be."

"Yeah, I'm not just talking about the makin' out. It's the bunch Hamilton runs with that oughta worry you and the girl's granddad." Brooks paused for a second. "They're responsible for just about all the drug dealing that goes on in this school."

Chapter 5

Phyllis stared at him. Worry suddenly felt like a trapped animal lunging around inside her.

"Drugs?" she repeated.

"That's right," Brooks said.

"Are you sure about that?"

"I'm around this school all day every day. I see what goes on in the parking lots, in the woods over there on the other side of the soccer pitch, in the out of the way corners inside the buildings . . . Do I have proof I can take to the cops? Not yet, maybe. But I know what goes on."

Phyllis had no reason to doubt him, other than his surly nature that might make him more suspicious than was called for, as well as what seemed to be a natural dislike for the kids. But none of that meant that he was wrong.

Like he said, he was in a position to see what went on.

"I just thought that the young man didn't really seem like the type—"

Brooks let out a contemptuous snort and waved a hand.

"You can't tell anything by looking at them! Well, some of the really bad ones you can, but I've seen plenty of the clean-cut types who are just as bad. Or even worse. I promise you, Hamilton's right in the thick of it. I'm not just talkin' about weed, either. That bunch is dealing pills, meth, maybe even harder stuff. Blue-haired weirdo or not, that girl doesn't need to be around that."

Under other circumstances, Phyllis might have been angry at him for calling Ronnie a blue-haired weirdo. And she probably would be upset about that, later. But right now she was too concerned with other things.

"I'll speak to Sam," she said.

"Good. Tell him to keep a tighter rein on the girl."

It wasn't easy to keep a tight rein on teenagers, and in many cases, not even desirable to do so, Phyllis thought. But this might be one of those times, considering Ronnie's recent history of erratic behavior and clashes with her parents.

Phyllis nodded to Brooks and walked toward the parking lot.

When she reached the Lincoln, Ronnie was slumped in the front seat on the passenger side, her head down and an angry glare on her face. Phyllis got in and closed the door, and Ronnie said without looking at her, "I suppose I'm in trouble now."

"I'm not your grandmother," Phyllis said. "If you're expecting me to scold you, you're going to be disappointed."

"But you're going to tell Gramps, and then *he'll* yell at me. He's liable to send me back to Pennsylvania." Ronnie's head came up. "But I won't go. I'll run away for real this time."

"Sam's not the sort to yell unless there's a really good reason. And I can't imagine him sending you away . . . unless he believed it was the best thing for you."

"And what about what I think is best?"

"Evidently that includes letting some boy paw you in an alcove."

"He didn't—! Chase wasn't *pawing* me. What an old-fashioned word."

"I'm old . . . and old-fashioned," Phyllis said. "And he *was* kissing you, wasn't he?"

"No, he wasn't," Ronnie insisted. She took a deep breath. "If you have to know, *I* was kissing *him*. Chase didn't start it. And I think he was just as surprised as you were when you walked up."

Phyllis frowned. "Are you telling me the truth?"

"Yeah. I was on my way out here to the parking lot when I saw him up there talking to somebody on his phone. I made a detour, okay? I went to talk with him, and maybe I got carried away—"

"You kissed him."

"All right, yeah, I already said I did, didn't I? He's just so . . . *cute* . . . and nice and brave . . ."

What she was hearing made Phyllis feel slightly relieved. Ronnie sounded like a lovestruck junior high girl now, instead of the ironic, hipster-y attitude she usually displayed. Phyllis said, "You have a crush on him, don't you?"

Ronnie glared down at the floorboards and muttered, "It's nobody's business if I do."

"It might be somebody else's business if you act on it."

"Gramps, you mean?"

"Actually," Phyllis said, "I was talking about Chase. You said he was surprised when you kissed him."

"Yeah, and he was already annoyed that I'd interrupted his phone call."

Because he'd been setting up a drug deal? Phyllis asked herself.

She didn't say that. Instead she asked, "He's never asked you out or anything like that?"

"Well . . . no. I talk to him every day, though. At least I try to."

"But he's not interested?"

"He's always nice! I'm sure he'll start to like me . . ."

Not all of Phyllis's worries had been eased, by any means, but at least she felt better about the situation now. Ronnie had a crush on Chase Hamilton and had been pursuing him, but from the sound of it, he didn't return her feelings. However, he was a teenage boy, so . . .

"I suppose when you kissed him, he didn't try to make you stop?"

"Well, no, not really, but like I said, I took him by surprise, and I suppose he would have gotten around to it sooner or later."

Probably later, Phyllis thought, if the security guard hadn't interrupted them. There was no telling how far things might have gone if Ray Brooks hadn't spotted them.

And there was still Brooks's accusation about Chase being involved with the kids selling drugs to consider, as well.

"You know that this boy doesn't have the best reputation, don't you?"

"What do you know about him?" Ronnie asked. "When you first walked up, you looked at him like you'd never even seen him before."

"That's not true. I knew I'd seen him around the school—"

"But you didn't know who he was!" Ronnie flung up her hands in frustration. "You're just going by whatever that guy Brooks told you!"

"*Mister* Brooks may have mentioned that Chase is part of a bad crowd—"

"A bad crowd," Ronnie interrupted her. She shook her head and laughed scornfully. "What, like the Sharks and the Jets?"

"You haven't read *The Outsiders*, but that reference you know?"

"The drama department at my old school put on *West Side Story*," Ronnie said. "Chase is not a member of a gang, okay?"

"But is he friends with people who are?"

"I don't know who all his friends are."

"Maybe you should," Phyllis said.

"And maybe you should—" Ronnie stopped herself.

Phyllis waited for her to go on. When Ronnie didn't, she said, "Maybe I should what?"

"Never mind," the girl muttered. "I'm sorry, okay? I shouldn't have got mad. I know you're just trying to help."

Phyllis suspected Ronnie was just parroting things she thought she'd want to hear. She was even more sure of that when Ronnie went on, "I wish you wouldn't tell Gramps about this. It's really no big deal, and there's no reason to worry him and get him all upset."

"What if Mr. Brooks makes an official report about it? If he writes up you and Chase, the school will have to notify your parent or guardian, and right now that's your grandfather."

Ronnie shook her head. "Brooks . . . *Mister* Brooks . . . won't write us up. He hardly ever does. It would be too much paperwork. He just likes to hassle the kids, everybody knows that."

Phyllis didn't, but her interactions with the security guard had been very limited. The general dislike for the man among the faculty seemed to be repeated among the student body, though.

"I can't promise not to tell Sam," she said. "But I suppose I don't have to tell him right away."

"Is this blackmail? Are you saying you won't tell him if I stay away from Chase from now on?"

"No. I'm just saying you need to think about what you're doing and maybe make some better choices."

Ronnie crossed her arms and frowned down at the floorboard again. "Sounds like blackmail to me."

"Think whatever you want," Phyllis said as she reached for the ignition key. "It's time we were getting home."

Ronnie didn't say anything else during the drive, and neither did Phyllis. When Phyllis stopped the Lincoln in the garage, Ronnie got out and closed the door maybe just a tad harder than was absolutely necessary and went into the house through the door into the kitchen. Phyllis followed her in and found Carolyn and Eve sitting at the kitchen table. Both women had cups of coffee in front of them.

"Well, that was certainly a thunderstorm that just blew through here," Eve commented. Raven was curled up her lap. She rubbed the cat's ears as she spoke. "Ronnie was mad about something, wasn't she?"

"I'm surprised she hasn't blown up before now," Carolyn said. "She hasn't really caused any trouble since she's been here, and for a teenage girl to be even halfway rational for that long is unnatural."

"There was . . . an incident after school today," Phyllis said.

"Did it involve a boy?" Eve asked. "I'll bet it had something to do with a boy."

Carolyn scoffed. "Not everything has to do with hormones, Eve. Some people think about other things."

Phyllis said, "Well, in this case . . ."

"See, I knew it had to be about a boy," Eve said. "What happened?"

Phyllis had heard Ronnie stomping up the stairs, so she knew the girl was out of earshot. Quickly, she gave Carolyn and Eve the details, leaving out only what Ray Brooks had said about Chase being involved with drug dealers. She didn't completely trust the man's opinion, and while she might wind up deciding to share that with Sam, she didn't see anything wrong with a little discretion at this point.

The part about Ronnie's crush on the boy, and the way she had kissed him, Phyllis knew to be true, even though she hadn't seen it with her own eyes. Ronnie had admitted what she'd done.

"I think I agree with Ronnie," Eve said. "A little making out is no big deal. That security guard overreacted."

"Of course you'd think that," Carolyn said.

"Well, they're teenagers, dear. What else do you expect them to do? They might as well be rabbits."

"Not *all* teenagers are like that."

"Some weren't, I suppose," Eve said with a sweet smile that didn't quite conceal the sting in the words.

Before Carolyn could respond, Phyllis said, "I'd appreciate it if you wouldn't say anything to Sam about this."

Carolyn looked surprised. "You're going to tell him, aren't you? He has a right to know the girl got in trouble."

"It wasn't that much trouble, and like Ronnie said, Brooks probably won't write it up. I mean, the worst he could accuse them of is a little PDA. They probably wouldn't even get detention for it."

Carolyn shook her head and said, "I think you should tell him, but it's your decision, I suppose."

"I promised Ronnie I would wait and think about it before I said anything to Sam."

"But you told us."

"I didn't promise not to do that. There's something else I want to do before I bring it up with Sam. *If* I bring it up with Sam."

Eve smiled. "You're going to investigate this boy Chase,

aren't you? Like he was a suspect in a murder!"

"Now hold on—" Phyllis began.

"Of course. It's a puzzle, and your detective instincts have kicked in. I can't say I'm a bit surprised."

Honestly, neither could Phyllis. Trying to uncover the truth about things seemed to be second nature for her now, and she didn't see where it would hurt anything.

She left her friends drinking their coffee and headed for the living room and the computer that sat on a desk tucked into a corner.

Chapter 6

In this day and age, not many people could live for seventeen or eighteen years and not leave some sort of digital record. Of course, "Chase Hamilton" wasn't an unusual name. Phyllis suspected that a search for it would yield page after page of hits that were totally unrelated to the young man attending Weatherford Courtland High School.

But there were things she could do to narrow down the results, like including the name of the town in the search. That didn't turn up anything, so she broadened out the parameters and looked for a Chase Hamilton anywhere in Texas. There were several, just as she expected, in different parts of the state. She found several social media and business networking pages for Chase Hamilton, but none of them matched the boy who had been with Ronnie in the alcove.

That was a little strange. She thought she should have found *something*. No one was a cipher. Not anymore. Why, if she searched her own name, she would find a lot more about her on the Internet than she liked the idea of!

She searched public records and online newspaper archives. Jimmy D'Angelo subscribed to a number of databases, and as a consultant to his law firm, Phyllis had access to them. She poured through those as well, her puzzlement growing as she failed to find any mention of Chase Hamilton. She knew he existed. She had seen him with her own eyes.

But increasingly, it appeared that this particular Chase Hamilton had left no digital footprint, and that just didn't seem possible to Phyllis.

She heard the door between the kitchen and the garage open and close, and then Sam greeted Carolyn and Eve. Thankfully, they honored Phyllis's request not to say anything to him about the incident at school just yet, and a moment later he came on into the living room and dropped the old-fashioned briefcase he carried onto the sofa.

Phyllis turned off the monitor as Sam came over and stood behind her. He rested his hands on her shoulders and said, "Ronnie catch a ride home with you all right?"

"She did," Phyllis said.

"I gave 'em a hand with football practice this afternoon, worked with the defensive backs some." Sam had coached both boys' and girls' basketball at Poolville, but during football season he had been an assistant coach for that sport, as well.

"How's the team looking?" Phyllis asked, glad for the opportunity to keep the subject from getting around to what she had been looking for on the computer. So far the football team had won two games and lost four, which according to Sam was a respectable record for a first-year school.

"They're startin' to come together, I think," he said. "They won't make the playoffs this year and probably not next year, either, but the year after that the players who are sophomores now will be seniors and will have some time together in the same system. They could be pretty good."

"I hope so." Phyllis pushed back the chair and stood up.

"I guess you talked to Frances Macmillan some more about the dance."

"Yes, we talked about what sort of snacks I'm going to make. She's very grateful that we're both going to be chaperones."

"I'm lookin' forward to it. It's always nice to see a bunch of kids havin' a good time. I hope Ronnie changes her mind about goin'. It'd be good for her to socialize a little more, I think."

Phyllis didn't say anything. She hadn't made any promises to Ronnie except that she wouldn't tell Sam right away. Well, she hadn't said anything to him about the incident when he came in, so technically she had lived up to that pledge and was free to bring up the subject now.

But that wouldn't be honoring the spirit of what she had told Ronnie, she thought, and besides, she was curious. She still had a hard time believing she hadn't come up with any more information about Chase.

"Maybe she'll come around," Phyllis said. "Right now I need to start thinking about supper, unless Carolyn already has something in mind."

"And I've got papers to grade. When we taught before, we didn't have to do so much gradin', did we? Seems like there's a lot more of it now."

"Paperwork always expands," Phyllis said. "It's a law of the universe."

After supper, she and Sam both graded papers while watching TV. Carolyn and Eve were in the room as well, and Eve commented, "I certainly don't miss that. There were a lot of TV shows I thought I watched, but then I realized I didn't know a thing that had happened because I was also grading papers at the time."

"We didn't have as much of that to do in elementary school," Carolyn said. "From what I hear, they do more of it now. I'm not sure how necessary it all is, though. Times have certainly changed."

"They've got a way of doin' that," Sam said. "Not to change the subject, but Ronnie sure was quiet durin' supper. She still didn't seem to care about goin' to the dance, even with you and me bein' there, Phyllis."

"Well . . . you wouldn't think that having her grandfather, and her grandfather's friend, there, would make a teenage girl more likely to want to attend a dance," Phyllis pointed out.

Sam frowned and said, "Dang it, I never thought about it like that. Did we make a mistake tellin' Frances we'd help out? Would it maybe be better in the long run if we backed out?"

Phyllis shook her head. "I don't *want* to back out. Carolyn and I have already been talking about recipes for the snacks. And like you said earlier, I enjoy watching the kids have a good time. If Ronnie doesn't want to be part of that, it's her own decision."

"Yeah, I know. You're right. I just worry about her, that's all."

Phyllis smiled and nodded as she said, "I think we all do."

Later, when Sam was out of the room, Carolyn said, "You're not going to tell him what happened, are you?"

"Not yet." Phyllis's curiosity about Chase Hamilton left her with an itch to scratch.

"When he finds out anyway, he's liable to be upset with you for keeping it from him."

Phyllis had considered that. She knew Carolyn was right.

Sam might be angry . . . but that wouldn't last long, especially after Phyllis explained the promise she had made to Ronnie. To Phyllis's way of thinking, trying to find out more about Chase really was looking out for the girl's best interests.

Carolyn started to say something else, but Eve touched her on the arm and said, "Quiet, now." Sam came back into the room a moment later.

"What'd I miss?" he asked.

"Great hilarity and frolicking," Eve said.

Carolyn snorted.

Later, after she had gotten ready for bed, Phyllis went out into the hall and looked along it at Ronnie's room. A line of light showed under the door. Phyllis gave in to an impulse, went down there, and knocked softly.

"What?" Ronnie answered.

"May I come in for a minute?"

At first Phyllis thought Ronnie was going to ignore the request, but then she said, "I guess so."

Phyllis opened the door and stepped into the room. Vanessa had shipped some of Ronnie's things down here to Texas, so she had been able to make the spare bedroom look at least a little like it was hers. There were photos of the family, including one of Ronnie with her older brother Vincent that was recently taken at his college. A quilt covered the bed that her grandmother made for her, and on the quilt were two stuffed animals, a bear and a ragged long eared dog.

She was sitting on the bed with her iPad leaning against her propped-up knees. Looking over the top of the tablet, she asked, "Am I in trouble?"

Phyllis shook her head. "No."

"No more than I already was, right? I could tell by the way

Gramps was acting when he stopped to say good night a little while ago that you haven't said anything to him."

"I told you I wouldn't until I'd had a chance to think about it. I'm still thinking about it." Phyllis paused. "How much do you know about Chase Hamilton?"

"What? What do you mean, how much do I know about him? He's really nice, what else do I need to know?"

Phyllis shrugged and said, "Did he grow up around here? Do you know anything about his family?"

"It's not like we've really talked that much . . ."

"You don't know *anything* about him, do you? You have a crush on him, and that's all you needed to know."

Ronnie set the iPad aside and swung her legs off the bed. "You were a teenager once, weren't you, Mrs. Newsom?"

"Of course I was."

"I guess it was so long ago you don't remember what it was like."

"I wouldn't go so far as to say that," Phyllis said as she shook her head. "If you mean, do I remember what it felt like to fall madly in love with someone . . . or at least *think* that I had fallen madly in love with someone . . . of course I remember that, too. I know how it can fill your mind and make everything else seem unimportant. But a lot of things *are* still important. You have to try to be clear-headed about the other person, Ronnie."

"I knew you wouldn't understand. Go ahead and tell Gramps whatever you want. I can't stop you."

Phyllis could feel the hostility and resentment coming from Ronnie and knew it wouldn't do any good right now to talk about this. She just said, "I really am on your side, whether you believe it or not."

Ronnie just turned away. Phyllis stepped back out into the hall and eased the door closed.

That didn't accomplish a thing, she thought as she went back to her room. Like it or not, in the morning she would get it over with and tell Sam what had happened. Because she was convinced now that Ronnie wasn't going to keep her distance from Chase Hamilton, and Phyllis had an undeniable hunch that more trouble was waiting in the future for the girl because of that.

Before going to bed, she opened her laptop to search just a bit more for information. On a whim, she entered Chase's name as well as the name of the Pittsburgh suburb where Ronnie lived with her parents.

For the first time, one of the results she got made Phyllis draw in a sharp breath and lean toward the screen. It was a police report from a local newspaper up there, with several mug shots and descriptions of people who had been arrested in the past week.

There he was, clean-cut but still guilty looking, listed as Chase Hamilton, 18, a senior at the same high school Ronnie had attended.

And he had been arrested for possession of illegal drugs with intent to sell.

Chapter 7

After making that discovery, there was no possibility of falling asleep any time soon, so Phyllis continued searching. She was able to access criminal court records for the Pennsylvania county in which Chase had been arrested. She looked for a record of him standing trial or reaching some sort of plea deal, but she didn't find anything.

Did that mean the charges against the boy had been dismissed? Could he have been arrested by mistake and actually was innocent?

That might be true, but not necessarily. Plenty of charges were dropped for lack of evidence or unwillingness of witnesses to testify, and the person arrested was guilty as sin anyway. The lack of criminal proceedings didn't absolve Chase of wrongdoing at all.

But there was such a thing as innocent until proven guilty, Phyllis reminded herself. She didn't want to be unfair.

Still, there was one undeniable fact: Chase Hamilton was from the same town where Ronnie had lived until recently.

Phyllis quickly double-checked something. Just as she'd suspected, the school district there had only one high school. That meant Ronnie and Chase both would have attended it. And yet Ronnie had acted as if she had never met Chase before coming to Weatherford.

Had they been a couple in Pennsylvania? Was *Chase* the real reason Ronnie had left home and come to Texas? She could have followed him down here. Would having a crush on him have driven Ronnie to such extreme measures?

Where teenage passion was concerned, who was to say what was possible? After all, there was a good reason why Shakespeare had written about Romeo and Juliet and found such dramatic possibilities in their doomed love affair, Phyllis reminded herself.

"The more things change . . ." she murmured, remembering what she had said to Sam that very morning.

She resumed searching, this time looking for anything involving that Pennsylvania high school and drug dealing.

A few more links to newspaper stories came up. Phyllis checked them out and saw that the previous spring, two 18-year-olds, Jonathan McKimmey and Richard Fleischman, had been convicted of possession of controlled substances with intent to sell and had been sentenced to prison terms. Both of them had been seniors at the same high school Ronnie and Chase had attended.

Chase was 18 at the time of his arrest, Phyllis recalled. Since he'd been a senior in Pennsylvania, clearly he hadn't graduated, or else he wouldn't be going to Courtland High School here in Texas. Being in jail probably would have a pretty bad effect on someone's academic career, she mused.

She laid out the scenario in her mind: Chase is arrested, isn't prosecuted for some reason, leaves Pennsylvania, and comes to Texas. Ronnie, convinced that she's in love with

him, follows him. That Chase would wind up in the same
town where Ronnie's grandfather lived seemed like quite a
coincidence, Phyllis thought, but it certainly wasn't beyond
the realm of possibility. If Chase had moved somewhere else,
Dallas or Houston, say, Ronnie might not have pursued him.
But if she'd found out that he was in Weatherford, that might
have seemed like an omen to her, a clear indication that she
should go there, too, and proclaim her love for him.

The biggest question remained: Had Chase come down
here and resumed his drug dealing ways at his new school?

Phyllis had no idea . . . but she knew someone who might
be able to tell her.

"Mornin', Mom," Phyllis's son Mike greeted her when she
called him early the next morning, before she started getting
ready to go to school. She knew that he would be up, since
his household would be on school time now as well. Her
grandson Bobby had started kindergarten this year.

"Is this a bad time?" she asked.

"Nope. Bob's eating breakfast, and my shift doesn't start
for a couple of hours. How are you? Nothing wrong, is
there?"

"No, not really. I just need to ask you a question."

"Shoot."

"What do you know about the drug situation at Courtland
High?"

Several seconds of silence went by at the other end of the
connection. Then Mike said, "No, I think the question is,
what do *you* know about the drug situation at the high
school? Because you wouldn't call me and bring that up if
something wasn't going on."

Phyllis was sitting at the small desk in her bedroom where

her laptop was. She rubbed her forehead for a second before saying, "Sam is going to be annoyed with me when he finds out I told so many other people before I told him, but something happened yesterday involving his granddaughter."

"Ronnie?" Mike said. "Wait a minute. She's a good kid, isn't she? I thought so when I met her and the times I've been around her since then. She wouldn't be mixed up with drugs."

"I wouldn't have thought so, either, but yesterday . . ."

She filled him in on what had happened. When she was finished, Mike asked, "What's the name of this security guard, the one who told you the boy was running with the drug dealers?"

"Ray Brooks."

"Hmm. Doesn't ring a bell. Some of those guys are former cops. I thought he might have worked for the PD or the sheriff's department, but I don't recognize the name. Of course, I don't know everybody who ever carried a badge around here."

"Do you think he might be right?"

"He'd be in a position to know," Mike said. "On the other hand, being a security guard is just like any other job—some of the people who do it are clueless."

"Well . . . my concern isn't based *entirely* on what Mr. Brooks told me."

Again, Mike was silent for a moment. Then he said, "What have you done, Mom?"

"I just searched some on the Internet," Phyllis said, trying not to sound defensive. In the past, Mike hadn't cared much for the way she poked her nose into murder investigations . . . especially since the time one of those cases had landed *her* in jail, charged with obstruction of justice. Despite that, however, it hadn't been very long ago that he had come to her and asked her to look into a murder case in which one of his old high school friends had been convicted. At least that one hadn't been an active investigation.

"What did you find?"

"The boy Ronnie was with, Chase Hamilton, was arrested for possession with intent, up in Pennsylvania in the same town where Ronnie and her parents live."

"You mean she knew him up there?"

"She must have. Although the school is big enough, with enough students, that I'm sure not everyone there knows everybody else. Still, it's a big enough coincidence that Chase wound up here in Weatherford, where Ronnie's grandfather lives. If there wasn't *some* previous connection between the two of them . . . no, that's just too much to swallow."

"I agree." Mike paused. "You told me one time that Ronnie came down here because she'd been having trouble with her parents."

"That's true. Vanessa and Phil said her behavior has been erratic over the past year, and she was hard to get along with."

"I hate to say this, but that sure sounds like she might be using."

"Or she's madly in love with this boy and out of her head because of that."

"Or both," Mike said. "You found something online about him being arrested? What happened with that?"

"I don't know. Two more boys from the same high school were convicted on the same charge and sent to prison. But there's no record that Chase ever went to trial."

Mike grunted. "The DA up there probably kicked the case for some reason. And the kid figured it would be a good idea for him to get out of town before they nailed him for something else."

"That sounds reasonable. But why Weatherford?"

The silence on the other end told Phyllis that her son was thinking about the question. After a few moments, he said, "If there was something going on between him and Ronnie up there, she might have told him about the little town down in Texas where her grandfather lives. She probably made Weatherford sound so sleepy and peaceful that the guy thought it was Mayberry or something, and all the cops would be like Barney Fife. That might have sounded like a tempting set-up to him."

"Weatherford hasn't been anything like Mayberry for at least thirty years," Phyllis said. "More's the pity, I think sometimes."

"Yeah, but it might sound like that to somebody up in one of those northeastern suburbs. They think we're all hicks down here, anyway."

"We got sidetracked," Phyllis said. "You still haven't told me what the drug situation is like at the high school."

"Not good," Mike told her. "You know Courtland's outside the city limits, so we handle things there, not the Weatherford PD. I've heard some of the guys who work Narcotics say that quite a bit of dealing goes on at the school. I mean, it's not like they're selling it openly in the parking lot or the cafeteria, but deals get done. Mostly weed, but some of the harder stuff, too. You want me to see what I can find out?"

"Could you do that without violating any sort of protocol?"

"I think so. I have a couple of buddies who work that detail. I'll ask around. The kid's name is Chase Hamilton, you said?"

"That's right."

"But you'd just as soon I kept Ronnie's name out of it, I imagine."

"Well . . . if you can do that."

"Of course," Mike said. "I'll call you later."

"I really appreciate it." The grandmother in Phyllis replaced the detective. "How does Bobby like kindergarten so far?"

"He loves it. His teacher's great, he gets along with the other kids, and you know he's smart and enjoys learning."

"Of course he does," Phyllis said without hesitation. "He's my grandson, isn't he?"

Mike laughed. "I'm not sure how much Sarah cares for it, though. She's sort of at loose ends with Bobby gone all day. He went to pre-school last year, of course, but that was only half a day and it's not really the same."

"The two of you could always have another baby, you know. I'm sure Bobby would love to have a little brother or sister, and I can certainly use another grandchild."

That suggestion brought another laugh from Mike. "To tell the truth, we've been thinking about it. But don't get your hopes up just yet. Having a kid means a lot of time and trouble, not to mention worry and heartbreak. Not all kids are as easy to raise and wonderful as I was, you know."

Now it was Phyllis's turn to laugh.

Chapter 8

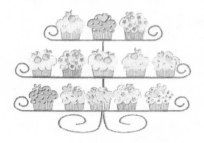

Phyllis enjoyed talking to her son, even though the subject of the conversation was mostly serious, but by the time she got downstairs for breakfast her mood was solemn again.

Ronnie had made it down first today, which was a little unusual, and was dressed and sitting at the table drinking a cup of coffee and eating a bagel. Looking at her, despite the blue hair, Phyllis could see the sweet and innocent girl she knew Ronnie was. *Hoped* Ronnie was. For Ronnie's own sake as well as Sam's.

But a lot of unanswered questions had cropped up, abruptly and unexpectedly, and they didn't paint a very good picture.

"Was Carolyn down earlier?" Phyllis asked.

Without looking up, Ronnie shook her head. "Nope. Haven't seen her this morning. I made the coffee. I hope that's all right."

"Of course it is. Thank you. Feel free to do anything in this kitchen you want to."

"Well, maybe not *anything*, right?" Ronnie said.

She had a faintly goading edge to her voice, but Phyllis didn't rise to the bait. Instead she said calmly, "You know what I mean. I'd love to see what kind of cook you are."

The moment the words were out of her mouth, she thought about a TV show they had watched and remembered that people who made methamphetamines were called "cooks". That wasn't what she had meant, of course, but at this point, elaborating on what she had said might make things even more awkward.

Ronnie didn't seem to have taken it the wrong way, because she said, "I'm not much of one, I'm afraid. My mom tried to teach me some, but I don't have the knack for it."

"Anybody can learn to cook," Phyllis said. "It's just a matter of practice . . . and a willingness to try new things and not be upset if they don't work out."

"Yeah, I bet you never had to worry about that. You've won awards and stuff. Everything you've ever made has probably turned out perfect the first time."

Phyllis chuckled. "As your grandfather would say, quoting John Wayne, not hardly. And please don't ask who that is."

"I know who John Wayne was," Ronnie said.

"Good. If you didn't, it might break poor Sam's heart."

He came into the kitchen a moment later and said, "My ears are burnin'. Are you ladies talkin' about me?"

"Not really," Phyllis said. "I was just explaining to Ronnie that not everything I've cooked has been good."

"I don't know about that," Sam said. "I've lived here a good number of years now, and I don't recall ever eatin' anything in this house that wasn't good."

"Yes, but you're biased, and I cooked for a long, long time before I ever met you, Sam Fletcher."

"I reckon that's true." He filled a cup with coffee, doctored it to his taste, and took a sip. "That's mighty good."

"Thank you," Ronnie said.

"You made it?"

"I did."

Sam looked around carefully, then said, "Don't tell Carolyn, but I think yours might be just a smidge better."

"I won't say anything," Ronnie promised, then glanced at Phyllis as if what she'd just said reminded her of the promise Phyllis made.

Phyllis kept her face expressionless as she poured her own cup of coffee. With everything she had found out so far, and the prospect of finding out more from Mike, she wasn't going to say anything to Sam until she had a more complete picture of the circumstances in her head.

Sam was in a good mood this morning, as usual. While he was eating breakfast, he said to Ronnie, "I'll make you a deal. Come to that dance at the school next week, and I'll pretend I don't know you the whole evening. You won't have your ol' grampaw crampin' your style."

"I never worried about that," Ronnie said. "I'm proud that you're my grandfather. I'm just not much on dances, that's all."

"You might make some new friends," Phyllis said. "You haven't been here that long. There must be a lot of kids your age you haven't met yet."

Ronnie frowned, and for a moment Phyllis thought the girl was going to argue with her. Then Ronnie seemed to remember what had happened the day before, and the knowledge that Phyllis held over her head, and she forced a faint smile onto her face and said, "I suppose I can think about it."

"I'd sure like it if you went," Sam said. "Not that I'm puttin' any pressure on you, you understand."

"Not hardly," Ronnie said with a smile. Sam's face lit up at hearing one of his favorite quotes, and in that moment, Phyllis hoped fervently that all her suspicions about Ronnie were wrong.

She was in the middle of her third period Pre-AP American History class when the phone in her pocket vibrated to let her know she had gotten a message. She waited until the students were busy doing a review paper to check it. Phyllis couldn't keep her eyebrows from rising slightly as she saw that the message was from Mike and asked her to call him as soon as it was convenient for her.

There was nothing about the message to indicate that it was urgent, but knowing what Mike had been looking into for her—plus the quickness with which he had gotten back in touch with her—made Phyllis anxious to find out what he had discovered. She felt like she had to wait, though, until this class was over. Then she could call Mike during the passing period between classes.

He answered his cell phone right away when she called. "Is this a good time?" she asked. "I know you're on duty."

"So are you, so to speak," he said. "But yeah, this is fine, there's nothing going on right now. I have to testify in a traffic case this afternoon, so I'm at my desk, typing up some notes for that. I reached out to those buddies of mine like I told you, and I also did some digging into that case up in Pennsylvania." He lowered his voice a little. "I might not have done this if it hadn't been Sam's granddaughter who's involved."

"I know what you mean," Phyllis said. "But it is. What did you find out?"

"Let's start with the Pennsylvania stuff. Chase Hamilton

and those other two guy you mentioned, McKimmey and Fleischman, were picked up for being the leaders of a ring supplying all kinds of drugs to the kids in their high school. McKimmey and Fleischman were also charged initially with assault and attempted murder because some competitor of theirs got his car shot up—with him in it."

"Oh, dear," Phyllis murmured.

"The other kid wasn't killed, and eventually those charges were dropped. Either the cops up there couldn't make the case, or else it went away as part of some plea deal. They wound up going away just for possession with intent."

"But Chase wasn't suspected of being involved with the shooting?"

"Not as far as I could determine," Mike said.

"What about the charges against him?"

"Dismissed. Don't know why. I'd have to call the DA's office up there and ask them, and I don't know if they'd tell me. Probably not. But Hamilton walked and, I guess, kept walking, because he seemed to drop off the face of the earth up there. He didn't go back to school and finish out his senior year."

"That's why he's going to school down here," Phyllis said. "Well, it's encouraging, I suppose, that he wants to finish his education."

"Or he wants to set up the same sort of operation here that he had in Pennsylvania," Mike said. "Even though Courtland is a new school and the school year hasn't been going on for all that long, there have been quite a few arrests for possession already. Not *on* the school campus, mind you. Away from there. But kids who go to school there are getting picked up with drugs on them. They're getting them some-where, and chances are that it's at school."

"Oh, I hate to hear that." Students had been coming into

the classroom for the next period while Phyllis was talking to Mike, and as she looked at them, she couldn't help but wonder which of them might have drugs on them at that very moment. She wasn't sure whether to feel sorry for them or be afraid of them. Things had changed so much since she was young and the most daring thing anybody did was sneak over the county line to buy a six-pack of beer.

"Don't worry, you're not in any danger. It's not like gang warfare is about to break out or anything."

"But what about Ronnie? If she's involved with one of the leaders, isn't *she* potentially in danger?"

Mike didn't say anything. Phyllis knew her son well enough to know that he was probably frowning right now.

After a moment he said, "You want me to have a talk with her? You know, somebody closer to her own age—"

"You're a man in your thirties with a wife and child. Not only that, you're a deputy sheriff. She might not think you're *quite* as ancient as Sam and me, but she's not going to consider you as anywhere near her contemporary."

He sighed and said, "Yeah, you're right about that. Look, I need to get back to work, but I'll dig deeper into this later. There may not be anything else to find, though."

"I appreciate that. And the bell's about to ring here, so . . ."

"Talk to you later, Mom."

Phyllis had been keeping her voice low enough that the students in the room couldn't hear her over the hubbub of their own chatter. But some of the more observant ones had noticed she was talking on the phone, and they must have recognized the look of concern on her face. A girl who sat near the front of the room asked, "Are you all right, Mrs. Newsom?"

Phyllis smiled and said, "Yes, dear, I'm fine." The bell rang, signaling the beginning of fourth period. "Now, I believe we were talking about the French and Indian War—"

A different girl said, "Shouldn't we call it the French and Native American War? Or the French and Indigenous Peoples War? Just because previous generations—and the textbook—used racist, derogatory terms, that's no reason we should."

"You can't blame the Indians for fighting the French, though," a boy said. "I mean, look how rude they are."

"The Indians?"

"No, the French!"

And this was a Pre-AP class, Phyllis thought. She had her work cut out for her.

Chapter 9

Phyllis's schedule called for her to have lunch at the end of fourth period. Technically it was still part of that period, but her class was over, which was good. When she taught in junior high, they had only A Lunch and B Lunch, so everyone had a complete class either before or after the midday meal. Enough students attended Courtland that three lunch periods were required, which meant dividing some classes in the middle, something that as a teacher Phyllis wouldn't have liked at all. It was difficult enough getting the students to settle down and concentrate once at the beginning of class; having to do that twice in the same period would be an even bigger chore.

She happened to know that Ronnie had C Lunch as well, so as she walked toward the faculty table with her tray, she scanned the heads of the teenagers sitting at the tables, searching for the girl's bright blue hair. She didn't spot Ronnie anywhere in the cafeteria.

She saw a familiar face at one of the tables. The day before, her eyes would have passed right over the dark-haired young man without any real notice. Today she recognized Chase Hamilton right away.

The table where he sat was full, but at first glance Phyllis didn't know any of the students, which meant they weren't in any of her classes. She always tried not to judge, but most of them, boys and girls alike, had a rough look about them, she thought. She knew that wasn't fair, but it was her impression.

Influenced, maybe, by what she had learned about Chase, she reminded herself.

"Hi, Phyllis." The cheerful voice distracted her. She looked around and saw Amber Trahearne sitting at the faculty table. The attractive young math teacher motioned to the empty space beside her. Phyllis didn't see any graceful way of refusing the invitation, and anyway, there was no reason to, other than the fact that Amber's perky attitude sometimes could be a little too much.

Phyllis set her tray on the table and said, "Hello."

"How are you doing today?"

"All right, I think." Phyllis wasn't, not really, but she wasn't going to share that with Amber.

"And how was Sam this morning?"

"I'm surprised he didn't tell you himself."

"Oh, I haven't seen him," Amber said with a casual wave of her hand. "Busy, busy, busy. Me, not him, although I assume he is, too. I saw him eating lunch at his desk when I came down here. Looked like he had a pile of papers to grade."

Phyllis hadn't expected to see Sam in the cafeteria today, in fact, because she had packed that lunch for him. Amber's assumption was right; Sam was trying not to fall behind on his grading.

"He seemed fine when I saw him," Phyllis said.

"Is he looking forward to the dance next week?"

"I think so."

"Frances told me you're going to be providing some of the snacks," Amber said. "I'm really looking forward to that. I've heard so much about what a great baker and cook you are."

"From Sam, you mean?"

"Well, of course! He brags on you all the time. Which makes sense considering that the two of you live together."

"Sam rents a room in my house," Phyllis said, trying not to sound stiff about it but not sure she succeeded.

"Sure, that's what I meant," Amber said. Phyllis wasn't sure she was being completely sincere, though. Maybe Amber was trying to find out just exactly what the relationship between Phyllis and Sam really was.

None of her business, that's what it was, Phyllis thought.

A change of subject was in order here, she decided. She asked, "Do you have a boy named Chase Hamilton in any of your classes?"

Amber frowned a little and looked puzzled. "As a matter of fact, I don't. All I teach are AP and Pre-AP level courses, and I'm not sure he'd be up to that. But he *is* in my home room, so I know who he is. Why do you ask?"

"Oh, it's nothing important," Phyllis replied with a shake of her head. "Sam's granddaughter said something about knowing him, and I just wondered what sort of boy he was."

"I couldn't really say. The school year's not that old, and I don't see him all that often. Would you like me to ask some of his teachers about him?"

"Oh, no, not at all. Like I said, it's not that important. I was just curious, that's all. Since there's the connection with Sam's granddaughter."

"And Sam rents a room in your house," Amber said.

"That's right."

Before Phyllis could say anything else, she was distracted by the feeling that someone was watching her. She turned her head and looked across the cafeteria. Ray Brooks stood beside the far wall with his shoulders leaned against it and his arms crossed over his chest. He wasn't exactly glaring in her direction, but he was certainly looking intently toward her.

Phyllis wasn't the only one to notice. Amber leaned toward her and said quietly, "He's kind of a creepy guy, isn't he?"

"You mean Mr. Brooks?" Phyllis said, even though she wasn't sure who else Amber might be talking about.

"Yeah. Look at him, scuttling away like a cockroach."

It was true that the security guard had straightened up and was walking out of the cafeteria. He wasn't scuttling, really, Phyllis thought, but he wasn't wasting any time, either. And he had reacted right after Phyllis had noticed that he was staring at her. Maybe he was embarrassed at being caught. Or maybe he just didn't want to provoke her into lodging a complaint about him with Principal Shula.

Another teacher came up then, sat down next to Amber, and began talking to her, so Phyllis was left to finish eating her lunch. Today she had crispy chicken tacos, baby carrots, and an apple with a glass of water.

A few minutes were still left in the lunch period when she saw Chase get up and leave the table where he had been sitting. He walked out of the cafeteria by himself.

Acting on a whim, and since she was finished anyway, Phyllis got up and followed him.

Chase walked past the floor-to-ceiling glass walls of the library toward a side corridor that led left to a classroom wing and right to the gym. He didn't so much as glance behind him, or he would have seen Phyllis, who figured she was at least fifty years too old to be skulking.

But she surprised herself by suddenly stepping behind a brick pillar when she spotted a flash of bright blue up ahead at the corner of the right-hand corridor. Ronnie was there. She said something to Chase, and then both of them disappeared around that corner.

Phyllis knew there were no classrooms along there, only a janitor's closet and the double doors at the end of the hall leading into the gym. It wasn't quite as private an alcove as the one where Ronnie and Chase had been the previous afternoon, but they could spend a few minutes there without much risk of being seen.

Phyllis started to turn away and head back to her classroom. If she tried again to interfere in Ronnie's life, she stood a good chance of making the situation worse.

On the other hand, she would never forgive herself if something happened to Sam's only grandchild and she could have prevented it somehow.

With that thought in her mind, she moved closer to the corner, being careful not to make too much noise as she walked.

When she could hear their voices, she slowed even more. In the past, she had been accused of meddling, of being a nosy busybody, and now she was about to add eavesdropping on a couple of teenagers to the list. Her concern for Ronnie overrode anything else, though, so she eased up to the corner, where she was out of sight but could hear what was going on.

"—got to cut this out, Ronnie," Chase was saying.

"But why?" she demanded. "Why deny what's going on between us?"

"Because there's nothing going on!" Chase sounded frustrated, even a little exasperated. "Look, I know what you think happened up there at home, but you're wrong."

At least they weren't making a drug deal, Phyllis thought, but she wasn't sure she understood what they were talking about.

"But Chase, you wouldn't have done what you did if you didn't care about me," Ronnie insisted.

If nothing else, this exchange confirmed that Ronnie and Chase *had* known each other in Pennsylvania.

"Sure I would have." Chase's voice hardened as he added, "I just felt sorry for you, that's all."

"You . . . felt sorry for me?"

Phyllis wanted to wince at the pain she heard in Ronnie's words.

"That's right. I mean . . . you're a good kid. Why wouldn't I want to give you a hand?"

"A kid," Ronnie repeated, still sounding miserable. "That's all I am to you? I'm a junior and you're a senior—"

"Yeah, but you know there were two grades difference between us before. I just didn't graduate, that's all."

"Two whole years," Ronnie said bitterly. "Are you really trying to tell me that's enough to matter?"

"That and the fact that I'm not your boyfriend. I never was."

Evidently Ronnie had been telling the truth about her being the one to pursue him. Given what Phyllis was hearing now, she had no trouble believing that Ronnie was the one who had initiated the kiss the day before, when Ray Brooks had caught them. Chase hadn't put a stop to it right away, but Phyllis supposed she couldn't blame him for that. What young man would object too much to being kissed by a pretty girl?

"You're horrible," Ronnie said.

"That's what I've been trying to tell you."

"I . . . I can't believe that I thought you really cared about me."

"I did care about you. Just not the way you convinced yourself I did. If I ever led you on, Ronnie, I'm sorry."

"Go to hell," she muttered.

Phyllis heard footsteps and turned to retreat toward the library. She reached the entrance and had one of the doors partially open by the time Ronnie hurried past behind her. Phyllis looked back over her shoulder and caught the girl's eye as if she had just been going into the library. Ronnie slowed for a second and Phyllis said her name, but then Ronnie hurried on, saying, "I've got to get to class."

So did Phyllis, but as she let the library door close without going in, she saw Chase come around the corner from the corridor where he had been talking to Ronnie.

If she was going to have a reputation as a meddler and a busybody, she might as well justify it, she told herself. She moved to intercept Chase, and when he stopped rather than run into her, she said, "Mr. Hamilton, I'd like to talk to you . . . in private."

He frowned. "You're not one of my teachers, Mrs. Newsom."

"No, but Ronnie is the granddaughter of my best friend. That's how I'm talking to you now, as Ronnie's friend, rather than a teacher."

He seemed to be thinking about it for a second, and then he drew in a deep breath and said, "Sure, I understand. Maybe it would be a good idea. Maybe you can talk some sense into the girl's head!"

"Give me a good reason to, and I'll try," Phyllis promised. "Let's go around the corner there, and you can tell me what's really going on."

Chapter 10

Phyllis checked the time as she and Chase stepped into the short hallway leading to the gym. She had only a few minutes before she would need to head back to her classroom, but what she was doing here might be important, too.

"How much has Ronnie told you about what happened up in Pennsylvania?" Chase asked.

"Not a lot," Phyllis answered, deliberately being vague.

"She never said anything about the two of us going to the same school up there?"

Phyllis raised an eyebrow in feigned surprise. She couldn't admit she already knew about that without telling Chase she'd been looking into his background, and she didn't want to do that. If he knew, he might decide not to tell her anything.

"She made it sound just the opposite, in fact, as if she didn't know you until she came down here."

"Yeah, well, that's not true. We weren't close or anything, but we knew each other up there. We were in a couple of classes together. I never really paid much attention to her, though, until that business with Shelby Vance started."

Now he was talking about something Phyllis actually knew nothing about. She hadn't run across the name Shelby Vance when she was searching for information about Chase on the Internet.

So she was sincere when she asked, "Who's Shelby Vance?"

"The most popular girl in school. And the head mean girl."

Over the years of teaching junior high, Phyllis had seen plenty of "most popular" girls. The cheerleaders. The athletes. The rich girls. The ones who had developed physically earlier than their peers.

Unlike the stereotypes found so often in movies and TV shows, many of those girls were smart, sweet, and genuinely nice young people. Some weren't, of course—enough so to give rise to that stereotype. According to what Chase was saying, Shelby Vance fit into that category.

"What's the connection between this Vance girl and Ronnie?" Phyllis asked.

"None at first. I mean, they moved in completely different circles. But then Shelby noticed Ronnie one day, and she decided to have some fun."

"But it wasn't fun for Ronnie," Phyllis guessed.

Chase shook his head. "You know how she is. She likes being an outsider, being different. It's not just her hair, it's her whole attitude, the way she considered herself apart from most of the people in school. And that comes across as looking down on them. It's like a red flag to a girl like Shelby, who has to feel like she's better than everybody else or her whole concept of herself collapses. She started making fun of Ronnie, and of course all her friends had to follow suit, and suddenly it was like Shelby was running this whole campaign of terror against Ronnie, not just at school but on social media and other places in town, wherever their paths happened to cross."

"You're saying Ronnie was bullied."

"Yeah, big time."

"I never heard anything about this. Did she tell her parents or any of her teachers?"

Chase scoffed and shook his head. "Ronnie's not the type who runs to some authority figure for help. She tried to deal with it herself. She asked Shelby to leave her alone. Of course, that didn't do a bit of good."

"It might have even made things worse," Phyllis mused.

"Yeah, maybe. Anyway, I kind of knew what was going on, but I didn't really pay much attention to it. I mean, Ronnie didn't run in my crowd or anything."

Your crowd of drug dealers, Phyllis thought, but she kept that to herself since Chase seemed to be opening up to her.

"Then Jerry Plemmons and his buddies started harassing her."

"Who?"

"Plemmons was Shelby Vance's boyfriend," Chase said. "If Shelby was the mean girl stereotype, then Plemmons was the dumb jock. Not really dumb, mind you, but he acted like it sometimes. And of course he did whatever Shelby told him to do. He and his friends started pushing Ronnie around. A couple of her guy friends tried to stand up for her, but they were, well . . ."

"Weirdos like her," Phyllis guessed.

Chase grunted. "Yeah. I probably wouldn't have thought of that word, but it's a good one. They got beat up, and that was the last time anybody tried to defend Ronnie."

"Until you got fed up with it and stepped in." It was a

guess on Phyllis's part, but given everything she knew, where else could this story be leading?

"That's right. I told Plemmons to back off and take his buddies with him, and he figured he'd whip me like he whipped those other guys."

"I suppose it didn't work out that way," Phyllis said, shaking her head.

"Not quite. I didn't hurt him enough to put him in the hospital, but he woke up sore and shaking for a week, I'll bet." Chase smiled a little, as if the memory was a fond one. "That was enough of a message for everybody else to decide it would be a good idea if they left Ronnie alone. It would have been fine with me if she had never heard about what happened—"

"But she did, and you were her hero," Phyllis said. "Her knight in shining armor. She would never think of it in those terms, but that was the way she felt."

"I guess. I wouldn't think of it like that, either." A wry laugh came from Chase. "Nobody ever considered me any kind of a hero before."

It was hard to be heroic when you were selling drugs and ruining other people's lives, Phyllis thought. But at the same time, she couldn't help but feel a small surge of gratitude that Chase had stepped in and put a stop to the bullying that targeted Ronnie as its victim.

"After that, some other things happened that didn't have anything to do with Ronnie, and I wound up leaving town," Chase went on. "But before I left, she made it pretty clear she had a crush on me, and she talked about how the two of us ought to run away together and come down here to Texas where her grandfather lived. She claimed we were meant to be together. I didn't believe that, of course. I didn't fall for her or anything. I just tried to help out a kid who was—and

no offense here—kind of pathetic. That's all." He shrugged.
"When I decided to leave town, I remembered her talking
about Weatherford. She made it sound like a pretty nice
place. So I thought I'd give it a try. Hey, it's a long way from
Pennsylvania."

"It never occurred to you that she might run away and follow you down here?"

"I swear to you it didn't, Mrs. Newsom." His expression
hardened. "The last thing I wanted was any of my trouble
from up there following me down here."

Phyllis could easily imagine that, considering how much of
his trouble had been with the law.

He seemed sincere, though, and she decided that she believed him . . . for now. She would keep an open mind,
though, and open eyes, as well, for anything that might con-
tradict what he had told her.

And none of his story, even if it was completely true,
meant that he wasn't dealing drugs here at Courtland High
School. Maybe he had some decency left in his character that
had led him to defend Ronnie. Phyllis was grateful for that. It
didn't absolve him of his wrongdoing.

But neither was it her job to bring drug dealers to justice.
The law would take care of that, as best it could. Her only
real goal was to keep Ronnie from being hurt.

"If you're telling me the truth about not having any . . .
romantic feelings . . . for Ronnie, I hope you'll continue
trying to discourage her."

"That's exactly what I want to do, and as far as I'm concerned, you can discourage her, too. It won't offend me. Like
I told you, I wish you'd try to talk some sense into her head."

"I intend to," Phyllis said. "In the meantime, you can keep
your distance from her."

"Yeah, believe me, that's not always easy to do. She keeps

ambushing me."

"Try," Phyllis said, and before she could add anything else, the bell rang for the end of C Lunch and the beginning of the passing period. She started to turn away, but she paused to say, "Thank you . . . for what you did for her."

"She's a good kid. She didn't deserve the crappy way they were treating her. I'd say that she ought to try to blend in more, but that just wouldn't be Ronnie, would it?"

"No," Phyllis said. "I don't suppose it would."

By the time Phyllis got there, all the students were in the classroom, waiting for fifth period to begin. She had to put everything that was going on with Ronnie and Chase out of her thoughts and concentrate on the lessons she needed to teach that afternoon.

When classes were over for the day, though, she allowed herself to think once more about the dilemma facing her. Sam still didn't know anything about what had happened. Phyllis had uncovered a great deal in the past twenty-four hours, and she could share all of it with him. She was sure he would be very interested, especially because the bullying Ronnie had undergone in Pennsylvania went a long way toward explaining her behavior problems over the past year. The girl had kept it all to herself, unwilling to share the burden with her parents. That was admirable in a way . . . but probably not very wise.

Even though Sam and his daughter and son-in-law probably would be upset to learn the truth, it might be a relief as well. At least they would know Ronnie hadn't been using drugs.

But then, as Phyllis sat at the desk in the now empty classroom and frowned, she realized that she *didn't* know that.

Everything Chase had told her could be absolutely true, and none of it eliminated the possibility of Ronnie having a drug problem. Phyllis closed her eyes, raised a hand to her temple, and moaned slightly.

"What's wrong? Got a headache?"

Sam's voice, speaking unexpectedly from the doorway, made her give a little start and jerk her head up. "What?" she said, then realized what he'd asked and went on, "No, I'm fine. Nothing at all to worry about. It was just a long day, that's all."

"Most of 'em are. And yet when you get to be our age, time seems to shoot by so fast."

"Yes, that's a paradox, isn't it?" Phyllis started gathering up the papers stacked in various places around the desk. This was Friday afternoon, and she'd have some grading to do over the weekend. But at least she didn't have to get all of it done by the next morning.

"One week until the Friday the Thirteenth dance, too," Sam said, reminding Phyllis that she probably should do some recipe experimenting over the weekend, to go along with the grading. "Still lookin' forward to it?"

"Of course," she said. "I'm not really superstitious. I hope Friday the Thirteenth turns out lucky for all of us."

Chapter 11

Phyllis set the plate of cookies on the kitchen table in front of Sam, Carolyn, and Eve and asked, "What do you think?"

Carolyn leaned forward, studied the cookies, and frowned. "There's something about them," she said. "That white icing, with the drops of red icing scattered around . . . it reminds me of something, but I can't think of what . . ."

"Blood!" Eve suddenly exclaimed. "Blood on the snow! That's the title of something, isn't it? Some mystery novel?"

"I don't know about that," Phyllis said, "but I call these killer sugar cookies. That's supposed to be blood."

Sam laughed. "When did you get so vicious? This is the way some of those Eighties horror movies started, and I didn't think you liked those."

"Well, I don't," Phyllis said. "But this is what I thought of when people kept talking about Friday the Thirteenth."

"Is that the one with the killer in the hockey mask?"

"I wouldn't know. I'm also doing chocolate mint brownies

decorated like black cats."

Eve said, "That's Halloween, isn't it?"

Sam said, *"That's* the one with the guy in the hockey mask!"

"Friday the Thirteenth is bad luck, and so are black cats," Phyllis said. "Supposedly. All the black cats I've ever known were very sweet."

She looked down at Raven, who was rubbing around her ankles.

Carolyn pointed at the cookies and said, "You can't serve these gruesome things at a school dance."

"I know. Frances Macmillan and I have already talked about that. I'll make plain sugar cookies for the dance. But I had this idea in my head and wanted to see how they would look and taste. So . . ."

Phyllis waved a hand at the plate in invitation.

"Thought you'd never ask," Sam said with a grin. He reached out and plucked two of the cookies from the plate.

Carolyn and Eve each took a cookie, as well. Carolyn had been trying to avoid foods with gluten in them, but recently she had been sticking more to a low-gluten, rather than a completely gluten-free, diet. She had found that eating a small amount of foods with wheat in them wasn't enough to make her arthritis flare up.

"That's mighty good," Sam said when he had eaten one of the cookies. "Aren't you gonna try 'em, Phyllis?"

She laughed. "I ate two when they were fresh out of the oven, as soon as I put the icing on them. I think they're good, too, but it's always nice to have other people agree. Of course, other than the icing they're just plain sugar cookies—"

"Nothing wrong with that," Sam declared.

"I'll second that," Eve said. "These are excellent."

"Very good," Carolyn admitted. "But I still think the

bloody icing is a bit much."

"You know what they say," Sam said. "If you're goin' over the top anyway, you might as well go way over."

"I never heard anybody say that in my life," Carolyn said.

"Well, now you have."

Eve said, "We don't have to wait until Friday the Thirteenth for the chocolate mint cat brownies, do we?"

Phyllis laughed and shook her head. "No, I thought I'd bake those tomorrow."

"Good," Sam said. "That'll give us time to finish off these cookies first."

That was on Saturday afternoon. Phyllis had been waiting all day for a good opportunity to present itself for her to talk to Sam about Ronnie, Chase Hamilton, and everything that had happened in Pennsylvania. So far that hadn't happened.

On Sunday morning, she baked the black cat brownies, and the rich, wonderful aroma of chocolate filled the house. That put Sam in a good mood to start with, and the brownies themselves, which everyone thought were delicious, only helped matters. Throw in a victory that afternoon by the Dallas Cowboys, and Sam was positively mellow that evening.

Now or never, Phyllis thought as she approached him after supper. Carolyn, Eve, and Ronnie were all upstairs, so Sam was alone in the living room except for Raven. He sat on the sofa with a Western paperback in one hand and the other hand rubbing Raven's ears as the cat lay curled up in his lap. He smiled as Phyllis sat down beside him. Their shoulders and hips touched companionably.

"Well, this was a pretty good day," he said as he lowered the book.

"I hope you still think so in a few minutes," Phyllis said.

A wary look appeared on Sam's face. "You sound like you've got some bad news to tell me," he said.

"It's not necessarily bad news. But it's news, I guess you could say. It has to do with Ronnie."

Sam stopped petting the cat. He picked up his bookmark, inserted it in the pages, and set the book aside. His expression was solemn as he said, "I'm listenin'."

"A few days ago—last Thursday, it was—when I was leaving the school that afternoon, I saw Ronnie outside."

"She rode home with you that afternoon, didn't she?"

"Yes, but this wasn't in the parking lot. She was in one of those little alcoves behind the gym where there's a service entrance. And she wasn't alone."

Sam's eyebrows, which were a little on the bushy side to start with, became more prominent as they lowered in a frown. "You're fixin' to tell me she was there with some boy, makin' out."

Phyllis couldn't contain her surprised reaction. "How did you know?"

"I didn't know, but it's easy enough to guess where you were goin' with that. And I can't say I'm all that surprised, either. Isn't that what teenagers do?"

Eve had made pretty much the same comment, although Phyllis wasn't going to mention that. She didn't want to tell Sam that she had discussed the matter with Carolyn and Eve before she said anything to him about it.

"I suppose that's right."

"She needs to be careful and not get carried away, of course. I know things are different now than when we were kids and they think they ought to get away with a lot more than we did, but there are still consequences if you make a mistake. Did you know the boy?"

"Not really, but I found out who he is. Ray Brooks caught them at it and threatened to get them in trouble. He told me about the boy."

"Brooks? The security guard?"

"That's right."

"Ronnie didn't get written up, did she? I didn't get a call from any of the vice-principals—"

"No, Brooks didn't do anything except warn them. But later he told me . . . the boy has a bad reputation."

Sam's frown reappeared, darker this time. "Bad how?"

"He . . . Chase Hamilton is his name . . . he runs with a group of students who are suspected of dealing drugs."

For a moment, Sam didn't do anything. Then, carefully, he picked Raven up and set the cat on the floor. He started to stand.

"Sam, wait," Phyllis said. "What are you going to do?"

Sam's voice was grim as he replied, "Have a talk with the girl."

He hadn't made it all the way to his feet yet. Phyllis put a hand on his arm to stop him and said, "There's more. You need to sit back down and listen to me."

Sam looked at her, then sank onto the sofa again beside her. "You say this happened last Thursday?"

"That's right." She knew what his next question was going to be.

"And you're just tellin' me about it now?"

"I promised Ronnie that I wouldn't tell you about it right away. She was very upset."

"She was upset at gettin' caught. Does she know about this boy bein' a drug pusher?"

"I'm not certain that he is. But I have a feeling Ronnie doesn't know anything about it."

Sam shook his head as if he hadn't heard her. "I was worried all along that she'd gotten messed up with drugs some-how, but I didn't want to believe it."

"Just listen, and I'll tell you the rest of it," Phyllis urged.

After a moment, Sam sighed and nodded. "Go ahead. And I'm not mad at you for not tellin' me until now. I know you were just tryin' to do right by the girl."

"I thought it would be a good idea to have more infor-mation, too, before I told you about the situation."

Sam cocked his head a little to the side and said, "I get it now. You wanted to carry out your own investigation."

"I guess I've gotten into that habit," Phyllis admitted. "Anyway, all I had to go on at first was what Ray Brooks told me, and to be honest, I don't like that man very much."

"I don't think anybody does. Go ahead."

For the next few minutes, Phyllis explained what she had found out about Chase Hamilton and his history as a student at the same high school Ronnie had attended in Pennsylva-nia. Several times, Sam started to break in, but he restrained the impulse and let Phyllis continue.

She told him about the information Mike had given her and finally about her conversation with Chase Hamilton himself on Friday after lunch. Sam's craggy features flushed with anger as Phyllis explained how the bullying directed at Ronnie had gotten her involved with Chase—and how her gratitude toward him had turned into an overpowering crush.

"And now this boy turns up down here in Weatherford the same time as she does?" he said when Phyllis was fin-ished. "That seems mighty fishy to me."

"It did to me, too, but Chase seemed honest enough when he told me why he came here."

"You reckon Ronnie knew he was here when she decided to run away?"

"There's no way of knowing without asking her," Phyllis

said. "I think it's possible that was just an honest coincidence and she didn't know Chase was here until she saw him in school. But think about it, Sam. If that's how it was, then Ronnie *must* have regarded that as an omen, a sign that the two of them are supposed to be together."

"Yeah, that's just the sort of grand, romantic notion a smart kid like Ronnie would get in her head, all right." Sam clasped his hands on his knees. His grip tightened visibly as he went on, "Do you think he's sellin' drugs to her?"

"I don't have any proof that he is or isn't . . . but when I talked to him, he seemed like he genuinely cared about her, just not in any boyfriend/girlfriend way."

"So he sells drugs to other kids, but not her."

"I don't have any proof of that, either. He hasn't been arrested for anything down here, and the charges in Pennsylvania were dropped."

Sam waved a hand and said, "You know that doesn't mean anything. He could've gotten off on a technicality."

"That's true."

Sam sighed again. "This is a lot worse than just her makin' out with some kid. This Chase Hamilton sounds like he could be bad news."

"I agree. That's why I knew I had to tell you, once I found out everything I did. I've just been trying to find the right time."

He shot a sharp glance at her. "If it had turned out different . . . if the boy was just a normal kid . . . would you have said anything? Or would you have kept it to yourself?"

Phyllis wished he hadn't asked that question, but she wasn't surprised that he had. Sam had a keen intellect behind that affable, folksy exterior. And she respected him and their friendship enough that she wasn't going to lie to him.

"I might not have told you about it. She's sixteen years

old, Sam. She can kiss a boy without her grandfather's permission."

"But not a drug-dealin' boy."

"No," Phyllis said, "as long as Chase has that cloud over his head, it would be better for Ronnie to stay away from him."

"The way she feels about him, how are we gonna get her to do that, short of lockin' her in her room and not lettin' her go to school?"

"That's a mystery I haven't solved," Phyllis said.

Chapter 12

The atmosphere was subdued at the breakfast table the next morning. Sam didn't say anything to Ronnie about the discussion he had had with Phyllis the previous evening. Phyllis knew that was because he hadn't figured out what to do about the situation yet. She was glad, though, that he didn't start blustering and laying down the law to Ronnie. That tactic would have backfired, almost certainly.

When Phyllis got to school, she found Frances Macmillan waiting outside her classroom. The other teacher wore her usual harried look as she said, "You're still going to volunteer at the dance this Friday, aren't you?"

"Of course," Phyllis replied. "I said I would."

"Some people's word evidently doesn't mean as much as yours does. I've had a couple of them drop out who said they would chaperone, which means I have to hustle up some replacements. I'm checking with everybody to make sure I'm not going to have to find even more."

"Well, you don't have to worry about me and Sam. We'll

be there." Phyllis smiled. "I made sugar cookies and brownies over the weekend, just to double-check my recipes." She didn't mention that she'd included the "blood-splattered" icing on the sugar cookies, since she wouldn't do that for the dance. "My friend Carolyn came up with the idea of taking little smokies and wrapping thin strips of dough in them to look like bandages. She calls them Mummies in a Blanket."

Frances stared at her for a moment, then said, "Oh, that's disgusting! But . . . the kids will like it, and I think we can get by with that one."

"She said she could make chocolate cupcakes with icing to look like bandages, too, and put eyes in them so they'll look like mummy faces."

"She must like mummies."

Phyllis had to laugh. "No, not really, and this sort of thing really isn't in Carolyn's usual nature. But she's making an effort to be helpful, and I think my friend Eve is egging her on a little, too. That *is* the sort of off-kilter thing Eve would come up with. She's a writer, you know."

"That explains it, I suppose. Those artistic types are always a little bit off."

"And she used to teach English."

"Oh, well, then, I'm not surprised."

Phyllis could only laugh as she said goodbye to Frances and went on into the classroom. A lot of things were still "hanging fire", as Sam would say, but for now it was time to concentrate on schoolwork again.

When Phyllis's lunch period arrived, she walked from the wing where her classroom was located over to the one where Sam's classroom was. She wanted to make sure they ate together today. Maybe he had figured out what he was going to do about Ronnie and Chase Hamilton . . . if there *was* anything he could do that wouldn't just make Ronnie's crush on the young man even stronger.

Maybe it was because she was thinking about Chase, but at first, she didn't realize he was walking along the hall in front of her. It was busy, of course, with dozens of kids on their way to lunch or their next class, and Chase didn't look back, so he didn't notice Phyllis behind him.

Phyllis knew he had lunch this period because she had seen him in the cafeteria the week before, but he wasn't going in that direction now. She caught her breath a little when she realized that he appeared to be heading straight for Sam's classroom. Did he think that Sam knew about him and Ronnie? Was he intending to confront Sam?

That prospect worried Phyllis. Sam could take care of himself, but he was getting on in years. Chase was young and had a reputation for trouble.

But then she relaxed a little as she saw Chase walk on past the door of Sam's classroom. Obviously, he didn't have a confrontation in mind after all.

Then he paused at the door of the next classroom and stood there for a moment, seemingly hesitating, before he grasped the knob, turned it, and walked inside. That classroom, Phyllis remembered, belonged to Amber Trahearne.

Chase was in Amber's home room, Phyllis recalled. Amber had told her that. So there was probably a perfectly good, school-related reason Chase had stopped by to see her between classes. Phyllis knew that.

The knowledge didn't stop her from angling closer to the door as she tried to see through the glass pane set into the upper half of it.

You're the world's worst snoop, Phyllis Newsom, she told herself. But as long as Ronnie was still involved with Chase—and she hadn't promised to stop pursuing him—and as long as Sam was Phyllis's best friend, Chase's actions weren't completely none of her business. Some might see her reasoning as convoluted, but it made perfect sense to Phyllis.

From the door, she couldn't see anything except a couple of rows of student desks. Amber's desk was set in one of the corners, out of sight from this angle. Amber and Chase had to be somewhere around there, or Phyllis would have been able to see them.

A feeling of unease stirred to life inside Phyllis. Despite his reputation, Chase had never been anything but polite when she was around. But he *had* been involved with some pretty unsavory characters at his old school, there was no denying that. Phyllis couldn't bring herself to believe that Amber would be in any danger from the young man, but worry nagged at her brain anyway.

Maybe she would just go in there, ask Amber to have lunch with her and Sam . . .

She reached for the knob, closed her hand around it, and tried to turn it.

Locked.

Phyllis's breath hissed between her teeth as she drew in air sharply. The door shouldn't have been locked, and no one had approached it from the inside while Phyllis was walking toward it a moment earlier. That meant Chase must have locked it when he went in. He shouldn't have done that. The reason couldn't be anything good.

"There a problem here?"

The question made Phyllis jump a little. She looked around and saw Ray Brooks standing there with his usual suspicious glare directed at her. She shook her head and said, "No, I was just going to ask Miss Trahearne a question, but her door's locked. I guess she's already gone to lunch."

Brooks just grunted, nodded, and moved off into the crowd of students, which was thinning now that the passing period would soon be drawing to a close.

Phyllis glanced at the locked door and thought, *Now why in the world did I do that?* This would have been the perfect opportunity to make sure Amber was all right. Brooks probably had a master key that would unlock any door in the school, including this one. He could have gone in there and checked to see what was going on.

And if he had, there would have been no way Phyllis could deny that she was spying on Chase. She wasn't sure why that possibility bothered her, but it did.

She saw a shadow move on the floor inside the classroom. Someone might be coming to the door. Phyllis turned away and took several quick steps toward Sam's room. No one would wonder why she was there.

She heard the door open and close behind her and risked a glance over her shoulder. Chase had stepped out of the classroom and now started along the hall, heading in the opposite direction. He didn't look back. Phyllis knew he had to be unaware that she'd been lurking just outside the door.

She paused with her hand on the door of Sam's room as Amber's door swung open once more. Amber stepped out and closed it behind her. In that moment before Amber realized she was there, Phyllis got a good look at the young teacher. Amber's face was flushed and she appeared to be breathing a little harder than usual. A few strands of her always carefully styled hair were awry. Her lips were slightly puffy, the lipstick smeared just a tad.

If Phyllis didn't know better, she would say that Amber had the look of a young woman who had just been doing some serious kissing.

But that was impossible, because apparently the only other

person in the room just now had been . . . Chase Hamilton.

"Oh, my goodness," Phyllis said under her breath.

She barely managed to get a smile on her face in time as Amber glanced in her direction, spotted her, and smiled as well. "Hi," she said, obviously believing that Phyllis had just arrived at Sam's door.

"Hello," Phyllis said, forcing her voice to remain calm and normal even though her mind was whirling. She had heard plenty about teachers becoming romantically involved with students, and for some reason it seemed to almost always be female teachers and male students. Amber never would have struck her as the type to do such a thing, though.

Maybe she was just misinterpreting the signs, she told herself. She hoped that was the case.

"Come to go to lunch with Sam?" Amber asked. She smoothed back those strands of hair that had gone astray and patted them into place.

"That's right."

Amber's smile was bright and friendly. "We can all go together."

The door opened while she was saying that. Sam grinned as he stepped out and asked, "Go where? Lunch?"

"No, Timbuktu, silly," Amber said.

Sam shook his head. "I think I'd rather go to lunch, if that's all right with you."

"Oh, all right, but I thought you had more of a spirit of adventure than that."

"I tend to do my adventurin' vicariously these days."

Sam started toward the cafeteria with Phyllis on his right and Amber on his left, clearly pleased to be walking along accompanied by the two women.

They reached the end of the hall, where it opened into a large, mall-like area in the center of the school, the hub from which the "spokes" of the different halls ran outward. The cafeteria was on the other side. As they emerged from the corridor, Phyllis looked over and saw Ray Brooks standing there, apparently leaning casually against the brick wall. However, his gaze was sharp and intent as he looked at them.

"Hello, Miss Trahearne," he said.

"Mr. Brooks," she replied. Phyllis heard the sudden stiffness in the younger woman's voice.

"How you doin' today?"

"Just fine," Amber said, not sounding sincere at all. She didn't slow down, so she, Phyllis, and Sam passed Brooks before the security guard had the chance to say anything else.

"That fella rubs folks the wrong way," Sam commented when they were out of earshot. In the hubbub of students going in for lunch, only Phyllis and Amber could hear his words.

"He can be pleasant sometimes," Amber said, "when he wants to be. The problem is that he usually doesn't think people are worth the trouble."

Phyllis remembered that moment the previous Friday when she and Amber had been sitting in the cafeteria and she had noticed Brooks staring at her with a peculiar intensity. She had thought then that his scrutiny was because of the run-in with Ronnie and Chase the day before.

But maybe Brooks hadn't been staring at her at all, she realized. Maybe his gaze had been directed toward Amber instead. Across the big room like that, she might not have been able to tell the difference, since she and Amber were sitting side by side. Was Brooks attracted to the young teacher? Amber was pretty enough she probably received a lot of looks like that.

And she had just said that Brooks could be nice when he wanted to. She'd sounded like she was speaking from experience, as if she and Brooks had had some sort of relationship in the past.

That was insane, Phyllis told herself. Amber was too sweet, and Brooks was too surly . . .

But there was no predicting such things, Phyllis reminded herself. After all, she had just been wondering if something could be going on between Amber and Chase Hamilton.

Not for the first time, Phyllis found herself glad that she was too old for such entanglements!

Chapter 13

The rest of the day went by peacefully enough. Phyllis didn't even see Ray Brooks or Chase again. The idea that there might be a relationship between Amber and Chase still nagged at her, but she wasn't going to come right out and ask Amber about it. Such things inevitably ruined a teacher's career, and because of that Amber would just deny it anyway, no matter what the truth was.

Ronnie rode home again with Phyllis, but this time she was waiting at the car in the parking lot, instead of making out with Chase in some alcove.

Chase's name didn't come up at supper, and Phyllis could almost believe that Sam had decided to let things stand as they were. She knew better, though. Sam was a deliberate man. He was just biding his time until he figured out exactly what he wanted to do.

After supper, Phyllis was in the living room grading papers. Carolyn and Eve were watching TV, some sitcom to which Phyllis was halfway paying attention as she worked.

All of them jumped a little as a metallic crash came from the kitchen, followed instantly by yowling and barking. "Oh, dear Lord!" Carolyn exclaimed as Raven streaked into the living room, launched into the air, bounced off the back of the sofa between Carolyn and Eve, landed on the coffee table, scattered the papers Phyllis had placed there, and slid off to fall in the floor with the lack of grace that cats occasionally demonstrated, to their great and utter humiliation.

Buck was right behind the black cat. The Dalmatian's loud, furious barking filled the air and assaulted the ears. Phyllis made a grab for his collar as he went by but missed.

Raven rolled over and came up on her back legs, balancing there as her front paws shot out toward Buck with all claws extended. Buck must have remembered what had happened before, because he came to a clumsy, skidding halt. Phyllis saw that his tail was wagging. This was all a game to him, she realized. He didn't want to hurt Raven; he was just chasing her for the fun of it. But animals sometimes got carried away, so this rough-housing needed to stop.

It wasn't a game to Raven. She leaped at Buck, swatting furiously with both paws. Buck jumped back so abruptly that he got tangled in Sam's long legs as Sam rushed into the room. Sam yelped, "Whoa!" and started to go down as he lost his balance.

Phyllis had already gotten to her feet. She grabbed Sam to steady him, and the impact made both of them stagger a little. Neither fell, though, which was a good thing because at their age, a tumble like that often meant a broken bone—or two.

"What in the world!" Carolyn said.

Eve moved in behind Raven, bent over, and scooped the cat from the floor, holding Raven so that she couldn't scratch her. Raven squirmed and hissed, but Eve hung on.

"Buck!" Sam said. "Get outta here!"

The dog retreated toward the kitchen. Sam turned to Phyllis and went on, "Thanks for catchin' me. I didn't hurt you, did I?"

"No, I'm fine," she assured him. "What happened?"

Before Sam could explain, Ronnie called from the top of the stairs, "What's going on? Is everybody all right?"

"Fine," Phyllis said again, raising her voice so Ronnie could hear her. "Just a little cat and dog commotion."

"Are they okay?"

"Yeah, don't worry," Sam said. To Phyllis he added, "Let me go put Buck back outside, and then I'll tell you about it."

He hurried toward the kitchen. Phyllis heard the door to the back yard open and close. When Sam returned a moment later, he was shaking his head ruefully.

"I sure am sorry about that," he said. "And don't worry, Phyllis, I'll clean up the mess in the kitchen."

"I'm not worried about any mess," she said. "I just want to know what happened."

"I was on my way out the back door to feed Buck . . . had his bowl in my hand and everything . . . when he caught sight of Raven behind me and decided to have some fun. I reckon he'd forgotten what happened last time, or else he was just excited and didn't care, right that minute. So he took me by surprise, charged inside, banged into my leg and made me drop his food bowl, and then took off after the cat. Y'all saw what happened after that."

"We certainly did," Eve said. She still had hold of Raven, who had settled down as soon as Buck was out of the room. She dropped the cat lightly on the sofa, where Raven curled up in a corner, started licking a paw, and looked very satisfied with herself.

Ronnie had come down to the bottom of the stairs and

stood looking through the arched entrance to the living room. "That's probably the most excitement this place has seen in a long time," she said.

Phyllis thought about the night she had found a bludgeoned body on the front porch and the time she had been attacked by a killer right next door. She could do without that sort of excitement. She was glad that neither Buck nor Raven seemed to have been hurt in this incident.

"And that's more than enough for tonight," Phyllis said.

By the next morning, she couldn't stand it anymore. She was up first, so she had the coffee brewing but was by herself in the kitchen when Sam came in, yawning. After she had told him good morning, Phyllis took the opportunity to ask, "Have you decided what you're going to do about Ronnie?"

"I'm gonna tell her to stay away from Chase Hamilton, and if she doesn't, I'll ground her. I may not be her legal guardian, but I figure I can do that much, as long as she's stayin' here with me."

"You don't think that will just make her more determined to pursue Chase?"

"Maybe it will. But sometimes you've got to take a stand and see how it plays out."

Phyllis nodded slowly. Sam wasn't the sort to let a situation fester for too long without taking action. Honestly, he had held off from confronting Ronnie longer than she had expected him to.

"Do you want me with you when you talk to her?"

"Yeah, I'd appreciate that." He smiled. "I'll be countin' on you to rein me in if I get too riled up. I don't want to say anything that'll make Ronnie think she did the wrong thing by turnin' to me for help."

"I don't believe she'd ever think that," Phyllis said as she put a hand on his arm for a second.

Carolyn came into the kitchen a few minutes later, followed almost immediately by Ronnie. Sam handed his granddaughter a cup of coffee and slid his arm around her shoulders for a quick hug, then said, "You and me got to have a talk."

Ronnie groaned. "This early in the morning?"

"Yep."

Carolyn filled her cup and said, "I think I'm going to take my coffee and go read the newspaper . . . such as it is, these days."

Phyllis knew her friend was making a discreet withdrawal so Sam could talk to Ronnie alone. She would have retreated, too, if Sam hadn't told her that he wanted her here.

Ronnie frowned suspiciously and said, "Uh-oh. I'm not going to like this talk, am I?"

"It won't be that bad. I just want to say a few things about this boy you think you like."

Ronnie's head jerked toward Phyllis. She glared and said, "You *told* him. You *promised!*"

"I promised not to tell your grandfather right away, until I'd thought about it," Phyllis said, remaining calm. "And I might not have told him if I didn't believe it was necessary."

"What's necessary about it? You're meddling in things that don't concern you."

"Don't get too feisty now," Sam warned. "I think a lot of Phyllis, and you're gonna show some respect for her. She's done a lot for me, and for you, too, in the time you've been here."

"I appreciate the place to live," Ronnie said grudgingly. "You know that, Mrs. Newsom."

"We all care about you, Ronnie," Phyllis said. "That's why

we don't want to see anything bad happen to you."

"Nothing bad is going to happen to me! Chase *helped* me. He saved me from those terrible bullies up there at home—"

"He was arrested for dealin' drugs," Sam said.

Ronnie's eyes widened. She stared at him for a second and then said, "How do you know—" Her head turned toward Phyllis again. "*You* told him. You're the big crime-solving detective. You . . . you investigated Chase!"

Phyllis started to say something, but Sam lifted a hand to stop her. "You're dang right Phyllis looked into the boy's background, and she had every right to do it. We're all just tryin' to look out for your best interests."

"Did you find out that all the charges against Chase were dropped?" Ronnie demanded. "Because he didn't *do* anything! Just because some of his friends were no good, it doesn't mean that he is."

"Yeah, but as soon as he got down here, he started hangin' out with the same sort of kids," Sam said. "That ought to tell you somethin' right there."

"It tells me that this is none of your business."

"You're sixteen years old and my granddaughter, so it dang sure *is* my business. And here's somethin' else for you to consider. You may be in love with this boy, but he's not in love with you. He felt sorry for you, that's all."

Phyllis tried not to wince. Sam had said that he wanted her to "rein him in", and she had failed to do so in time. The hurtful words were already out, and the pain and anger on Ronnie's face were unmistakable.

Ronnie's expression closed off abruptly, though, as she said, "What do you want me to do?"

"Well, I think you should stop runnin' after this boy. Chances are, he's gonna wind up in trouble, and you don't want to be anywhere around him when he does."

"Is that an order?"

"I'd rather consider it me askin' you to do something for me . . . and because it's the right thing."

"And if I don't, what happens? You'll ground me?"

"I might, if it comes to that."

"You're not my parents."

The sneer in Ronnie's voice as she said that grated on Phyllis's nerves. She would have had a hard time controlling her temper, and she was proud of Sam for doing so. He sounded cool and collected as he said, "Stay away from Chase this week. Go to the dance Friday night. Maybe you'll meet somebody you like better. Just let things simmer down some, and maybe we'll talk more about this later."

"You mean you'll change your mind about Chase?"

"I don't know about that. There's a lot of evidence piled up against him."

"Yeah, it always comes back to the evidence, doesn't it? Well, sometimes the evidence is wrong!"

Ronnie turned on her heel and stalked out of the kitchen without looking back. Sam called after her, "You didn't have your breakfast!"

"I think breakfast is the least of her worries right now, Sam," Phyllis said with a sigh. "We'd better let her go. She'll cool off and see that you're trying to be reasonable."

"Maybe. Maybe not. We *are* talkin' about a teenage girl, you know."

"An intelligent teenage girl who loves her grandfather. That will count for more than you think it might."

"I sure hope you're right," Sam said. He sighed heavily and sat down at the table.

"She has a point about one thing, you know," Phyllis said. Sam looked up at her and cocked a quizzical eyebrow. She went on, "Sometimes the evidence is wrong. Sometimes the truth we think we see isn't true at all. We've run into that more than once."

"Yeah, but don't forget the old sayin' about who are you gonna believe, me or your lyin' eyes?"

Phyllis didn't have a response to that. Every fact she had turned up pointed to the fact that Chase Hamilton was a bad kid.

And the only thing he had on his side was the lovestruck faith of one girl . . .

Chapter 14

A tense air hung over the house for the next couple of days, whenever Phyllis, Sam, and Ronnie were all there. It made Phyllis think of an armed truce during wartime. Of course, the wrath of a teenage girl was nothing like having a whole army poised to wreak death and destruction . . . but it felt a little like that anyway.

As far as Phyllis could tell, Ronnie was honoring Sam's request to stay away from Chase Hamilton. She went with Sam to school every morning and returned home in the afternoon with either Phyllis or Sam. While she wasn't very outgoing, she didn't give either of them the silent treatment. She was just more subdued than usual.

But that left hours every day when she was at school, and they couldn't really keep an eye on her there since they had their own classes to teach. Phyllis would have liked to think that Ronnie couldn't get into *too* much trouble while she was at school, but Phyllis's decades as a teacher—plus memories of things that had gone on when she was a student herself—

told her that kids could get up to all kinds of mischief, even within the four walls of a school building.

Phyllis hadn't told Sam of her suspicions about Chase and Amber. He'd already had his talk with Ronnie, and there was no need to muddy the waters with that. As long as Ronnie stayed away from Chase, it didn't matter what was going on between those other two—if anything. Phyllis knew she could have been wrong.

Thursday afternoon, after she had done what was necessary to prepare for the next day's classes, she walked across the building toward Sam's classroom. She hadn't gotten a text from Ronnie about which one of them the girl was going home with, so she thought it would be a good idea to see if Sam had heard from her. The door was open, and when Phyllis reached it, she saw Ronnie sitting at one of the desks in the front row, working on some assignment while Sam finished with his chores.

Ronnie glanced up, saw Phyllis, and set aside the iPad she was using to make notes. "I'm sorry," she said. "I should have let you know I was riding with Gramps. I just forgot."

Phyllis smiled and said, "That's all right." It appeared that Ronnie had also forgotten, at least for the moment, to feel resentful toward her, and Phyllis welcomed that. "I just thought I'd check. Anyway, I never mind seeing the two of you."

"And you're a mighty welcome visitor any time you come around—" Sam began. He stopped short as angry voices were raised somewhere nearby. The commotion sounded like the prelude to a fight. There hadn't been any students in the hall when Phyllis walked through it a moment earlier, though. Actually, the shouting seemed like it was coming from next door.

Amber's room.

Sam stood up and moved quickly to the door. Phyllis was right behind him. He paused and motioned to Ronnie, who had gotten to her feet as well.

"You just stay right here," he told her. "Whatever that's about, you don't need to be mixed up in it."

"Maybe you don't, either," Ronnie said. "I don't want you to get hurt."

"I'm just gonna take a look and see what's goin' on. If somebody's botherin' Amber . . ."

He left the rest unsaid, but Phyllis knew what he meant. If someone was bothering Amber, Sam would step in to defend her. But, she reminded herself, Sam would step in to help anybody who was in trouble, not just Amber Trahearne.

They stepped out into the hall. The door of Amber's classroom was open, and now Phyllis could tell for sure that was where the angry voices came from. She was a little surprised that both of them were male, and a little familiar. It didn't sound like Amber was taking part in the argument, whatever it was.

No one else was close by in the corridor. Some kids were visible in the mall, at the far end of the hall, but they didn't act like they had noticed what was going on. Sam and Phyllis went to the door of Amber's room and looked in.

"—done, kid. You're gonna be expelled, but before they kick you out of this school, I'm gonna kick your ass!"

"Back off, man. You don't want to do this."

"The hell I don't!"

Phyllis and Sam had moved far enough into the room now to see the two figures confronting each other with fists clenched and angrily jutting jaws. Chase Hamilton and Ray Brooks stood in front of Amber's desk. Amber was behind the desk, leaning forward so that her hands rested on it. Her face was taut with concern.

"Please," she said, her voice low but urgent. "There's no need for this."

"The hell there isn't," Brooks blustered. "I come in here and find this little son of a bitch with his tongue down your throat." A sneer twisted the security guard's face. "I'd figure he attacked you . . . but I've been watching the two of you and I know better!"

"Shut up!" Chase said. "You don't know—"

"I know enough," Brooks went on. "I know it doesn't matter if you're over eighteen, you're a student and she's a teacher and this is illegal! You're both gonna be in all kinds of trouble for this!" He closed in on Chase, who backed away slowly but stopped when he reached one of the desks. "Now you're gonna get what's comin' to you, kid."

"Hold it!" Sam shouted in his best teacher's voice. The heads of the other three jerked around. From the looks of it, they had been so caught up in their drama that they hadn't noticed when Phyllis and Sam came in.

"Butt out, Fletcher," Brooks said. "This is none of your business."

"You go beatin' up on a student and I'll make it my business. It's bad enough you're threatenin' him and sayin' those things to Miss Trahearne."

"You're gonna defend her? She's fooling around with a student. That doesn't make her anything but a—"

Chase leaped at him, grappled with him before he could continue.

It was less of a fight and more of an awkward dance as the two of them staggered back and forth, bumping into desks as they wrestled. They probably weren't going to do much damage to each other as long as that continued, but at any second they might start throwing punches, and then things could get a lot more serious in a hurry. Phyllis remembered what Chase had said about hurting the bullies up in Pennsylvania.

She watched anxiously as Sam shoved his arms between them and thrust them apart. He might not have been able to keep them that way if Amber hadn't come around the desk and grabbed Chase from behind. He started trying to pull away from her, then stopped abruptly as if unwilling to do anything that might hurt her.

Phyllis worried that Brooks might throw a punch and accidentally hit Sam as he blocked the path of the stocky security guard. Brooks's fists were up and ready, but he didn't lash out. Instead, his face twitching with rage, he backed off a little and gradually lowered his fists.

Amber said, "You need to get out of here, Ray, right now!"

"Why? So you can go back to messing around with a student?"

"Stop saying those ugly things."

"I know what I saw! Didn't take you long after I broke up with you, did it, Amber? But with a kid? Is Hamilton the only one?"

Even under the tense circumstances, Phyllis noticed what Brooks said. He and Amber had dated? That was news, although she had begun to speculate about that very thing.

"You're crazy," Amber said. "You need to just leave me alone, Ray. Whatever was between us is over, and nothing's going to change that."

Brooks laughed. It was an unpleasant sound. "You think I want you back? Knowing what I know now, I wouldn't have you on a bet. But I'm not gonna let you get away with it, either. You or the kid. He's probably just as much to blame for it as you are."

"You better just shut up—" Chase said, but Amber

moved in front of him now.

"You don't know what you're talking about," she told Brooks, and her voice was cold with anger. "Make any wild accusations about Chase and me that you want to. I'll deny all of it."

"I saw you—"

"You made up the whole thing because you're mad that I broke up with you," Amber overrode his protest. "Not that many people know that you and I dated, but a few do. Enough to make sure everybody finds out, and who do you think they're going to believe, Ray? Most of the people around this school can't stand you! They're going to believe me."

"You bitch."

"Just go on. Swallow your pride and forget about this. We'll all be better off if you do, I promise you."

"So you think the two of you should get away with it? With all of it?"

Amber smiled. "There's nothing to get away with. It's just a figment of your imagination, Ray."

Only it wasn't, Phyllis thought. She had heard the anger in Ray Brooks's voice and knew it was genuine. He had seen something to set off that reaction, and Phyllis was convinced that he had walked in on Chase and Amber in each other's arms, just as he'd claimed.

Of course Chase didn't have any interest in a blue-haired, angst-ridden teenager. He had Amber.

But none of that made Phyllis like Ray Brooks any better, or feel sorry for him. Nor did it improve her opinion of Chase—or Amber, for that matter. In fact, the whole thing made her feel a little dirty.

Brooks raised his hand and pointed at Amber. "I don't care what you say, I'm tellin' Shula. There are laws about this kind of stuff, you know."

Amber looked like she was going to say something else, but before she could, Brooks turned and stomped out of the classroom.

Turning to Phyllis and Sam, Amber gave them a weak smile and said, "I'm sorry you had to get mixed up in this, that you had to see and hear all that . . . that craziness."

"Is what he said true?" Sam asked bluntly.

"Oh, Sam," Amber said with a look of dismay. "Don't ask me that."

"I reckon that's our answer then," Sam said. His rugged features were set in stony lines. "I'm just glad nobody got beat up."

He headed for the door. Phyllis looked at Amber and Chase, unwilling in a way to leave them here together. But there was nothing she could do, she told herself. They would have to sort all this out themselves. She remembered something she had heard some of the kids say.

Not my circus. Not my monkeys.

Maybe those were pretty good words to live by, she thought as she put a hand on Sam's arm and they went to the door.

When they stepped out into the hall, Ronnie was standing there, just a few feet away, and all it took was one look at the girl's stricken face for Phyllis to know that she had overheard the whole thing.

Chapter 15

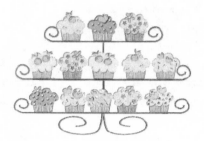

Phyllis put out a hand toward Ronnie and said her name. Ronnie didn't respond, though, other than to turn away abruptly and run along the hall away from them. Sam uttered a heartfelt, "Dadgum it! You reckon she heard what Brooks was accusin' Amber and Chase of?"

"I think it's pretty clear she did," Phyllis said.

"She idolized that boy, whether he deserves it or not. Which it sure looks like he doesn't, in more than one way. But now she's finally seen he's got feet of clay."

"She never would have believed it if we told her," Phyllis pointed out. "She's so used to defending Chase that her instinct would have been to deny anything bad about him. So maybe it's a good thing she overheard, even though it's painful for her right now."

Sam sighed. "Maybe. But all Chase would have to do is tell her it's not true, and she'd go right back to defendin' him."

"You're probably right about that," Phyllis said. "But maybe not. We'll have to wait and see."

"Yeah. Where do you reckon she went?"

"I don't know. I'll go see if I can find her."

Sam glanced back at the door to Amber's classroom and said, "I ought to go try to talk some sense into those two, but I just can't work up the enthusiasm for it. What they do is their own look-out."

"I feel the same way," Phyllis said with a nod.

Ronnie had disappeared into the mall by now. Phyllis headed in that direction while Sam went back into his class-room. When she reached the mall, she paused and looked around but didn't spot the tell-tale blue hair. There were several different ways Ronnie could have gone from here, and Phyllis wasn't sure which one to try.

"Excuse me," a voice said. "Are you looking for Ronnie Ericson?"

She looked around and saw a boy standing there. He was young, probably a freshman or sophomore, slender with dark brown hair. He was a little better dressed than many of the students, in slacks and a button-down shirt. Phyllis was cer-tain he wasn't in any of her classes and didn't recall seeing him around the school, but there wasn't anything particularly memorable about him.

"Who are you?" she asked.

"Walter Baxter," he said, which sounded to Phyllis like a name out of a 1950s TV situation comedy. "If you're looking for Ronnie, Mrs. Newsom, she went that way." He pointed along the corridor that led to the band hall.

Phyllis gave in to curiosity and asked, "How do you know who I am?"

"I know who all the faculty members are. I realize you're a long-term substitute and not the actual teacher of record for your classes, but as far as I'm concerned you're part of the faculty."

"And you know Ronnie?"

A faint pink color rose in his cheeks. "She's in a couple of my classes."

Walter Baxter was blushing, Phyllis realized. He probably wouldn't be doing that unless he liked Ronnie.

"And I know you and Coach Fletcher are friends and she's his granddaughter and is staying at your house," Walter went on. "She looked upset when she came through here, and then you came along right after her, so I figured you might be looking for her."

"You're an observant young man," Phyllis told him.

"I try to be. You have to know what's going on in the world to get ahead in it."

"That's a good attitude to have. Thank you, Walter."

She turned away, but he said quickly, "If there's anything else I can do—"

"No, that's all right. I appreciate your help." Phyllis didn't think Ronnie would want a potentially love-struck under-classman around right now.

She left Walter in the mall and headed toward the band hall. She could see all the way along the corridor and didn't spot Ronnie anywhere, but there were a couple of smaller halls that crossed this one.

She found Ronnie in the second of those cross corridors. The girl stood with her back against the wall. Her shoulders slumped and her head drooped forward. She wasn't crying at the moment, but her face bore the streaks of drying tears.

"Ronnie . . ." Phyllis said.

She looked up and asked, "Is it true?"

"About Chase and Miss Trahearne?"

Ronnie said again, "Is it true?"

"I'm not absolutely certain, but I believe it is."

"She didn't deny it, you know. She told Brooks that she

would, if he accused her, but she didn't actually deny it just now."

"No, she didn't. That doesn't mean it's true, but—"

Ronnie lifted both hands and covered her face as if she were about to start sobbing again, but no sound came from her except a long sigh. When she lowered her hands, she shook her head and said, "I should have listened to you and Gramps."

The last thing in the world Phyllis wanted to do right now was say *I told you so*. Instead she said, "Sometimes it's hard to know what the right thing is. And I'm not just talking about when you're a teenager. That never ends."

Ronnie summoned up a faint smile. "You don't ever get old enough to have all the answers?"

Phyllis smiled, too, and said, "If you do, I must not be that old yet!"

Ronnie grew solemn again. "Chase is going to get in trouble now, isn't he? It isn't just a matter of whether it's true about him and . . . and Miss Trahearne. He fought with Brooks."

"It wasn't much of a fight—"

"But Chase attacked him. I was peeking around the edge of the door and saw it. Brooks will complain to Mr. Shula and get Chase kicked out of school. He may even call the police and try to have him arrested."

"I'm not sure the police will want to get involved in what was nothing more than a scuffle."

"But Chase could still be expelled." Ronnie stepped away from the wall. "I know I should be mad at him right now . . . I *am* mad at him . . . but he really was nice to me last year. And I guess I can't blame him *too* much. I mean, Miss Trahearne is so freakin' gorgeous! I'm sure she came on to him, and he couldn't help it."

She was already trying to talk herself out of being angry with him, Phyllis thought. She wasn't really surprised. A crush like the one Ronnie had on Chase Hamilton was pretty resilient.

"I know it's a lot to ask," Ronnie went on, "but could you talk to Mr. Shula? I know the two of you used to work together, and I'm sure he'd listen to you, Mrs. Newsom."

"You want me to ask him to go easy on Chase?"

"He can punish him. Just don't kick him out of school."

Phyllis didn't say anything for a moment. Chase being expelled might be the solution to the problem. Ronnie wouldn't be around him all the time anymore. Her feelings for him might fade.

Or she might feel that he'd been treated unfairly, and that sympathy might make her crush even stronger.

One thing was certain: Ronnie was reaching out to Phyllis right now because she was hurting, and Phyllis didn't want to refuse her that help.

"I'll talk to Mr. Shula," she said. "But I can't promise anything."

"Thank you!" Ronnie took her by surprise then, throwing her arms around Phyllis and hugging her. That was the first time that had happened. "If there's anything I can do to pay you back . . ."

"Just look at things with clear eyes from now on," Phyllis said. "Don't let yourself be blinded by your feelings."

Even as she said it, she knew how difficult that was even for people with many decades of life experience. For a teenager, it was almost impossible to put feelings aside and be pragmatic. Even if Ronnie just made an effort to do so, though, it might help.

"I can do that," Ronnie said. "Should I ride home with you today?"

"Why don't you go with your grandfather?"

"Do you have something else you need to do?"

Phyllis said, "I suppose I'll go talk to Mr. Shula. I suspect Mr. Brooks has already been there, as angry as he was the last time we saw him."

"That guy is the worst!"

Phyllis didn't know that she would go so far as to say that, but she didn't feel any natural liking or sympathy for Ray Brooks. Logically, though, he hadn't really done anything wrong. Chase and Amber were the ones who had crossed the line, she thought.

Phyllis and Ronnie walked together to the mall, where Ronnie went toward the hall where Sam's classroom was located while Phyllis turned left toward the main offices.

The secretary wasn't at her desk in the outer office, but Phyllis heard voices coming from the hall that led to the principal's office. She knew she was butting in, but she had told Ronnie that she would do what she could to help Chase.

Sam might not appreciate that. He'd probably be fine with it if Chase was kicked out of school. But Phyllis could only follow her instincts.

The door to Tom Shula's office was open. Shula stood behind the desk, Ray Brooks in front of it.

Shula looked past the security guard toward the door. He was a medium-sized man in his fifties, mostly bald with a fringe of brown hair around his ears and the back of his head. He said, "I'm sorry, Phyllis, I'm a little busy right now—"

"She's here to stick up for that little weasel," Brooks broke in. "That little blue-haired tramp is the granddaughter of the guy she's shacked up with. Everybody knows that. The girl probably begged her to put in a good word for Hamilton."

Shula's voice was sharp as he said, "Watch your mouth, Ray. We respect other people in this school."

"Yeah, Amber and the Hamilton kid have probably been respectin' the hell out of each other."

"That's enough! Do you want to file a formal complaint?"

"You bet I do," Brooks said. "I want him expelled and the slut fired."

"Write it up," Shula said. "Write it up and submit it, and I'll take it under consideration."

Brooks glared. "That's it?" he demanded. "You're gonna sweep this under the rug?"

"I said I'd take it under consideration."

"And I'll take it to the damn school board—*and* the cops!"

"I'm asking you not to do anything for the time being, until I've had a chance to look into the incident." Shula glanced at Phyllis. "You were a witness to what happened, is that right?"

She nodded and said, "I saw most of it."

"Have you got a minute so I can ask you some questions?"

"Of course."

Brooks looked back and forth between them and practically snarled. "It's a whitewash, that's what it is. Don't think I don't see what's happenin'."

"Just give me a chance, Ray, that's all I ask," Shula said.

Brooks glowered for a moment longer, then blew out a disgusted breath and stomped from the office. Phyllis was glad to see him go. Brooks reminded her of a feral animal.

When the security guard was gone, Tom Shula sighed and waved Phyllis into the chair in front of the desk. He slumped behind it and asked, "Was it really as bad as Brooks made it out to be? Are Amber and the Hamilton boy . . .?" He held out a hand and wobbled it from side to side.

"I don't have any proof one way or the other about that."

"But you have an opinion," Shula prodded.

"I think . . . there *might* be something going on."

Shula shook his head and said, "I was hoping he was mistaken about that. Legally, if he files a complaint, I'll have to report it to the authorities and this will become a matter for the police. What about the fight?"

"It wasn't much of one," Phyllis said. "I don't think a single punch was thrown. It might have come to that if Sam hadn't stepped in, but as it was, Brooks and Chase just wrestled around for a few seconds. Neither of them even fell down."

"Still, even a scuffle between a student and a school employee is serious business."

"I know it is. Just like I know you'll do whatever you have to do, Tom. But as for that part of it, I really don't believe it rose to the level of justifying Chase being expelled."

"I'm not going to expel him."

That flat statement surprised Phyllis. "You're not?"

Shula shook his head. "Nope. Not right away, at least. We'll let things play out and see what Brooks does. The weekend is coming up. Maybe he'll cool off and let the whole thing slide."

"Maybe," Phyllis said, even though she didn't think that was very likely, from what she had seen of Ray Brooks.

"He'll be here for the dance tomorrow night. Maybe that'll cheer him up. It's overtime pay, after all. Lucky Friday the Thirteenth for him."

Chapter 16

Sam was alone in his room when Phyllis got back there.

"What happened with the principal?" he asked. "I know you found Ronnie, and she asked you to talk to him."

"Tom isn't going to expel Chase," Phyllis said. "But if Brooks lodges a formal complaint against Chase and Amber, he'll be legally required to turn the case over to the authorities."

"And that district attorney of ours will try to make political hay out of it, the same way he always does."

"Probably." Phyllis paused. "I imagine you're disappointed that Chase isn't going to be kicked out of school, at least not right away."

Sam leaned back in the chair behind his desk and sighed. "To tell you the truth, I'm not sure how I feel. If he was gone, then I wouldn't have to worry so much about Ronnie."

"Where *is* Ronnie, by the way?"

"She stopped here, said she was going to the library for a few minutes to pick up something for an assignment, and then she'd meet me at the pickup."

Phyllis felt a stirring of unease. She said, "You believed her?"

Sam's forehead creased in a frown. "Yeah, given her track record, maybe that wasn't the smartest thing to do. I'm ready to go. I'll see if I can't hunt her up."

"I'll come with you," Phyllis said.

As they left the room, she glanced toward Amber's room. The door was closed and the light was off, she saw.

"Did Amber stop and say anything to you before she left?"

Sam shook his head. "I got to admit, I'm sorta glad she didn't come in while Ronnie was there. That would've been a mite awkward."

"More than a mite, I'd say. Whatever has been going on between her and Chase, Ronnie blames her for it."

"Well, she's older . . . and in a position of responsibility and authority. When you're a teacher, you can't do anything that might be seen as takin' advantage of that."

"Chase doesn't strike me as the sort who would be easily taken advantage of."

"No." Sam's voice hardened. "If everything we suspect about him turns out to be true, he's more of a predator himself."

"That's why I thought it might be better if he *was* expelled. I didn't know what to do when Ronnie asked me to speak up for him with Tom Shula."

Sam shrugged. "She would've hated you if you hadn't. This way, you talked to Shula, but whatever happens is out of your hands now."

"I told him it wasn't much of a fight."

"And that was the truth. Can't blame you for that."

They passed the library on their way toward the back of

the building. It stayed open for an hour after the end of classes every day, so it would be closing soon. Right now, though, the door was still propped open. Sam paused and said, "I want to go in and find out if Ronnie stopped here like she said she was."

Phyllis followed him in. The librarian was at the desk, along with one of the student aides. When Sam walked up, the woman asked, "Can I help you, Coach Fletcher?"

"I was wonderin' if my granddaughter was in here durin' the last little while. The blue-haired girl?"

The librarian smiled. "There's more than one blue-haired girl who goes to school here, I'm afraid."

The aide said, "I know the one he means, Mrs. Booth." The girl told Sam, "Yes, Ronnie was here, about fifteen minutes ago. She checked out a couple of books."

"Thanks."

"You're welcome, Coach."

As they left the library, Phyllis said to Sam, "You were afraid she had gone off somewhere with Chase, weren't you?"

"Well, under the circumstances, I reckon it was a possibility."

"I think she's probably still too mad at him right now for that. She'd still stand up for him against anyone else, but the idea that he rejected her in favor of a teacher had to wound her pride considerably."

"But she'll get over it, won't she?" Sam asked.

"I think that's likely."

They emerged from the building a couple of minutes later. From where they were, Phyllis could see Sam's pickup in the parking lot, and it was no trouble to spot Ronnie sitting in the passenger seat, doing something on her phone. Phyllis knew that Sam had given her a key to the truck, so she could go ahead and get into it whenever she was riding with him and reached the parking lot first. It was cool enough today, nearing mid-October, that it would be comfortable sitting in the pickup with the windows rolled down.

"Looks like you were right," Sam said. "There she is, and I don't see that Hamilton boy around anywhere."

"She could be texting him on her phone," Phyllis said.

"Yeah, but there's no way for us to police that, short of takin' away her phone, and like you said, she's probably lettin' him stew for the time being."

"Except he won't be stewing. He's not romantically interested in Ronnie, remember? In a way, having his affair with Amber out in the open might be a relief to Chase."

"He probably doesn't know how stubborn Ronnie can be."

"No," Phyllis said, "he probably doesn't. But I expect we'll all find out soon enough."

With everything that had happened, it was difficult to concentrate on baking, but the smell that filled the house when Phyllis got home made it easier. Carolyn had baked a small batch of her mummy cupcakes as a test, and the aroma of fresh cake made Phyllis's mouth water.

While Phyllis tried one and found that it tasted as good as it smelled, she told Carolyn and Eve what had happened after school. Carolyn was outraged, just on general principles since she didn't know Amber or Chase.

"I keep hearing about such things, and I just don't understand them," she said. "Thank goodness I taught elementary school, where you don't have to worry about sordid behavior like that."

Eve said, "No, at that grade level you just have to worry

about the teachers fooling around with the students' parents . . .
especially some of those hot single dads."

"Good Lord! Are you insane? That never happens."

"Really, dear?" Eve smiled. "I suppose I must be mistaken
about some of the stories I've heard."

Phyllis let them continue wrangling about it while she got
ready to bake the sugar cookies and brownies she would need
for the dance the next evening. She didn't want to leave that
to do between the end of the school day and the dance that
night.

Sam and Ronnie came in a short time later. Ronnie went
upstairs right away, but Sam had to stop in the kitchen to
sample one of Carolyn's cupcakes.

"Is she all right?" Carolyn asked quietly.

"She's still upset, but she'll be okay," Sam said. "She
might've got her heart broke a little bit, but she's a tough
girl."

Eve said, "I've had my heart broken many times. It stings
for a little while, and then you get over it."

Phyllis wasn't sure she looked at the situation as blithely as
Eve did, but her friend had a point. At Ronnie's age, emotions were extremely intense but seldom long-lasting.

Try explaining that to a broken-hearted sixteen-year-old,
though.

Phyllis had to put that out of her mind and turn her attention to baking. They ate Slow Cooker Texas Chicken and
Dumplings for supper since the oven was going to be in use.
Carolyn had put it on to cook in the slow cooker that morning after Phyllis and Sam left for work. The house smelled
heavenly when they came in. By that evening, she had the
cookies and brownies baked, cooled, and placed in plastic
storage containers so it would be easy to load them into the
car and take them to the dance on Friday night.

"I expect you not to raid these," she told Sam, who was sitting at the kitchen table sipping a cup of decaffeinated coffee. "They're for the kids tomorrow night."

"I'll leave 'em alone," he promised, "but it won't be easy."

"I'm not sure how you could still be hungry. You went back for thirds on Carolyn's chicken and dumplings. You can have whatever's left over."

He laughed. "The chicken and dumplings were too good not to go back for thirds. And it's funny you really think there's gonna be anything left over after you turn a bunch of hungry teenagers loose on those goodies."

"Well . . . probably not. But if you want to nibble on the various snacks while you're chaperoning, I'll pretend not to notice."

"Deal," he said.

The morning of Friday the Thirteenth dawned with an appropriate gloominess. A thick gray overcast hung in the sky, and the breeze that send the clouds scudding along had more than a hint of coolness in it. After the hot Texas summer, it actually felt good to Phyllis as she walked from the parking lot toward the school.

That good feeling evaporated as she saw the three figures loitering near the door where she usually entered the school. She recognized one of the boys as Chase Hamilton, but she didn't know the other two. Phyllis thought they were part of the group she had seen sitting with Chase at lunch.

She hesitated and pondered turning around to return to her car. Sam would be coming along soon, and she could wait and walk in with him.

But Ronnie would be with him, and Phyllis wasn't sure it would be a good idea for her to see Chase right now.

Anyway, she just couldn't bring herself to believe that Chase meant her any harm. Despite everything she had learned about him, her instincts told her that she was safe around him.

Those other boys might be a different story, though, and there were two of them and only one of Chase.

Phyllis had gone too far to turn back, though. She couldn't outrun them if they wanted to catch her. All she could do was forge ahead and see what happened.

"Mrs. Newsom," Chase said as he moved to block the door and forced her to stop. "I need to talk to you."

"I'm not sure that we have anything to talk about, Mr. Hamilton."

One of the other boys, who had long, straggly, light brown hair, laughed and said, "Mr. Hamilton. Anybody ever call you that before, Chase . . . except for some teacher who's scared of you?"

"I got this, Riley," Chase snapped. "I don't need any help."

"I'm not so sure about that," the other boy said. He was bigger than either of the other two, with heavy shoulders. A first glance might take him for a big, dumb jock, but Phyllis saw intelligence in his eyes—along with hostility.

Chase ignored the other two and went on, "I just want to ask you about Ronnie. She won't answer my calls or return my texts. Is she all right?"

"As far as I know, she is," Phyllis said. "She's just angry with you . . . and for good reason."

Chase scowled. "I wouldn't say that. I told you before, I'm not interested in her except as a friend. I made that very clear to her. She just won't listen."

Phyllis heard a note of frustration in the young man's voice. She could understand him feeling that way. Once

Ronnie got an idea in her head, she didn't want to let go of it.

Chase went on, "Would you tell her I talked to you and asked about her?"

"I don't know if that would be a good idea. To be blunt, Mr. Hamilton, I don't think you should have any more contact with her at all."

"That's all right, Chase," the boy called Riley said with a smirk on his narrow face. "You got Miss Trahearne to *have contact with*. I think you got the better end of the deal."

"Shut up, Riley," Chase said wearily. He looked at Phyllis again and continued, "I just want Ronnie to know that I never meant to hurt her. That was the farthest thing from my mind. I mean that, and you can tell her or not, whatever you think best."

Phyllis nodded and said, "I appreciate that. I need to get to class now—"

"Hamilton!"

The loud, harsh voice made all of them look around, and Phyllis felt her apprehension grow even stronger. Ray Brooks was striding toward them with anger twisting his face. There was no way this was going to turn out well, Phyllis thought.

Chapter 17

"What are you three doin' back here?" Brooks demanded as he walked up to them.

"Going into the school," Chase said. "That's what we're supposed to do in the morning, isn't it?"

"Don't smart off at me. That's the faculty parking lot."

The biggest of the three boys pointed toward the east end of the school campus. "There's a student lot right over there. It's just about the same distance whether we go in the front or the back, and our first classes are around here on this side of the school. Anybody can go in and out here, right?"

"You got an answer for everything, don't you, Duncan?" Brooks sneered for a second, then turned his attention to Phyllis. "Are they botherin' you?"

"No," she said. "I was on my way in and we just stopped to talk for a minute."

She didn't mention that she'd been nervous at being confronted by Chase and the other two boys. Brooks would seize any excuse to cause trouble for Chase and his friends. Phyllis didn't particularly want to cooperate with that vendetta.

Brooks looked like he didn't believe her—or at least didn't want to believe her—but after a moment he nodded and said, "All right, you can go on in. You three troublemakers stay right where you are."

"We're not making any trouble," Chase said, "and we've got to get to class."

"Are you arguin' with me, kid?"

"No. Just saying we need to get to class."

Phyllis said, "I'm sure it'll be all right, Mr. Brooks. I'll keep an eye on them and make sure they go on where they're supposed to be."

"Yeah? How do I know you can do that?"

Phyllis drew in a deep breath and squared her shoulders. "I was a teacher before you were born, Mr. Brooks," she said coolly. "I think I know how to keep an eye on students."

Brooks looked like he wanted to grind his teeth together, but after a moment he muttered, "All right, all right. I know you punks think you can get away with anything you want around here, but that ain't the way it is. Now move along."

"Sure, officer," Riley said with a mocking tone in his voice. The big young man called Duncan took hold of his arm and steered him toward the door. Chase looked like he wanted to say something else to Phyllis, but instead he turned and followed his friends into the school.

"I'm not surprised you stuck up for them," Brooks said to Phyllis. "You didn't back me up with Shula yesterday, did you?"

"I just told Mr. Shula what I saw happen in Miss Trahearne's room."

"You mean how that kid attacked me?"

Phyllis kept her voice level as she said, "I told the truth and answered all of Mr. Shula's questions. Now *I* have to get to class, too."

Brooks just grunted and turned away. Phyllis went on inside, halfway expecting to see Chase lingering nearby in hopes of talking to her again. He was nowhere in sight, though, and neither were Duncan or Riley.

A harassed-looking but clearly excited Frances Macmillan was waiting outside the door of Phyllis's classroom. "This is the big day," she said. "Friday the Thirteenth."

"I have everything ready that I baked," Phyllis said. "Carolyn will finish the snacks she's making during the day, and she'll have them ready for me to bring this evening with everything else."

"I'm glad to hear it. None of the other volunteers have backed out, so I'm hoping that everything is going to go very smoothly."

"I hope so, too," Phyllis said. She also hoped that Ronnie would come to the dance, and that things on that front would start to settle down. She thought of something else and asked, "Is Amber Trahearne still going to be one of the chaperones?"

"As far as I know," Frances said. "Why wouldn't she be?"

She didn't seem to know what had happened after school the day before, which was a little surprising to Phyllis. Gossip in a school traveled practically at the speed of light. The fact that Frances didn't know told Phyllis that Tom Shula was doing a good job of keeping a lid on things.

It might have been better, though, if Amber *had* backed out. If Chase attended, it would lead to tension, and there had been more than enough drama recently without making it worse.

But in answer to Frances's question, Phyllis just said, "Oh, no reason. I was wondering, is all. I know that she and Sam have become good friends."

"You don't have to worry about that." Frances leaned closer and lowered her voice to a conspiratorial tone. "From what I hear, Amber goes for younger men, if you know what I mean."

So maybe the gossip *had* started making its way around the school. Amber might be the target of some stares and whispers tonight. But that was her problem, as well as the price she'd have to pay for giving in to her impulses.

If that was the only price, Amber would be lucky, Phyllis thought.

The day went by quickly, with no more incidents involving Ronnie, Chase, Amber, or Ray Brooks. In fact, Phyllis didn't even see any of them except Ronnie, who was sitting by herself in the cafeteria during lunch. A part of her wanted to go over and sit with the girl, but she knew Ronnie wouldn't want that so she sat with Sam instead, as usual. Amber didn't come to lunch; Phyllis supposed she ate in her classroom. Quite possibly she didn't want to face them after what had happened the day before. Not wanting to embarrass her, Sam hadn't stopped in at her classroom to say hello as he often did.

By the time Phyllis got home, she had put all those thoughts out of her head and concentrated only on getting ready for the dance. Carolyn had the containers of mummy cupcakes and mummies-in-a-blanket ready to go. She had also made little cups of cheese crackers with ranch seasoning, explaining to Phyllis, "These will go good with the mummies-in-a-blanket and will give the students another option that isn't so sweet."

"They'll probably eat some of those things," Eve said, "but the cupcakes and cookies will disappear first, I'll bet."

"No bet," Sam said. "You can't underestimate a kid's sweet tooth." He grinned. "Or an old man's."

"Hands off until we get there," Phyllis warned him. "Did Ronnie say for sure whether she's going?"

"I think she is. She mentioned it on the way home. Said she didn't like gettin' dressed up. I told her just to wear whatever's comfortable."

Carolyn said, "Telling a teenage girl something like that can cause trouble. You know some of them like to dress to shock people."

When Ronnie came downstairs, though, she wore jeans with some fashionable rips in them and a lightweight jacket over a black lacy top. The outfit wasn't fancy, but it looked good on her and Phyllis was pleased there was nothing really extreme about it.

"You look beautiful, dear," Eve told the girl.

"Yeah, you do," Sam agreed.

"Thanks," Ronnie said with a shrug. "Not that it'll matter. Nobody's going to ask me to dance, anyway."

"You might be surprised," Phyllis told her, thinking of Walter Baxter and wondering if the boy was going to be there. Of course, Ronnie might not want to dance with a freshman or sophomore. But from what Phyllis had seen, students these days were a bit less conscious of things like that than they had been when she was young and no upper-class girl would be caught dead even acknowledging an underclassman's existence.

Sam and Phyllis went upstairs to change into something a little nicer than their everyday work clothes. They met in the hall.

"Don't you look nice," Sam said, helping her slip on the purple jacket that matched her slacks. She was wearing a lilac shell under it that matched her low-heeled shoes.

Looking Sam over, Phyllis remarked, "Thank you. You're looking pretty dashing yourself." He had on black slacks with a crisp white shirt. Tieless, of course.

Phyllis and Sam decided they would all go together in Phyllis's Lincoln. There was plenty of room in the back seat for all the goodies they would be taking, as well as Ronnie. They ate a light supper, just some small salads, and then loaded everything in the car.

The overcast had hung around all day, but there was no rain in the forecast. The air was cool but slightly oppressive. Phyllis parked in front of the school this time instead of going around back to the faculty lot, because the front entrance was closer to the cafeteria and they wouldn't have to carry everything as far.

There were already quite a few cars in the parking lot, and even though the dance didn't officially start until seven o'clock, some students were already hanging around in the mall, waiting for the cafeteria doors to open.

Phyllis didn't see Chase Hamilton among them. A dance like this probably wasn't the sort of thing that would interest Chase and his friends, although they might well be in the parking lot selling drugs. Phyllis told herself she didn't have any proof of that, but the thought crossed her mind anyway.

Ronnie was carrying a couple of the plastic containers. She said, "Will they let me in the cafeteria since the dance hasn't officially started yet?"

"You're helping us with the snacks," Phyllis said. "I don't think anyone is going to tell you that you can't come in."

Sam said, "You might want to come back out here and hang around with these other kids once we get everything inside, though. That'd be fine if that's what you want."

"We'll see," Ronnie said.

One of the cafeteria doors swung open before they

reached it. Walter Baxter stood there, holding it for them.

"Hello," he said. "Do you need some help?"

"No, I think we have it," Phyllis said. "What are you doing here, Walter?"

"Inside the cafeteria, you mean? I help with the sound system."

Somehow they didn't surprise Phyllis.

Walter smiled shyly at Ronnie and went on, "Hi, Ronnie."

She frowned and said, "Walter, isn't it?"

"Yeah. I'm in your Language Arts and Astronomy classes."

"Yeah, sure. How're you doing?"

"Oh, I'm fine." Walter swallowed hard, causing Phyllis to wonder if he was trying to work up the courage to ask Ronnie if she'd dance with him later. But Ronnie walked on past without another look at him, leaving him with a look of disappointment on his face.

Quietly, Sam said, "Don't worry, son. She's only got eyes for somebody else right now, but that won't last forever."

"It won't?"

"Trust me."

Sam went on into the cafeteria. Phyllis smiled at Walter as she went past and thanked him for holding the door. "My pleasure," he said.

Frances Macmillan was already there, of course, bustling around and trying to check on a dozen different details at once. Some of her student council kids were helping her, and a handful of teachers were also on hand.

Phyllis saw Ronnie break stride and realized that the girl was staring across the big room at Amber Trahearne. Amber met Ronnie's gaze for a second, then looked at Phyllis and Sam, then turned away. Under the circumstances, Phyllis might have expected Amber to dress down a little, but instead she looked stunning in a silk blouse, short skirt, and higher heels than she would have ever worn to teach class.

Ronnie looked angry, so to distract her from the sight of Amber, Phyllis moved up beside her and said, "I think all the snacks need to go up there on that table in the front of the room."

"Yeah, I guess," Ronnie said. She turned her gaze away from Amber and walked with Phyllis and Sam toward the table.

Frances met them there. "This is wonderful. I'm so glad you're here. Just put everything on the table. The punch should be arriving shortly."

"Everything goin' all right?" Sam asked.

Frances blew hair out of her face, laughed, and said, "So far!"

"Let's hope it stays that way," Phyllis said.

Chapter 18

Phyllis watched Sam's head bobbing slightly in time to the music. She tended to like the music they had grown up with in the Fifties and Sixties, and Sam did, too, she knew, but he was wide-ranging in his tastes and was familiar with quite a bit of the current music. As she had heard him say, he could listen to almost anything.

She had no idea what the title of this song was or who sang it, and she couldn't make out any of the lyrics. But it had a catchy tune. You could dance to it, as the kids on *American Bandstand* used to say, 'way back when.

The cafeteria was full of students, some of them dancing but many just standing around socializing. A lot of them were doing things with their phones, too. Phyllis couldn't grasp the idea of coming to a dance only to stand around looking at a cell phone screen, but she had long since given up understanding the almost mystical connection between kids and their phones.

The dance had gotten underway on time, with several

hundred students streaming through the cafeteria doors bent on enjoying themselves. By that point, the table was loaded down with snacks in addition to the ones Phyllis had brought, as well as a large bowl of punch. At the far end were a couple of ice chests with canned sodas and bottled water in them.

Although some of the kids had visited the table for food and drinks, it hadn't been busy so far. They had their minds on dancing, flirting, and talking. Phyllis tried to keep an eye on Ronnie and see how she was doing, but that was difficult with such a crowd. After a while, Phyllis had to give up. The best she could do was hope that Ronnie was having a good time.

She stayed near the table, but Sam circulated around the room more. Phyllis saw him talking to Amber once, but the conversation lasted only a moment. When he drifted back to the table, Phyllis asked him, "What did Amber have to say?"

"Not much," Sam replied with a shake of his head. "She just said she was sorry for any trouble she had caused. I told her she needed to think about what she was doin'. She said she would and promised that things were gonna change. She said there wouldn't be any more problems." Sam paused, then went on, "I can believe it, too, because Chase is here and the two of 'em didn't go anywhere near each other."

"Chase is here?" Phyllis said, surprised.

"Yeah, I spotted him over in the corner with a couple of other boys. Tall, skinny fella with long hair, and a big one who looked like he ought to be a football player but probably wasn't."

Riley and Duncan, Phyllis thought. Their presence seemed even more unlikely than Chase's. The dance was open to any and all students, though, so she supposed they had every right to be here.

Actually, she was more worried about something else. "Do you know where Ronnie is?" she asked.

"I saw her a few minutes ago. She was nowhere near Chase, if that's what you're thinkin'. She was talkin' to that nerdy little kid who opened the door for us when we came in."

"Walter Baxter," Phyllis said.

"Yeah, I guess. I don't know him."

"Neither do I, really. At least Ronnie's staying away from Chase."

"Or she hasn't realized he's here yet," Sam said.

Phyllis frowned. She could have done without him pointing out that possibility.

A short time later, Tom Shula came in and stopped at the table to pick up a couple of cookies. He grinned at Phyllis and said, "It's sure been good having you here while we get this new school off the ground. Are you certain you don't want to un-retire and come back permanently? That way we could have goodies like this around all the time."

Phyllis laughed and shook her head. "Sam and I have been glad to help out, but I think we'll be even happier to get back to retirement once Frank and Molly come home. Have you heard anything from them recently?"

"Frank's in a clinical trial that seems to be working pretty well. Conventional treatment wasn't doing much good, you know."

"I know. I'm glad to hear that there's some hope."

"There's always hope, I guess," Shula said.

Phyllis would have liked to think so, but she had lost too many friends and loved ones to believe that. Still, that was no reason to stop fighting. Sometimes, miracles happened.

"I just wanted to stop by and see how things were going," Shula continued. "I'll go tell Frances what a great job she's done."

"I'm sure she'd appreciate that."

The principal waved a hand and moved off into the crowd, munching on one of the cookies he had picked up.

Phyllis felt like somebody was watching her and turned her head to see Ray Brooks walking slowly along the wall at the side of the cafeteria. He wore his usual surly expression. Phyllis looked away and ignored him. She wasn't going to let Brooks get under her skin. He could resent her for not supporting him with Tom Shula all he wanted to. She didn't care.

Eve's prediction was right. The cookies and mummy cupcakes disappeared first, but the mummies-in-a-blanket and ranch cheese crackers proved popular, too. As the evening went on, more students began to visit the table for snacks. Teenagers were always hungry, Phyllis recalled from when Mike had been that age.

The next moment, those thoughts were gone from her head. She saw Ronnie moving toward one of the rear corridors that led out of the cafeteria. The students weren't supposed to be roaming around the school, so everything was off-limits except the cafeteria and the mall. To enforce that, a teacher/chaperone was posted at the entrance to each of those side corridors.

However, no adult was standing near this one, Phyllis noted. Something must have happened to distract whoever was supposed to be there.

Phyllis looked around. She couldn't be sure because there were too many kids in here, but she didn't see Chase anywhere in the cafeteria. He and his friends could have left already, she told herself.

But it was just as likely that they had snuck out the way Ronnie was attempting to. In fact, Ronnie might be on her way to meet Chase right now.

Phyllis glanced along the table. Frances and another teacher stood at the far end. They could handle anything that came up. She looked for Sam but didn't see him. Another turn of her head showed her Ronnie again, disappearing into that corridor.

She was going to have to go after the girl, Phyllis realized. She had a legitimate reason to do so: Ronnie was breaking the rules by leaving the cafeteria that way.

Phyllis had just taken a step away from the table when a crash sounded behind her.

She turned around quickly and saw the punch bowl lying in pieces on the floor behind the table. A pool of red punch spread around the debris. In front of the table, a horrified-looking girl cried, "Oh, my God, I'm sorry! I didn't mean to bump the table. I just tripped! I didn't know the punch bowl was so close to the edge."

Frances hurried over to her and said, "That's all right, dear, I saw the whole thing. I know it was an accident." She glanced at Phyllis. "I think I saw Mr. McCracken going around the back way toward the band hall just a little while ago. Can you go see if you can find him, Phyllis?"

"All right," Phyllis said. George McCracken was one of the custodians at the high school and normally worked at night like this. He would have what was needed to clean up the mess.

Of course, the hallway leading from the back of the cafeteria to the band hall was on the other side of the big room from the corridor where Ronnie had gone, so if Phyllis went to find him, she couldn't check on the girl. But it wouldn't take long, she told herself as she hurried out of the cafeteria to do as Frances had asked.

She didn't see Mr. McCracken anywhere as she went toward the band hall. When she reached it, she pulled open one of the double doors and looked inside. The room was dark.

"Mr. McCracken?" Phyllis called. No answer.

She looked the other way along the hall that led all the way to the lobby just inside the school's front entrance. The custodian wasn't in sight.

Maybe he had gone in a different direction once he was back here. Part of the school was built on a hill, and a nearby set of stairs led down to a tiny, isolated corner where three classrooms were tucked away. Mr. McCracken could be down there in what some students had dubbed The Dungeon, cleaning those rooms.

She started toward those stairs. She had to go around a couple of corners to get there. The music coming from the cafeteria was already muffled by distance and the labyrinth of corridors, and as she turned those corridors the sound faded even more.

She heard a rapid, irregular patter of footsteps somewhere nearby and looked over her shoulder. She didn't see anyone, but she realized just how gloomy it was, here in the far back reaches of the sprawling building. The lights in the halls were set up on motion detectors at night, so they came on whenever someone walked through them, but they went off when the movement was gone. So all the halls between Phyllis's location and the cafeteria were dark.

Except for one ahead of her where the lights suddenly came on. She caught her breath and paused for a second, then continued on resolutely.

Ronnie came around the corner and stopped short at the sight of her.

"Mrs. Newsom," she said. "What are you doing back here?"

"A better question is what are you doing?" Phyllis responded. "Students are supposed to stay in the cafeteria or mall."

"I know." A guilty look came over Ronnie's face. "It's just that . . . I saw Chase come back here, and I thought maybe I could talk to him one more time, and we could get things settled between us . . ."

"There's nothing to settle. You're a smart girl, Ronnie. You know he doesn't want to be your boyfriend."

"But if I could just get him to see how good we'd be together!"

Phyllis didn't want to be cruel, but she said honestly, "I don't believe that's ever going to happen."

"You can't be sure of—"

From the corner of her eye, Phyllis saw a light flick on, illuminating the top of the staircase off to her left. The light wasn't actually in the stairwell, but it came from the hallway below.

Someone was down there. Mr. McCracken . . . or Chase Hamilton?

And if it was Chase, what was he doing in The Dungeon?

"We'll talk about this later," Phyllis said. "I'm looking for Mr. McCracken, the custodian. The punch bowl got broken and there's a mess he needs to clean up."

"I'll help you find him. Although I haven't been able to find Chase."

Phyllis started to tell Ronnie to go back to the cafeteria instead, but then she realized it was possible the girl might run into Chase along the way. Better to keep Ronnie with her, she decided.

"All right, come on." They walked toward the stairs. Their footsteps echoed hollowly in the empty hallways. Phyllis wondered briefly if it had been Ronnie she'd heard a few moments earlier. She didn't think so. Those hurrying footsteps had sounded as if they came from a different hall.

The light downstairs went out before they reached the stairwell. Phyllis frowned. If Mr. McCracken was down there cleaning he should have been moving around enough to keep the light on. Unless he was inside one of the classrooms, then the light might have gone off, she reasoned.

Then it came on again.

Something about the way things were happening made a chill run down her back. She was at the top of the stairs now, so she stopped and called, "Mr. McCracken?"

A strange sound came from below. It might have been a human groan. Ronnie exclaimed, "What was that?"

The lights went off again.

"Ronnie," Phyllis said, "I'm starting to get the feeling that something is wrong. Go back to the cafeteria and find your grandfather."

"What are you going to do?" Ronnie gestured toward the stairs. "Go down there and see what it is we heard? It might be a . . . a monster!"

"You don't believe in monsters."

"Right now, I don't *disbelieve* in them."

Phyllis wasn't sure she did, either.

The light in the downstairs hall came on.

"Ohhhhh, shoot," Ronnie said in a half-whisper. "Let's both get out of here."

The pained noise sounded again. Phyllis said, "Someone down there is hurt and needs help. You stay right here. I'll go down and have a look."

Ronnie seemed to want to argue, but she didn't. She nodded and said, "Okay. Just be careful."

"I intend to," Phyllis said. She started down the stairs. There was plenty of light for her to see where she was going.

When Phyllis reached the bottom of the stairs, she stopped on the last step and leaned forward to peer around the corner.

About twenty feet away, a man lay face down on the tile floor. As Phyllis watched in horror, he groaned again and tried to heave himself up on hands and knees. He lifted his head just enough for Phyllis to recognize him as Ray Brooks—and recognize the lines of mortal agony etched into his face as well.

Then his strength deserted him and he toppled over onto his left side. He rolled onto his back. His arms flopped out loosely at his sides. The light from the fluorescent fixtures on the ceiling shined down on the spreading patch of red on the front of his shirt. A trail of crimson ran down the hall where Brooks had crawled along and tried to get to his feet, only to fail.

The amount of blood and the limp way his arms had fallen told Phyllis that Ray Brooks was probably dead.

Chapter 19

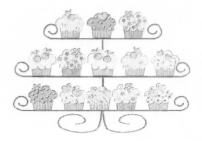

This wasn't the first time Phyllis had seen a body, but the sight was still enough to make her heart beat heavily. She put her left hand against the brick wall of the stairwell to steady herself.

"Mrs. Newsom!" Ronnie called from the top of the stairs, making Phyllis jump a little. "What is it?"

Without turning her head, Phyllis told the girl, "Go find your grandfather, right now." She hoped Ronnie could hear the urgency in her voice.

Then a thought occurred to her, and she cried, "Wait! Come down here."

She was remembering those footsteps she'd heard. Could that have been killer fleeing from the scene of the murder? If that was true, he could still be somewhere close by, waiting to see if his crime was going to be discovered. Ronnie might run right into him . . .

Ronnie edged down the steps, obviously nervous. "What's down here?" she asked.

Phyllis had taken out her cell phone. She checked for service and saw that there was only one bar. The school had its own wi-fi network, though, and she was able to connect to it. She thumbed Sam's number and lifted the phone to her ear, listening to it ring on the other end.

While she was doing that, she motioned for Ronnie to stop a couple of steps above her. Phyllis looked past the girl at the top of the stairs. Thoughts flooded her mind. She was just assuming that Ray Brooks had been murdered, she told herself. She hadn't seen what happened.

But it seemed unlikely that anyone could injure themselves that badly, either accidentally or on purpose, without using a gun, and Phyllis hadn't heard any shots back here.

So the assumption that there was a murderer on the loose was justified enough to warrant plenty of caution.

At the same time, since this part of the school was built against a hill, there was only one way in or out of The Dungeon: these stairs. If the killer came back, she and Ronnie would be trapped down here.

The smart thing would have been for both of them to get back to the cafeteria and seek help as quickly as they could. But to do that they would have to leave the body here, and Phyllis knew how important it could be to the investigation that the crime scene remain undisturbed.

All that went through her mind in the time it took for Sam's phone to ring three times. He wasn't answering, and Phyllis wondered if he could even hear it ringing over the sound of the music in the cafeteria . . .

"Phyllis? Where are you?"

The sound of his voice in her ear made her close her eyes for a second and heave a sigh of relief. Then she said, "Sam, do you know where The Dungeon is?"

"The what? Wait . . . That little downstairs hall at the back of the school where there are a couple of classrooms?"

"That's right. Ray Brooks is back here, and he's been hurt. There's a good chance that he's . . . dead."

"Good Lord! Are you sure?" Then before she could answer, he went on, "No, never mind. Are you all right?"

"I'm fine. But Sam . . . Ronnie is with me."

She heard him catch his breath. Then he said, "Get out of there, both of you, right now."

"We need to stay and keep an eye on the crime scene. Find Tom Shula and both of you get back here. Tell Frances or someone else to call 911."

"I'm on my way. Phyllis, you stay on the line, just in case . . ."

His voice trailed off, but Phyllis knew what he meant.

Just in case the killer came back, so she could identify him.

"I'm here," she said, but he didn't respond. She could hear his breathing, though, and found herself hoping that the stress wasn't going to cause him to have a heart attack.

Ronnie's eyes had widened in shock when Phyllis said that about Ray Brooks being dead. She moved to the side, as if she intended to edge her way around Phyllis and take a look for herself. Phyllis put out her free arm to stop her.

Less than a minute passed before Phyllis heard shoe leather slapping the floors above them . . . but it was a long minute. Then Sam called, "Phyllis!"

"Down here!"

Sam appeared at the top of the stairs, still clutching his phone in his left hand. Tom Shula was right behind him. Both men looked upset.

Sam paused long enough to tell Shula, "Stay here and keep an eye out for the cops." Then he clattered down the stairs, spread his arms, and gathered both Phyllis and Ronnie to him in a rough embrace. "The two of you are all right?"

"Yeah, we're fine, Gramps," Ronnie said as she tried to

work her way free. "Nothing happened to us. We just . . ." She swallowed hard. "Well, it was Mrs. Newsom who . . . found the body."

He let go of them and stepped down into the hallway. After peering along it for a couple of seconds, he jerked his head in a nod and said, "Yeah, that fella's dead, all right. I can tell from here that he's not breathin'."

"Don't get any closer to him, Sam," Phyllis cautioned. "You don't want to disturb any evidence. It's bad enough we've walked on these steps, and I'm pretty sure I had my hand on the banister as I came down. I probably ruined any fingerprints that were on it."

Sam shook his head. "Doesn't matter. Kids and teachers go up and down these stairs all the time. There's bound to be such a mess of fingerprints on the banister, nobody could ever make any sense of 'em, even those super forensics folks on TV."

No doubt he was right about that, Phyllis thought. Still, she would have been more careful if she had known that a crime had taken place down here.

"Can you tell what kind of wound that is on his chest from where you are?" she asked.

Sam leaned forward and craned his neck to study the corpse. After a moment, he shook his head and said, "Not for sure. I'd have to guess it's some kind of knife wound, though. I don't see any powder burns on his shirt."

"I didn't hear any gunshots, either," Phyllis said.

"There's somethin' else," Sam said, and Phyllis could hear the consternation in his voice. "Somethin' around his mouth, but I can't tell what it is. It looks sort of like . . . cookie crumbs."

No, Phyllis thought. Not cookie crumbs. Not her . . . killer sugar cookies.

At least Carolyn wasn't here to speculate over whether Brooks had been poisoned by the cookies Phyllis had made. Not that anybody would have taken such a theory seriously, considering all the blood Brooks had lost. Still, that was just the sort of thing Carolyn would have said in this situation.

Maybe Sam was mistaken, Phyllis thought. Maybe those *weren't* cookie crumbs he saw. That was something the sheriff's department homicide investigators would be able to determine once they examined the body. They would glean every bit of evidence they could find.

Ronnie was still trying to work her way around to where she could see the dead man, Phyllis noted. She said, "Why don't you go back up there with Mr. Shula, dear?"

"You think I'm morbid just because I want to see him?" Ronnie asked.

"I didn't say that."

"I've seen dead bodies before, you know. I've been to funerals."

"We all have," Phyllis said. "But that doesn't mean you should be looking at this one."

Ronnie sighed and said, "Oh, all right." She started to turn away, but Phyllis stopped her as something else came to her.

"Wait a minute. You said you saw Chase leave the cafeteria and come back here to this part of the school?"

"Yeah, I—" Ronnie stopped abruptly and her eyes got big again. "Whoa! No way. You can't believe that *Chase* had anything to do with this."

"You know he and Brooks didn't get along. They had plenty of reason to dislike each other."

"Brooks *hated* him. You know that. But Chase just wanted the guy to leave him alone. He wouldn't hurt anybody."

"What about those bullies he beat up when he was defending you?" Phyllis asked.

"That was different. They were asking for it. They forced him into it."

Sam said, "Same kind of thing could've happened here. They could've been arguin', and Brooks tried to get rough. He's bigger, burlier than Chase. If Chase had a knife, he might've had to use it to defend himself."

And then run away when he realized what he had done, Phyllis thought. That would explain the rapid footsteps she had heard when she was looking for Ronnie. The gait had been erratic because the person was hurrying, maybe even stumbling a little in shock over what had happened.

From the top of the stairs, Tom Shula called, "Here come the cops."

Ronnie looked intently at Phyllis and said, "Please don't say anything to them about Chase. You know he didn't do this. He couldn't have."

"I'll have to answer their questions honestly," Phyllis said. "But I didn't see Chase back here. You're the one who saw him coming in this direction."

"You got to tell 'em the truth, honey," Sam said to the girl. "You go to lyin' when they question you, and you'll be in trouble. I won't stand for that."

"You're just trying to make it so they'll blame him for killing Brooks," Ronnie said. "You think that'll solve all your problems with me!"

Phyllis said, "We all just want to get to the bottom of what happened here."

Ronnie flung her hands out and said, "Well, then, solve the case! You're the big fancy detective! Find out who murdered Brooks, and you'll see it wasn't Chase."

The wheels of Phyllis's brain were already turning over, had been ever since she had seen Brooks collapse and die. But she had nothing to work with except the obvious: a young man with a history of violence and a reason to hate the victim had been seen in the vicinity of the crime. It wasn't eyewitness testimony, by any means, and it was much too early for any forensic evidence to come into play, but Phyllis knew the simplest explanation was also the most likely to be right.

Whether it was self-defense or cold-blooded murder, Phyllis didn't know, but the simplest explanation was that Chase Hamilton had killed Ray Brooks.

Chapter 20

A couple of uniformed sheriff's deputies appeared at the top of the stairs. Phyllis had hoped one of the deputies to respond to the call might be Mike, but she knew that was unlikely. In fact, she didn't recognize either of them. One was a young man, the other a young woman. The male deputy motioned for Tom Shula to stay back while the woman started down the stairs toward Phyllis, Sam, and Ronnie. Her right hand was on the butt of her holstered service weapon.

"You folks just stay right where you are, where I can see you," she said. "Where's the body?"

Sam pointed. "Right over there. Ronnie, scoot over so the deputy can get by."

The deputy moved past Phyllis and Ronnie and stepped down into the hallway beside Sam. She didn't get any closer to Ray Brooks than that, but keen eyes took in the entire scene for a long moment. Then she called up to her partner, "Jerry, we're going to need the crime scene unit and a homicide team."

"Got it," the other deputy said. He spoke into the radio microphone clipped to his shoulder, putting in the call.

The woman looked at Phyllis, Sam, and Ronnie and asked, "Did any of you touch the body?"

"No, none of us got any closer than we are now," Phyllis replied. "I saw him first. My friend's granddaughter was with me, but she stayed at the top of the stairs."

"I still haven't seen him," Ronnie put in.

The deputy said, "That's all right, you don't need to."

"That's what everybody keeps saying."

The deputy ignored that and asked, "Do any of you know who the victim is?"

"We all do," Phyllis said. "His name is Ray Brooks. He was a security guard here at the school." She drew in a breath. "When I first saw him, he was still alive. He was lying on the floor and tried to get up, but he didn't make it and fell, then rolled over like he is now." She had to swallow before she added, "I assume that was when he . . . died."

And she had seen the last of the man's life run out, she thought. She hadn't liked Ray Brooks, but witnessing his death had left her shaken.

"I'm going to need names for all of you," the deputy said.

"I'm Sam Fletcher," Sam said. "This is my granddaughter Ronnie. Veronica Ericson."

"And I'm Phyllis Newsom. Sam and I are substitute teachers here, and Ronnie is a student."

"You all have IDs?" the deputy asked. Then, before they could answer, she went on, "Wait. Newsom. Any relation to Mike Newsom?"

"He's my son," Phyllis said.

"Then you're that woman who—" The deputy stopped. Her eyes narrowed with suspicion. Clearly, she had heard of Phyllis and her involvement with previous cases. "You're sure you didn't disturb the body?"

"I know better, Deputy," Phyllis replied with a trace of crispness in her voice.

"Okay. All of you can go back upstairs and wait with my partner for the homicide investigators to get here."

"You agree that it looks like murder, then?"

"I don't know anything," the woman said. "It's not my job to even have an opinion."

Phyllis and Ronnie went up the stairs first, followed by Sam. They gathered at the top with Tom Shula, the four of them moving to the side a few feet away from the stairwell.

"My God, this is awful," Shula said. "What in the world happened? What was Ray Brooks doing back here, anyway? No one was supposed to be in this part of the school during the dance." He frowned at Phyllis and Ronnie. "How did the two of you happen to find him?"

"It's a long story," Phyllis said. "I'm not sure we should be going into it until we've had a chance to talk to the detectives."

"I just . . ." Shula shook his head. "I'm just having a hard time understanding all this. I mean, the school year has gotten off to a pretty good start, and since this is a new school you want everything to go well, right off the bat, so the proper tone is set . . ." His gaze intensified. "Does this have anything to do with the fight Brooks got into with that Hamilton kid?"

"No!" Ronnie said before Phyllis could stop her. "It couldn't have anything to do with that."

Phyllis could tell that her quick, emphatic response just made Shula more suspicious. She said, "I think we should just wait for the investigators to get here."

Shula continued frowning at Ronnie, but he didn't say anything else. An uneasy silence hung over the corridor near the stairwell. The male deputy stood at the top of the stairs and watched the four civilians, which didn't do anything to decrease the tension.

The sheriff's department responded quickly and efficiently. Crime scene technicians descended on the scene, followed minutes later by a pair of homicide detectives, both male. Phyllis didn't know either of them.

She wondered if the dance was still going on. The kids had to have seen the officers entering the school. By now speculation would be rampant.

Except on the part of the killer. Considering how quickly everything had happened, Phyllis believed there was a good chance whoever had murdered Ray Brooks was still in the school.

Not surprisingly, the detectives split up the four of them to question them. Phyllis found herself with one of the investigators in a nearby classroom. The man was big and blond and red-faced and looked more like he ought to be at the wheel of a tractor in a field rather than investigating a murder.

"I'm Sergeant Appleton," he introduced himself. "You're Mrs. Newsom?"

"That's right."

"Mike Newsom's mom? The one who's solved all those murders before?"

"Mike is my son," Phyllis said. "I've been lucky enough to figure out a few things in the past."

Appleton grunted. "You planning on figuring out this one?"

"Not at all," she said.

But then, she had never actually *planned* on getting involved in those other cases, either.

"You're the one who found the body?"

"That's right."

"How did you happen to do that?"

"I'm one of the volunteers chaperoning the Friday the Thirteenth dance out in the cafeteria. I saw one of the students heading back into this area and I knew no one was supposed to be back here, so I came to check on that. Also, I was looking for Mr. McCracken, the custodian who's here tonight, because the punch bowl got knocked over and broken, and we needed someone to clean up the mess."

"Did you find the custodian?"

"No, and I still don't know where he is."

And that was vaguely troubling, Phyllis thought. She hoped nothing bad had happened to George McCracken. He had always been friendly to her while she was working here at Courtland High.

"This student you mentioned," Appleton went on. "Are you talking about the girl with the blue hair?"

"Yes."

"Do you know who she is?"

"Her name is Veronica Ericson. She's the granddaughter of my friend Sam Fletcher, who's also a long-term substitute teacher here at the school."

Appleton's pale eyebrows rose. "Sam Fletcher," he repeated. "Your sidekick who's helped you solve those other crimes."

"Sam is my friend," Phyllis said firmly. "Not my 'sidekick'."

"Okay. So the girl is his granddaughter. And you followed her because you didn't want her getting in trouble for leaving the dance and wandering off into an area that's off-limits to the kids."

Phyllis nodded. "Yes."

"So what made you look down there in that hall where the

body is? Was that where Miss Ericson was?"

"No, she was in the hall right outside here. I had found her and was talking to her when we noticed the lights going on and off down in the Dungeon." At Appleton's startled look, Phyllis added, "That's what the students call that little hall. Anyway, at night the lights are on a motion detection system so they come on when anyone walks into a hall and go off when there's no movement. The way the lights down there were acting was so odd that I thought I ought to have a look." Phyllis paused. "It seems to me that what must have been causing it was Mr. Brooks crawling and trying to get up, then collapsing and lying still enough that the sensors thought he was gone."

"That makes sense," Appleton agreed. "So, Ray Brooks, the victim. Do you know anyone who had a reason to want him dead?"

That was the question Phyllis hadn't wanted to answer. Ronnie didn't want to believe that Chase was guilty. To be honest, Phyllis didn't want to believe that, either, no matter that Ronnie had accused her and Sam of that very thing. But she couldn't avoid telling the truth.

"There's a student here, a young man named Chase Hamilton. He and Mr. Brooks have had some trouble recently. I know he was in the building tonight, at the dance."

Appleton pounced on that, just as Phyllis knew he would. "What sort of trouble?" the detective asked.

With practiced efficiency—she had been interrogated before—Phyllis told the investigator what had happened during the past week, culminating in the scuffle between Chase and Brooks the day before. Appleton listened intently and made notes, and every time he scribbled something in his notebook, Phyllis felt like that was another brick in the wall of guilt that was being built around Chase Hamilton.

"Anybody else?" Appleton asked when Phyllis was finished. "What about this math teacher? Miss Trahearne? You said she and the victim used to date. Is she here tonight?"

"She was volunteering at the dance, too. I don't know where she is right now. Probably still in the cafeteria."

"Maybe there was a lover's quarrel between her and Brooks. He wanted her back and got rough . . ."

Phyllis shook her head. "Amber broke up with him a while back, and she didn't want anything more to do with him. She wouldn't have gone down there with him. He would have had to force her, and I think I would have heard her screams."

"What about other people who work here at the school? Was Brooks well-liked?"

Again, Phyllis had to be honest. "I don't think he got along well with anyone. He always seemed to be angry, and for the most part everyone tried to stay out of his way. If he had any real friends among the teachers or staff, I didn't know about it."

"Just because a guy doesn't have any friends doesn't mean he has a lot of enemies," Appleton said.

"No, it doesn't."

"But it increases the odds." Appleton looked at his notebook, then up at Phyllis again. "What could you tell about the wound?"

"Nothing, really. I saw a lot of blood, that's all. Sam said it must have been a stab wound of some kind."

"No guess as to the murder weapon?"

Phyllis shook her head. "None at all."

"Anything else you can add?"

"Not that I can think of," Phyllis said.

Appleton took a business card from his pocket and handed it to her. "If you do think of anything, I'd appreciate a call."

"Of course." Phyllis stood up from the student desk where she'd been sitting. "I'm free to go?"

"Yes, ma'am."

She started to turn away, then paused and said, "Victor Appleton."

The detective looked up, seemingly a little surprised. "You saw my name on the card?"

"No, I remembered you. I'm sorry I didn't remember earlier. It's just that there were so many students over the years. How long has it been?"

"Since I was in eighth grade?" Appleton laughed. "Longer than I want to count up."

"Refresh my memory. Were you a good student?"

"I got C's. B's if I was lucky. But I wasn't a troublemaker. I hadn't got my full growth yet, so I was a pretty scrawny kid. Just kept my head down most of the time."

"Well, I hope you enjoyed the class."

"The way I recall it, I did. But that was a long time ago."

Phyllis smiled. "It's good to see you again. I just wish it were under better circumstances."

Appleton closed his notebook and nodded. "That's what people usually say when they're talking to me."

Chapter 21

When Phyllis came out of the classroom where Appleton had questioned her, she saw Sam a few yards away, leaning against the wall with his arms crossed. He straightened from the deceptively casual pose as Phyllis came toward him.

"You all right?" he asked her.

"Of course. Being interrogated isn't anything I haven't gone through before."

"Yeah, me, too. A few years ago, who'd have thought we'd be so familiar with murder investigations?"

"Certainly not me," Phyllis said.

"Well, some people don't find their true callin' until later on in life."

His tone was light, but Phyllis could see the worry in his eyes. She asked, "Where's Ronnie?"

"That other detective is talkin' to her. He called her in when he finished with me."

Phyllis nodded. They had been kept separate until they could be questioned. That was standard procedure. Of course, if they'd wanted to lie and work out a shared story, they had had time to do that before the authorities arrived.

The two deputies who had answered the original call were still there, standing near the top of the stairwell keeping an eye on things while technicians came and went from the crime scene. Tom Shula was in the corridor, too, pacing back and forth, obviously disturbed by having a murder take place in his school. A moment later, Appleton stepped out of the classroom and said, "Mr. Shula, if I could ask you a few questions . . .?"

"Certainly," Shula said. "The sooner we get this catastrophe cleared up, the better." He went into the classroom with the investigator.

Phyllis watched them go, then asked Sam, "What was Tom doing when I called you and yelled for help?"

"What was he doin'?" Sam said with a slight frown. "I don't know. When you said to bring him along, I looked around until I found him. Didn't take long. He was doin' something with the sound system. I guess they'd had a problem with it. Don't know what he'd been doin' before that." Sam's keen gaze played over Phyllis's face. "You don't think *Tom* could've had somethin' to do with what happened to Brooks?"

"Right now I don't know enough to have an opinion on anything," Phyllis said. "But with that crowd in the cafeteria, and all the music and the lights, it would have been hard to say where someone was all the time." She thought again about the hurried footsteps she had heard. Even though this part of the school was something of a maze, someone who knew it well could cover the distance between here and the cafeteria in a fairly short period of time.

But other than the friction between Brooks and Shula she had witnessed the day before in the principal's office, she didn't know of any reason why Shula might want the security guard dead.

Besides, she had known Tom Shula for years, and the idea that he could be a murderer just seemed so far-fetched as to be ridiculous.

A little commotion made Phyllis and Sam both turn toward the front of the school. Chase Hamilton was walking along the hall toward them, flanked by two uniformed deputies, one of whom held Chase's right arm. He looked upset, which came as no surprise. He wasn't cuffed, but he was definitely in custody, at least for now.

At that moment, Ronnie came out of one of the other classrooms, followed by the second homicide investigator. She stopped short at the sight of Chase, then exclaimed, "Oh, my God! They've arrested you!" She turned to the detective who had questioned her and went on, "This is so wrong! Chase would never hurt anyone. He didn't do anything to Mr. Brooks, I'm sure of it!"

The deputy who had hold of Chase's arm brought him to an abrupt stop before he could get too close to Ronnie. She took a step toward him, but Sam moved to intercept her. He didn't touch her, just got in her way.

"We don't need to be interferin' with the investigation, honey," he told her. "Let's give these folks a chance to do their jobs."

"But they're going to blame him for what happened!" she protested. "You know they are."

Chase said, "It's all right, Ronnie. I didn't do anything. You don't have to worry."

Appleton stepped out of the other classroom with Tom Shula and told the deputies, "Bring him in here." He looked at Ronnie and added, "Nobody's been arrested yet, Miss Ericson. We're just asking questions and trying to figure out what happened here."

"I don't believe you. Chase didn't do this—"

Sam put an arm around Ronnie's shoulders and steered her away. Phyllis went with them but looked back over her shoulder to see the deputies escorting Chase into the classroom. Appleton and his partner followed them in, and the door closed.

One of the deputies farther along the hall stepped into the path of Sam, Phyllis, and Ronnie, causing them to halt momentarily. The man said, "You folks can go back to the cafeteria, but don't leave the school until you've been told it's all right."

"Is everyone being detained?" Phyllis asked.

"Everyone who was here as soon as the scene was secured after the homicide call came in."

Phyllis nodded and thought about the time involved to make that happen. Everything had taken place pretty quickly once she and Ronnie found Ray Brooks's body, but the possibility that the killer had slipped out of the school before the authorities arrived couldn't be ruled out.

The deputy moved aside and they walked on to the cafeteria. The music had stopped—Phyllis could tell that before they ever got there—and a subdued atmosphere hung over the big room as they stepped into it. Students and teachers were huddled in small groups, and a hum of low-voiced conversations filled the air. Deputies were posted at all the exits to make sure no one left.

Frances Macmillan saw them come in and hurried over. She looked even more flustered and harassed than she usually did.

"Do you know what's going on?" she asked. "The police won't tell us anything, they just say we have to wait here until we're told it's all right to leave. Can they do that?"

"They can if they're conducting an investigation," Phyllis said.

"An investigation into *what?* There are all sorts of rumors flying around. Most people seem to think it was a drug bust or something like that, but somebody even said they thought somebody *died*. That would be terrible."

Ronnie started to say something, but Phyllis put a hand on the girl's arm to stop her. The investigators probably wouldn't want everyone in the cafeteria gossiping about the murder. It would be best not to say anything.

Besides, there might well be one person here who knew exactly what had happened. Phyllis looked around the room, trying to study all the students and teachers without being too obvious about it.

Unfortunately, no one was wearing a sign that read *KILLER*.

Frances wasn't the only one who had seen them walk into the cafeteria. Walter Baxter came up to Ronnie and asked, "Can I get you anything? Something to drink? I'd offer to fetch some punch, but unfortunately that's moot now since the punch bowl broke."

"No, I don't want anything," Ronnie said. She didn't thank Walter for the offer or even glance in his direction as she spoke. Phyllis saw Walter's lips tighten a little, but other than that he didn't show any reaction to the casual dismissal.

Sam was looking around the room. He said, "I see Amber over there. Think I'll go make sure she's okay."

Frances frowned after him as he walked off. She said to Phyllis, "Doesn't that bother you?"

"What, Sam checking on Amber?" Phyllis shook her head. "No, because it's Sam. She helped him when he started this long-term sub job, and he considers her a friend. And now that I look at her, she does seem a little upset." She turned to

Ronnie. "Let's go see what's wrong."

"What's wrong is that—" Ronnie began, then stopped short at a stern look from Phyllis. "I know, I know."

"Know what?" Frances asked. "Something bad is definitely going on here, and you know what it is, Phyllis. I'm supposed to be in charge of this dance, so I think I have a right to know, too."

"I'm sorry, Frances. But for now, it's probably better not to say anything."

Frances looked like she was going to continue arguing, so Phyllis took hold of Ronnie's hand and the two of them followed Sam across the cafeteria. Walter Baxter tagged along behind them. Phyllis could have told him he was wasting his time, but she supposed he would learn the lesson better if he figured it out for himself.

They came up to the spot near the far wall where Sam and Amber stood, talking. Amber summoned up a weak smile as Phyllis, Ronnie, and Walter joined them. Phyllis noticed that Amber was in her stocking feet and was carrying her shoes.

"What happened?" she asked.

"Oh, it's ridiculous," Amber replied, "and I know I shouldn't be so upset about it, but when the police came in everybody got scared and upset and I was afraid it was going to turn into a riot. I was trying to calm the kids down and one of them bumped into me and made me stumble and break a heel." She held up one of the expensive designer shoes, which indeed had the high heel barely hanging on. "It's ruined! I know something terrible must have happened or there wouldn't be all these officers here, and I shouldn't be worried about a stupid shoe . . . but it was just so *cute* before this happened."

Phyllis managed not to sigh in exasperation. Having seen a man die tonight, she didn't think Amber should be upset about something so trivial, either. But of course Amber hadn't seen Ray Brooks breathe his last and didn't even know that he was dead.

That thought made Phyllis feel a twinge of guilt at keeping the news from the younger woman. Based on everything she had seen, she didn't believe Amber still had any feelings for Brooks, but she supposed that was possible. The two of them had dated, after all, at least for a little while.

Appleton and the other investigator hadn't specifically told them not to say anything about what had happened. She was considering telling Amber what she had found when Ronnie suddenly gasped beside her.

"Oh, no!" Ronnie said. "They can't! They just can't!"

Amber raised a hand to her mouth in shock as she looked in the same direction Ronnie was looking. Phyllis and Sam turned to see what was going on, too.

Chase and the two deputies who had been escorting him earlier had reappeared and were on their way through the cafeteria, followed by Appleton and the other detective. A stunned silence spread through the entire room as everyone noticed what was different this time.

Chase's hands were cuffed behind his back.

Chapter 22

"No!" Ronnie said. "They can't do that!"

She started toward Chase and the deputies, but Sam took hold of her arm to stop her.

"I know you're upset, but gettin' in a fight with the law won't do any good. It won't help Chase, and it'll just get you in more trouble than you know."

She tried to pull away from him, but his grip was too strong. "You don't understand! They're arresting him! But I know he's not guilty. He didn't kill Mr. Brooks, he just couldn't have."

That settled the question of whether or not to tell Amber what was going on, Phyllis thought. And everyone else nearby, for that matter, because Ronnie was upset enough that her voice was pretty loud. Surprised, excited talk started immediately as the news began to go around the room.

Amber reacted strongly, her precious shoes forgotten as she let go of them and they thudded to the tile floor at her feet. Her eyes were wide with disbelief.

"Ray?" she said. "Ray is dead?"

"I'm afraid so," Phyllis said. "I found his body back in that little downstairs hallway."

"That's crazy. What could have happened to him down there? There's nothing that could hurt any—" Amber broke off and started shaking her head. "Wait. Chase is being arrested. The police think that he . . . No! I don't believe that! He's not a . . . a murderer."

That was one thing—maybe the only thing—Amber and Ronnie agreed on.

"Might not be murder," Sam said. "Those two had had trouble. Could be they got into it again, and things went farther this time. That'd make it manslaughter, or maybe even self-defense."

"Except he didn't do it," Ronnie said, tight-lipped.

"But they have him in handcuffs," Amber said, staring toward the exit where Chase and the officers from the sheriff's department had left the cafeteria and gone out of sight by now.

"Just because he's been taken into custody doesn't mean he'll be charged with murder," Phyllis said. "That won't be determined until later in the investigation."

Walter said, "Or unless he confessed."

The others all turned to look at him, which made him take a step back and add, "I'm just saying that's a possibility."

"No, it's not," Ronnie told him coldly. "Chase wouldn't confess to something he didn't do."

Frances Macmillan joined them and said to Phyllis in an accusing tone of voice, "You knew about this. You knew Ray Brooks had been killed."

"I'm sorry," Phyllis said. "I believed the detectives would want that kept quiet for the time being." She shrugged a little. "Clearly, at this point it doesn't matter."

Phyllis saw one of the deputies still posted at the exit lean his head toward the shoulder where his radio was. A moment later the man raised his voice to be heard over the continuing hubbub in the room.

"You're all free to go," he told the students and teachers assembled in the cafeteria, "but as you leave you're going to need to give your name and phone number to the officers at the front door, in case we need to get in touch with you again."

That announcement started a bit of a stampede toward the exit. The deputy held up his hand to slow the exodus.

"Take it easy," he said. "There's no need to rush. All the excitement is over."

The excitement might be over, Phyllis thought, but the ordeal was just getting started for Chase Hamilton.

Before leaving, Phyllis went to the table where the snacks had been. Frances had gone back there, too, and while she still seemed a little miffed, she said, "Everything you brought went over really well. In fact, it's all gone. I thought the cookies and cupcakes would disappear first, but as it turned out, a couple of the cookies were the last things left. Somebody got them just a little while before all the trouble broke out."

Phyllis looked at the puddle of spilled punch, which had turned into a sticky mess with pieces of broken glass in it.

"No one ever cleaned that up," she said. "Have you seen Mr. McCracken?"

Frances shook her head. "I wonder where he's gone to."

"You remember, I went to look for him earlier—"

"And found a dead body instead." Frances sighed. "I know. But you never found Mr. McCracken."

"No, I didn't. Whose punch bowl was that?"

"Mrs. Chamberlain's. The art teacher."

"Is she going to be upset that it was broken?"

"I don't think so. It's not a family heirloom or anything like that. She told me she bought it last year." Frances frowned and added, "I suppose the student council should reimburse her from the money we made on the dance. It was going to be a pretty successful fundraiser, you know. I'm just sorry we'll probably never get to have another one."

"Why not?"

"Who's going to want to come to a dance if there's a chance there's going to be a murder?"

Phyllis didn't have an answer for that question.

As she gathered up the containers she had brought her snacks in, she wondered if she ought to find one of the deputies still in the building and say something about George McCracken's mysterious disappearance. She would hate to think that the kindly custodian had fallen victim to the killer as well, and even now, his body might be hidden in some out-of-the-way place.

But while she was thinking about that, Tom Shula walked into the cafeteria again, and this time, Mr. McCracken was with him.

The white-haired man had a miserable look on his face, not like anything was wrong, necessarily, but more like he was embarrassed. Phyllis set the stack of plastic containers back on the table and went over to them.

"Mr. McCracken," she said, "are you all right?"

"Yeah, sure, Missus Newsom," he said, clearly not wanting to meet her eyes.

Shula said, "I found him in the band hall just now."

"But I looked in the band hall," Phyllis said with a frown. "I called your name, Mr. McCracken."

"He didn't want to answer you," Shula said. "And he wasn't really in the band hall, but in one of those little practice rooms on the side. Evidently he had a bottle hidden in there."

"Just a little bottle," McCracken said, shuffling his feet and shrugging. "And it's not like I ever got drunk, Mr. Shula. Just a nip now and then to help get through the nights workin' here." He finally looked at Phyllis. "I'm sure sorry I didn't answer you when you called me, Missus Newsom. I heard you, but I'd just slipped in there and taken a drink, and I was afraid you'd smell it on my breath if I came out then. So I figured I'd wait a while, and then when I started to come out, I heard a bunch of people talkin' and it sounded like somethin' bad had happened, so I, uh, I went back in the practice room to wait some more."

"I was going to tear the school apart to find you if I had to, George," Shula said. "I was afraid something had happened to you, too."

Phyllis said, "So was I. In fact, I was just thinking about reporting that you were missing to one of those deputies."

"Mr. Shula told me what happened." McCracken shook his head. "Sure hated to hear it."

"Were you and Ray Brooks friends?" Phyllis asked.

"No, I hated the nasty son of a—Beg pardon, ma'am. But Brooks and me, we didn't get along very well. He said some things about custodians that got me mad. Called us puke-moppers and toilet-scrubbers." A defiant look appeared on the older man's face. "Well, maybe so, but somebody's got to do them jobs. Brooks sure wouldn't have been happy if they didn't get done, let me tell you."

"No, I don't imagine he would have been," Shula said. "None of us would have."

"Anybody who stops to think about it knows that what

you do is important, Mr. McCracken," Phyllis added.

"I appreciate that, ma'am." McCracken shot a glance toward Shula. "Are you gonna fire me because of what you found out?"

"About the drinking?" Shula took a deep breath. "I ought to. But I probably won't. You need to make certain that it never happens again, though."

"It sure won't," McCracken said as he shook his head solemnly. "I can promise you that, Mr. Shula." He looked over at the spilled punch and pointed. "I'd better get to cleanin' that up before it dries even more."

"Is it going to leave a stain on the floor?" Shula asked.

"Maybe. But not if I can do anything about it."

McCracken started to walk off, no doubt heading for one of the supply closets to get something he could use to clean up the spill, when Phyllis stopped him.

"Mr. McCracken," she said, "when you were going to the band hall earlier, after you left the cafeteria, did you see or hear anybody back in that part of the school?"

"You mean, did I see Brooks?"

"Or anybody else."

"No, ma'am." McCracken lifted a hand and rubbed the silvery beard stubble on his chin. "Come to think of it, though, the light was on in that main rear hall, and in the side hall down at the other end from the band hall. So somebody could've come through there just a minute or two earlier."

"And at the far end of that other side hall is the stairwell leading down to The Dungeon."

Shula made a face and said, "I wish people wouldn't call it that. I don't want to be the principal of a school with a Dungeon in it." Then he laughed humorlessly and added, "But what does it matter now? I'm the principal of a school where a murder took place."

"You didn't see anything," Phyllis said to McCracken, "but did you *hear* anything? Voices? Footsteps?"

McCracken didn't answer immediately, but after a couple of seconds he said, "Maybe some rats tippy-tappin' along in the wall. Hard to say, the way those halls echo when they're empty."

"Rats!" Shula repeated. "We have rats already? The school just opened."

"Any place there's a kitchen, you're gonna have to fight the rats. There's just no gettin' around it. The school's been open long enough to attract 'em."

"But nothing else?" Phyllis said. "No people?"

McCracken shook his head again. "No, but I wasn't really payin' that much attention, you know. I had somethin' else on my mind."

"That bottle," Shula said.

A shame-faced look came over McCracken's weatherbeaten features again. He all but hung his head as he said, "Yeah, I'm afraid so."

"Thank you anyway," Phyllis told him, even though he hadn't given her any information she didn't already know. This time when he shuffled away, bent on cleaning up the spilled punch, she didn't stop him.

She wondered if later, when the forensics team was through, he would have to clean up the spilled blood.

She could understand why he might need a drink after that.

Chapter 23

Sam and Ronnie were waiting near the cafeteria's main exit. Phyllis picked up the empty snack containers again and went to join them.

"You need some help with those?" Sam asked.

"No, they're lightweight and no problem." Phyllis smiled. "The one thing that went well tonight. The snacks Carolyn and I made were popular."

"You know Carolyn's gonna have somethin' to say about somebody gettin' killed while you were around."

Phyllis sighed. "I know. But it's not my fault. It just seems to work out that way."

They walked out of the school, pausing at the front entrance to give their names and phone numbers to one of the deputies on duty there. The man entered the information into an electronic tablet and then nodded that they could continue.

"Where have they taken Chase?" Ronnie asked as they headed toward Phyllis's car.

"The county detention center is on Fort Worth Highway," Phyllis said. "We'll pass it on our way home."

"But don't get any ideas about stoppin'," Sam told his granddaughter. "They won't be lettin' Chase have any visitors tonight except his lawyer."

"His lawyer!" Ronnie exclaimed. "That's it! You can get that lawyer you work for to help him. He's really good, isn't he?"

Phyllis said, "From what I've seen, Mr. D'Angelo is an excellent attorney. We don't actually work for him, though, except as consultants now and then."

"But you know him," Ronnie insisted. "He'll help Chase, if you ask him to."

"Chase is the one responsible for asking for an attorney. They'll make sure he knows he's entitled to one."

Although Phyllis didn't see how anyone could be unaware of their Miranda rights in this day and age when they were repeated on TV shows all the time.

Ronnie caught hold of Sam's arm. "Please, Gramps. I'm sure Chase is alone and scared."

"What about his folks?"

"He doesn't have any family. Not down here, anyway. He said something about living with, like, an aunt or uncle or maybe some cousins, up in Pennsylvania, but I'm pretty sure both of his parents are dead. He's eighteen, so he didn't have to get anybody's permission to move down here. Well, I guess he's probably nineteen by now, but you know what I mean."

Phyllis thought about it and said, "He may not have enough money to hire a lawyer, which means he'll get a public defender. I know some of them do fine work . . . but Jimmy is better."

"Yeah, I reckon you're right about that," Sam said in

grudging agreement. "I suppose it wouldn't hurt to give him a call. It's not too late, is it?"

"Lawyers are like doctors. They get called out at all hours of the day and night."

They had reached Phyllis's car. She put the empty containers on one side of the back seat. Ronnie got in on the other side. Phyllis told Sam, "You drive, and I'll call Mr. D'Angelo."

"Thank you, Mrs. Newsom," Ronnie said. "I know both of you think I shouldn't have anything to do with Chase, but I don't want to see him . . . what's the old-fashioned word? . . . railroaded for something he didn't do."

"Nobody wants to see that," Phyllis said.

As they started back to the house, which was located on a side street a few blocks south of the courthouse square, Phyllis took out her cell phone and called Jimmy D'Angelo. The lawyer's office and cell numbers were on her list of favorites. She thumbed the icon for his cell.

D'Angelo answered almost right away. "Phyllis!" he said in his usual jovial, booming voice. "What can I do for you?" Before she could answer, he laughed and went on, "There hasn't been another murder, has there?"

"As a matter of fact, there has," she said.

A sudden silence reigned on the other end of the call.

But not for long. D'Angelo asked, "Have you been arrested?"

"No, of course not."

"Sam?"

"No."

"One of your friends?"

Phyllis said, "I'm not surrounded by murderers!"

"Given your history, I think it was a reasonable question," D'Angelo said.

"But it *is* a young man Sam's granddaughter knows," Phyllis went on. "A student at the high school where Sam and I are substitute teaching. His name is Chase Hamilton. I don't know that he's actually been arrested, but he was taken in for questioning, at the very least. And he was handcuffed."

"That's not a good sign," D'Angelo said. "Where did the crime take place?"

"At Courtland High, the new high school on Farm Road 730 northwest of town."

"He'll be at the county lock-up, then, since it's out of the city limits and the sheriff's department is handling the investigation. Do you know if he already has legal representation?"

"I have no idea," Phyllis answered honestly.

"Well, I'll run over there and find out." He laughed again. "I've already got a reputation as an ambulance chaser, not that I care. Of course, in this case, the ambulance will be going to the morgue, not the hospital."

"Yes, I suppose so."

"I'll give you a call once I know something. You'll still be up?"

Phyllis looked around at Ronnie's face as the girl watched her from the back seat. The light from the Lincoln's dashboard was enough to reveal how anxious and worried Ronnie was.

"We'll be waiting to hear from you," Phyllis said.

Carolyn and Eve were both in the living room watching TV when Phyllis, Sam, and Ronnie came in. Phyllis had dropped off the empty plastic containers in the kitchen.

Raven was curled up in Eve's lap, apparently sleeping, but the black cat opened one eye and gave the newcomers a hostile look that said nobody had better disturb her or cause

Eve to get up.

"You're home already?" Carolyn said as she muted the TV. "I'm no expert on school dances—Lord knows it's been long enough since I went to one—but they must end earlier than I thought they would. It's not even ten o'clock yet."

"This one got interrupted—" Sam began.

"The cops arrested Chase for murder!" Ronnie broke in, unable to contain her rampaging emotions.

Carolyn's eyebrows arched. "Murder? At the high school?"

"I'm afraid so," Phyllis said.

"Who was killed?" Eve asked. She continued to scratch Raven's ears.

"The security guard. Ray Brooks."

"The one you had trouble with," Carolyn said. "Let me guess. Was he poisoned?"

"No, he . . . Wait," Phyllis said. "You don't think *I* had anything to do with it?"

"It's a reasonable question," Carolyn insisted, unknowingly echoing Jimmy D'Angelo. "Not you personally, of course, but people have put poison in things you baked in the past."

"Stabbed, from the looks of it," Sam said. "A mighty ugly business."

"And they arrested Ronnie's drug dealer friend?"

"He's *not* a drug dealer!" Ronnie said. "Oh! Nobody ever listens to me!" She turned toward the hall and the stairs, ready to stomp out of the room, but paused and said to Phyllis, "You'll let me know when you've talked to Mr. D'Angelo again?"

"I will," Phyllis promised.

"Thanks." Ronnie left the room, still angry but not as upset as she had been a moment earlier.

Eve said, "You know you're going to have to tell us all

about this."

"I know." Phyllis sank wearily onto the sofa, and Sam sat down beside her. Carolyn turned off the TV. Whatever they had been watching couldn't compete.

For the next several minutes, Phyllis told them what she knew about the evening's events, with Sam adding some detail now and then. Carolyn and Eve had heard grim recitals like this numerous times before, so they didn't say anything until Phyllis was finished.

When the story was concluded, Carolyn said, "The young man certainly sounds guilty to me."

"But there were no eyewitnesses," Eve pointed out.

"At least none that we know of right now," Phyllis said.

"And you've always been the one to be skeptical of the authorities, dear," Eve went on to Carolyn.

"With good reason," Carolyn said. "How many times have we seen the police arrest someone who turned out later on to be innocent?" She shrugged. "In this case, though, it really seems obvious. I mean, given the young man's history."

Phyllis glanced through the living room's arched entrance to the foyer and the stairs. Ronnie had already gone up to her room, and Phyllis was glad of that. Otherwise she'd probably be in here arguing with Carolyn, which wouldn't be good for anyone.

Eve said, "What about you, Phyllis? Do you think Chase Hamilton killed that man?"

"I don't know," Phyllis said. "I don't really understand it, but for some reason I hope he didn't. I have to agree with Ronnie. Despite everything I've found out about his past, he just doesn't seem like a murderer to me."

Eve nodded. "Well, there you go. I trust your instincts. You haven't been wrong about such things yet, have you?"

Maybe not, Phyllis thought, but there was always a first

time.

She was saved from having to say that by her cell phone ringing. She looked at the screen and said, "It's Mr. D'Angelo." She thumbed it. "Hello."

"Hey, Phyllis, it's me," the lawyer said. "I went over to the detention center and asked to see the Hamilton kid. They told me they'd already kicked him."

"What?"

"They turned him loose."

"But they took him out of the school in handcuffs, right in front of everybody."

"It happens," D'Angelo said. "The cops think they've got the right guy, and then they talk to him some more and decide that he's not good for the crime after all. Or they still think he's the right guy, but they don't have enough evidence to charge him. Could go either way, and in this case I don't have any way of knowing which. I talked to that guy Appleton. Looks like a hayseed, but let me tell you, he's the great stone face. I got nothin' out of him."

"So what happens now?"

"They'll keep investigating. If they still consider Hamilton a person of interest, they'll watch him to see if he tries to run. Other than that, he's in the clear . . . for now." D'Angelo paused. "Do you want me to see if I can talk to him anyway, offer him my services in case they pick him up again?"

"Is that ethical?"

"Well . . ."

"No," Phyllis decided. "For now let's just wait and see what happens."

"Okay. If you need me, you know where to find me."

"Thank you, Jimmy."

"Any time," D'Angelo said.

Phyllis broke the connection and turned her head to see

Ronnie standing in the opening between the living room and the foyer. She had changed into a cotton nightshirt that came down to her knees. It had a bunny on it, and for a second Phyllis thought she looked like a little girl.

"Was that the lawyer?" Ronnie asked.

Phyllis nodded. "He said that Chase had been released by the time he got there."

"They let him go?" Ronnie looked and sounded as surprised as Phyllis had been by the news. "Does that mean they don't think he did it after all?"

"Maybe." Phyllis was going to be honest with the girl. "Or they can't prove it yet but will still try to."

"Then somebody else has to prove that he's innocent by finding out who really killed Mr. Brooks. And I can't think of anybody better to do that, Mrs. Newsom, than you."

Chapter 24

Truthfully, in the back of her mind Phyllis had been expecting that from the moment she had seen Ray Brooks lying on the floor of the Dungeon and realized he was dead. Once again circumstances—or fate, or whatever you wanted to call it—had conspired to place her at the center of a murder case, and someone close to her needed her help. She couldn't turn her back on Ronnie's plea.

But there was nothing else she could do tonight, and she said as much. Ronnie hectored her to promise that she'd save Chase, but Phyllis wouldn't go that far.

"I'll look into it," she said, and then she managed to talk Ronnie into going back upstairs. She didn't know if the girl would be able to sleep or not, but she ought to try, anyway. Phyllis knew she intended to. The strain of the evening had wearied her.

A while later, when she was already in her pajamas but hadn't gone to bed yet, a quiet knock sounded on her door. She opened it to find Sam standing there in his bathrobe and pajamas.

"Talk to you for a minute?" he said.

"Of course. Come in."

Phyllis closed the door behind him. He looked at her, shook his head, and said, "I sure am sorry you got dragged into a mess like this again."

She smiled. "You would think I'd be used to it by now, but somehow I'm not."

"You know you don't have to investigate just on account of Ronnie askin' you to."

"I can't let her down, Sam. But I may not be doing her any favors. If it turns out that Chase is guilty . . ."

"You said you didn't think he is."

"I could be wrong," Phyllis replied. "Despite what Eve said."

Sam scraped a thumbnail along his jawline as he frowned. "I hate to say it, but Ronnie might be better off in the long run if it turns out that fella *is* guilty. He's got a mighty shady background. Shoot, everything you find out about him says that he's a bad character."

"Yes, it certainly does," Phyllis mused.

"Anyway, he's three years older than her, and to tell you the truth, he seems even older. And he's not interested in her, like that. She's wastin' her time swoonin' over him, just like that little freshman Walter's wastin' his time makin' calf eyes at Ronnie." Sam sighed. "Lord, if people could just be lucky enough to fall for the right one the first time around, it'd sure make life simpler."

"And a lot less messy," Phyllis said, "but messy is good. That's what gives life some of its flavor. You wouldn't want everything to work out just right all the time, so that there's never any struggle. Struggle is how people develop character."

"That's true," Sam admitted.

She put a hand on his shoulder and laughed softly. "I haven't heard anybody talk about swooning and making calf eyes for a long time."

"Well, I'm an old geezer. That's how I talk."

"Not too old," Phyllis said.

It was the weekend, so at least Phyllis, Sam, and Ronnie didn't have to get up and go to school the next morning. In fact, Ronnie slept in and didn't come dragging downstairs until nearly eleven o'clock, still in the nightshirt, with her hair tousled from sleep.

She came into the kitchen where Phyllis and Carolyn were and said, "It wasn't all just a bad dream, was it?"

Phyllis didn't have to ask what she meant. She said, "No, I'm afraid it wasn't."

"Well, I could have hoped . . . Is there coffee?"

"Still a little. I can make some fresh."

Ronnie shook her head. "No, that'll do." She got a cup from the cabinet and went over to the coffeemaker to pour. When she had sat down at the table, she asked, "Where's Gramps this morning?"

"He went to the lumberyard to pick up a few things for some project he's working on."

Ronnie jumped a little, then looked under the table and said, "Oh, it's just you, Raven. Sorry, I didn't know you were under there." She reached down, scooped up the black cat, and put Raven in her lap. She petted the cat with one hand and held the coffee cup in the other.

Phyllis and Carolyn were cleaning the kitchen. Phyllis was squeezing a lemon she'd cut in half into a bowl of water. She popped it into the microwave and set the timer for 3 minutes.

She set a second timer for ten minutes so she wouldn't start working on something else and forget to wipe out the inside of the microwave. The sound of the doorbell made Phyllis turn away from the counter.

"Are you expecting anyone?" Carolyn asked.

"No, not at all."

Ronnie set her cup down and dumped Raven on the floor, which made the cat hiss in protest, and got to her feet. "Maybe it's something about Chase," she said. "Maybe it's that lawyer."

She hurried out of the kitchen before Phyllis could stop her. Carolyn blew out a breath and said, "My goodness, she's obsessed with that boy. She seems to think the whole world and everything on it revolves around him."

"When you're that young and that much in love, I don't suppose you can think anything else," Phyllis said. She brushed off her hands on the apron she wore over her jeans and followed Ronnie toward the front door.

Ronnie had it open by the time Phyllis got there. She was a little surprised to see Mike standing on the porch, but once she stopped and thought about it, she wasn't surprised at all.

"Come on in," she told her son, who wore his deputy's uniform and probably was on his way to or from a patrol shift.

Ronnie stepped back to let him in. "Hi, Mike," she said. She suddenly looked a little self-conscious, as if she'd just remembered that she was wearing her nightshirt, and she turned and retreated toward the stairs.

"You probably know why I'm here, don't you?" Mike said as he and Phyllis walked into the living room.

"I'm a good enough detective to figure that out." She smiled. "You came to warn me to stay out of the investigation into Ray Brooks's murder."

"That homicide investigator, Vic Appleton, talked to me this morning. He's heard about your reputation, of course. Probably everybody in the department has. He just doesn't want you getting into any trouble."

"You mean he doesn't want me interfering," Phyllis said. "Did he tell you anything about the case?"

Mike laughed, but he didn't sound particularly happy. "You're determined, aren't you?"

"I didn't say I was investigating. Can't I just be curious?"

"Not lately," Mike replied with a shake of his head. "I guess I can't complain too much, though. You've kept some innocent people from going to prison, and it hasn't been that long since *I* was the one who asked you to help out a friend of mine. I get the impression that Appleton is really touchy about this one, though. He seems to be playing everything closer to the vest than usual. I didn't hear even a whisper of speculation about the case around the department this morning. He's got the lid on tight."

"Does he, now?" Phyllis said.

Mike cocked his head slightly to the side and asked, "What does that mean?"

"Nothing. Like you said, it's just unusual."

Mike looked like he didn't fully believe her but knew the futility of trying to press her to say more. Instead he said, "I just wanted to let you know that Appleton isn't going to cut you any slack . . . even though you were his teacher a long time ago."

"He told you about that, did he?"

"Yeah, he mentioned it." Mike shrugged. "He didn't seem to be holding any grudges against you because of it."

"I'd like to think that *none* of my former students have any old grudges against me." Phyllis laughed. "That's probably a little too much to hope for, though, isn't it?"

"Some people hate school and everything about it, including all their teachers. There's no getting around it. And some of them probably never forget it."

Phyllis knew he was right, and it was a shame people felt that way. It came with the territory, though.

"Can I get you anything?"

"Nah, I've got to get to work." Mike leaned forward and kissed her cheek. "See you, Mom."

Phyllis went with him to the door and watched him walk out to his patrol car. As Mike drove away, Ronnie asked from behind her, "Did he know anything about Chase?"

Phyllis turned and saw that the girl had put on jeans and a t-shirt.

"He was just telling me that the investigator in charge of the case doesn't want me looking into it."

"But you're going to anyway, aren't you? I mean, the cops telling you to butt out never stopped you before. I know. I've read Eve's book."

"That book is fiction," Phyllis said.

"Yeah, but it's based on you and Gramps. Anyway, I've read enough about the real cases to know you don't back off just because somebody tells you to. You keep poking into things until you figure out the truth."

Phyllis saw such desperate hope in the girl's eyes that she couldn't do anything except nod. "There are a few questions that are nagging at me," she admitted. "Nothing in the way of actual evidence, mind you, just things that seem a little . . . off-kilter. Things I'd like to know more about."

Ronnie nodded. "That's what it's going to take to clear his name. Those detectives have made up their minds that Chase is guilty, so the only things they'll look for are the ones they think will make their case. They're not even trying to find out what really happened anymore."

"We don't know that," Phyllis said. However, she had a feeling that Ronnie was right, that Appleton and his partner had zeroed in on Chase to the point they weren't considering anyone else as a serious suspect.

"So what do we do?" Ronnie asked. "How do we go about finding the real killer?"

"*We* don't do anything. I'm sure you have schoolwork to get caught up on this weekend. The best thing you can do as a student is to use your time wisely."

Ronnie flung out her hands and said, "How do you expect me to concentrate on something like school when Chase is in so much trouble?"

"Chase isn't your responsibility. Your grades are." Ronnie looked like she was going to argue, so Phyllis went on, "But there is one thing you can do. People of your generation seem to be able to find out almost anything about anybody. I'm guessing that you know where Chase lives."

"What, you think I'm some kind of stalker or something?" Ronnie tried to sound offended by what Phyllis had suggested, but she didn't pull it off very well. After a moment she sighed and admitted, "Well, yeah, I do."

"Tell me."

"Are you going to go see him?" Eagerness leaped back into Ronnie's voice as she asked the question.

"I need to talk to him. And before you even ask, no, you can't come with me."

"Why not? I want him to know it was my idea for you to help him."

"I think the young man is probably smart enough to figure that out on his own," Phyllis said. "Just give me his address."

"I don't know the actual address. But he has his own apartment, and I can tell you how to find the place and which apartment is his."

"Because you've spied on him."

"I wouldn't call it spying, exactly . . ."

Phyllis brushed aside that protest, and Ronnie told her how to find Chase's apartment. Then the girl asked, "You're not going by yourself, are you?"

"Why would you worry about that if you're so convinced he's innocent?"

"He *is* innocent. I'm not worried about Chase." Ronnie caught her lower lip between her teeth and chewed at it for a second before she continued, "It's those guys who hang around with him. I've seen them there at his place a few times. *They're* the ones I don't trust. Alan Riley and Jason Duncan."

Phyllis filed that information away in her head. She had known the boys' last names, but not their first names.

"I'll wait until your grandfather gets home," she said.

"I have Chase's phone number, too, if you want to call him first."

Phyllis shook her head. "No, I'd rather that he didn't know we're coming."

An idea had formed in her head, starting out as a vague notion but gradually taking on more shape as she thought about it, and she believed the best way to confirm it would be to confront Chase Hamilton with her theory without any warning.

And if she was right, it might well change everything she had believed about the case.

Chapter 25

Sam got back from the lumber yard a short time later. Phyllis heard the garage door go up and went out there to see him carrying in several boards.

"Can I give you a hand with those?" she asked.

"Naw, I got 'em. I'm gonna lean 'em over there in the corner until I get a chance to cut 'em, if that's all right."

"Of course it is. More shelves?"

"Yeah. You know the old sayin': You can't have too many books, you just don't have enough shelves."

"You're the only one I've ever heard say that," Phyllis pointed out.

"Well, I'm old, so it's an old sayin'."

When he had placed all the boards in the corner, she said, "There's something you can do to help me, if you don't mind."

"Of course not. You know I'll do anything in my power for you. What do you need?"

"I want you to go with me to see Chase Hamilton."

Sam's bushy eyebrows drew down. "You're gonna go see that kid? How come?" He held up a hand to stop her before she could answer. "You're gonna do like Ronnie asked and try to solve the case."

"She's miserable with worry over that boy, Sam."

"Worry that I'm not convinced he deserves." Sam propped a hip on the front fender of Phyllis's Lincoln and crossed his arms. "Has she been workin' on you today, tryin' to make you feel sorry for her so you'll help Chase?"

"Not really. But Mike stopped by this morning."

"To ask you to stay out of it, I imagine."

"To let me know that Victor Appleton doesn't want me poking around in the case." Phyllis shrugged. "But why should this case be any different than all the others?"

A short bark of laughter came from Sam. "Mike should know by now he can't make you do anything. Tellin' you *not* to do something is liable to just make you more determined. I figured that out a long time ago. It's easier for me to help you do whatever it is, so you're liable to be safer."

"And that's exactly why I want you to go with me to Chase's apartment," Phyllis said.

"With that boy's background, I'd worry about him, too."

Phyllis shook her head. "Like I've told Ronnie—and you—I don't believe that Chase is a murderer. I don't think I have anything to fear from him. But there's no getting around the fact that he's been known to associate with some unsavory characters."

Sam grunted. "I guess you're bound and determined to go talk to him?"

"I am."

"Then I'm comin' with you, all right. When did you want to go?"

"Now is all right with me. I realize it's nearly lunchtime . . ."

"That's all right. When we're done, we'll go to that Chinese buffet. Haven't been there in a while. Sound like a good idea?"

"It's definitely a plan," Phyllis said. "Let me go get my purse and tell Carolyn we won't be here for lunch."

"We can take my pickup, since it's parked in the driveway."

That was fine with Phyllis, and a few minutes later, they were on their way.

Chase lived in an apartment complex just off Santa Fe Drive, not far from the hospital and medical district. Holland Lake Park, the scene of another murder that had involved Phyllis, lay in the other direction. Phyllis had no trouble giving Sam directions to where they were going, and they arrived less than fifteen minutes after leaving the house.

"You know, he may not be home," Sam said as he parked in the complex's lot.

"He may not be, but we can always come back later if we need to. Ronnie gave me his number, but I didn't want to call him."

"So Ronnie knows where he lives, *and* she's got his phone number." Sam shook his head. "The girl's been sneakin' around spyin' on him. How's she even been doin' that? She doesn't have a car."

"I'm sure she has friends who might help her out," Phyllis said.

"Yeah, teenage girls are always suckers for some romantic yarn. Ronnie probably made it sound like she and Chase were Romeo and Juliet."

"I don't doubt it for a second. That should be Chase's apartment on the second floor, three down from the south end."

They got out of the pickup and climbed the stairs. Phyllis

took a good look around. She heard children shouting in play somewhere, and a TV was playing, but she didn't see anyone. There was no sign of Alan Riley or Jason Duncan, but they could be in Chase's apartment.

There was only one way to find out. They stopped in front of Chase's door. Sam raised his hand and looked at Phyllis. She nodded. He rapped his knuckles sharply against the panel.

The door stayed closed. No response came from inside.

"Not here?" Sam said.

"Try again," Phyllis told him. She could see that there was a peephole built into the door. Chase might be inside looking at them right now, trying to figure out if he wanted to answer or not. She put a determined expression on her face. She wanted him to realize that they weren't going to go away any time soon.

Sam knocked again, a little harder and louder. A moment later, Phyllis heard a chain lock being taken loose. The door opened a few inches. Chase looked out. He was dressed in a sweatshirt and jeans.

"Mrs. Newsom," he said. "Mr. Fletcher. What are you doing here?"

"I'd like to talk to you, Chase," Phyllis said. "It's important."

He shook his head. "I don't have anything to say. I've told both of you, you don't have to worry about me and Ronnie. There's nothing going on, and there won't be anything going on."

"It's not about Ronnie. It's about you."

"No offense, but my life's not any of your business." He started to close the door. "Now, if you'll excuse me—"

"Are you alone, Chase?"

Evidently, that question took him by surprise, because he

stopped with the door still open and frowned. "What do you mean, am I alone?"

"Your friends Alan and Jason aren't here?"

Chase's frown deepened. "Why do you care about them?"

Phyllis lowered her voice. "I don't want to say the wrong thing where they could hear it."

"What the—What are you talking about, Mrs. Newsom?"

Phyllis knew she had to run the risk. She said, "I don't want them to find out that you're actually an undercover police officer."

It was a toss-up which of the men looked more shocked as they stared at her. But Chase didn't deny what she had just said. Instead, after a moment he stepped back, opened the door wider, and said in a taut voice, "Please, come in."

Phyllis did so, with Sam following close behind her. She looked around. The apartment's living room was cluttered, even messy, but no more so than anyone would expect from a nineteen-year-old young man living alone.

Although she suspected that in reality, Chase was at least a few years older than nineteen . . .

He closed the door, turned to look at his visitors, and shook his head. "What in the world would make you say such a crazy thing as that, Mrs. Newsom?"

"It would explain a great many things," Phyllis said. "For example, why you were arrested in Pennsylvania with the other leaders of that drug ring, but the charges against you were dismissed mysteriously."

"Nothing mysterious about it. The cops couldn't make the case, and the DA decided not to go ahead with it. Happens all the time. So they turned me loose."

"The way they let you go last night after leading you out of the school in handcuffs, in front of everyone at the dance? I know you were out of the sheriff's department almost as soon as you went in there, because you'd already told Victor Appleton and the other investigator who you really are when they questioned you in that classroom."

That was mostly a guess on Phyllis's part, but she thought it was a good one. Besides, she had seen the look in Chase's eyes when she had thrown her idea out there. He had been shocked and more than a little alarmed, and if he really wasn't working undercover, he would have just laughed and told her she was crazy without ever inviting them in.

"You've got this all wrong," he said.

"Do I? You've been careful to keep Ronnie at arm's length because she's underage and you're a grown man. But when you were attracted to Amber Trahearne, you were willing to act on that."

"Lots of high school guys have fooled around with female teachers. You know that."

"That's true," Phyllis said. "But once I thought about it, I realized you're more well-spoken than most high school boys I've known. You let your guard down when we were talking in the hall that day, when you told me about everything that happened with Ronnie in Pennsylvania and how she reacted to it. You were talking like one adult to another. And it would explain why I'm convinced you didn't kill Ray Brooks. It's your job to uphold the law, not break it."

"You're reading an awful lot into some feelings."

"Of course I am," Phyllis said. "That's what tells you more about people than anything else. You're bound to know that if you're working undercover."

"I'm not . . . Oh, hell!" Chase blew out a breath, stared at her, shook his head, and then sighed again.

"Who knows about it?" Phyllis said. "Sheriff Haney, I'm sure. And probably Tom Shula, since you're working in his school. But I'm betting that was all, until you told Detective

Appleton last night."

"I didn't tell Appleton," Chase snapped. "Shula did." He rolled his eyes, evidently disgusted with himself. "And now I've just admitted it, haven't I?"

Sam said, "You never had a chance, son. Once she believes she's figured somethin' out, she locks onto it like a pit bull."

"Months of effort almost turned out to be a total waste when Shula blew my cover like that. If I'd had a chance to talk to him first, I would have told him to keep quiet. I never would have told Appleton. I would have let them arrest me and hold me until some public defender arranged bail. But he thought he was helping me out, I guess." Chase laughed. "The funny thing is, just because I'm on the job doesn't mean Appleton's convinced I'm innocent. When they kicked me last night, he told me that if I killed Brooks, he's going to nail me for it."

"But you didn't kill him, did you?" Phyllis said.

"No. Why would I? Because he's a jerk and he caused trouble about me being with Amber? There's all kinds of jerks in the world. I wouldn't risk all my work to bring down the drug operation at Courtland just to get even with one of them."

"Then that *is* what you're doing? Trying to put the drug dealers out of business?"

"Yeah." Chase waved toward a sofa. "You might as well sit down. I guess since you figured out most of it, you deserve to hear the rest of it."

Sam moved aside some clothes that were piled on the sofa, and he and Phyllis sat. Chase went around a counter into the apartment's kitchen/dining room and picked up a chair. He brought it back with him, turned it around, and straddled it.

"My name really is Chase Hamilton," he said. "I'm twenty-three. The department up in Pennsylvania recruited me right out of the academy to go into the high school Ronnie attended. Everything I told you about what happened with her and those bullies was true."

"So you really did just want to help her?"

"Yeah. Sort of against my better judgment, I might add. But I couldn't help it. I felt sorry for her."

Sam said, "I appreciate you stickin' up for her, son."

"Well, I might not have if I'd known everything it was going to lead to . . . Nah, who am I kidding? I would have." Chase paused and took a breath. "But then it was all over—the operation up there, I mean—and I figured I'd never see her again. Everything went so well, the department wanted me to get out of town for a while, so maybe they could use me again. I remembered Ronnie talking about Texas and figured that was far enough away. My chief worked out a deal with the chief in Fort Worth for me to come down here for a while. Then Sheriff Haney asked for the loan of somebody who could go undercover at Courtland . . . and I guess you know the rest of it."

"Does Amber know who you really are?" Sam asked.

"Good Lord, no. That was never planned. It just sort of . . . happened. And it was a stupid mistake on my part, too. I've already told her it can't go on. Something like that could get us both fired."

Phyllis said, "It may cost her her job anyway, if the rumors get around."

Chase shrugged. "There are always rumors. We were careful. Nobody can prove anything. Not even you saw anything that's actually incriminating, Mrs. Newsom."

"I suppose that's true," Phyllis admitted. "As long as you and Amber both deny that there's anything going on between you, the school district won't be able to fire her."

An uneasy silence hung over the room for a moment. Then Chase asked, "So what happens now? What are the two of you going to do?"

"About your undercover assignment?" Phyllis shook her head. "Nothing. That's not really any of our business."

"I'm glad you can see that much, anyway."

Sam said, "As long as you steer clear of Ronnie. I don't want her gettin' mixed up in anything dangerous."

"Believe me, Mr. Fletcher, neither do I," Chase said. "And you don't have to worry about anything happening between me and her. I mean . . . she's sixteen years old."

"Yeah. You'd do well to remember that."

Chase looked at Phyllis again and said, "But that still leaves Ray Brooks's murder. That could foul everything up."

"I don't see how," Phyllis said. "Everyone saw you being taken out of the school in handcuffs. By now the whole student body will know that you're the leading suspect in the murder. I would think that would give you more . . . What do they call it? Street cred? . . . than just about anything else."

Chase shook his head. "Riley and Duncan won't want to attract that much attention. They'll drop me now. Another week or two and I would have had all the others who are involved and the evidence needed to bust them. Now that's not going to happen unless Brooks's murder is solved."

"Well, then, we'll just have to see what we can do about that," Phyllis said.

Chapter 26

She and Sam drove away from Chase's apartment a short time later. They had promised not to say anything to anyone about who he really was.

"That's all I can ask, isn't it?" he asked before they left.

"It's not going to do any good to reveal it," Phyllis said. "That wouldn't bring us any closer to finding out who killed Ray Brooks."

Chase shook his head and said, "I'm a cop, you know. It rubs me the wrong way for a civilian to be investigating a murder. I don't want either of you to get hurt."

Sam said, "We've gotten pretty good at lookin' out for ourselves."

"If we find anything that's solid, we'll let Victor Appleton know right away," Phyllis promised.

Chase laughed. "I'd insist that you stay out of it, but for one thing, it wouldn't do any good, and for another . . . I could use the help, if we're being honest here." He frowned in thought, then went on, "You know, while Appleton was questioning me, he had some of the things they took off of Brooks's body lying on the desk in that classroom. I didn't get a close look at them, but I saw there was a business card with the name Oak Trails on it. Does that mean anything to you?"

Phyllis considered for a moment and then shook her head. "I don't think I've ever heard of it."

"Me, neither," Sam said. "You're sure it came from Brooks's body?"

"It was in an evidence bag," Chase said, "and one edge was stained with blood. I think it must have been in his shirt pocket."

"We'll look into it," Phyllis said.

Now, as Sam drove away from the apartment complex, Phyllis pulled out her phone and launched a search for Oak Trails. That brought up a lot of results, so she narrowed it down by adding Weatherford to the search terms.

The first link on the list made her frown in surprise.

"I've found it," she told Sam. "It's a drug and alcohol rehabilitation clinic."

"A drug rehab place? You reckon maybe Brooks had a drug problem? That might explain why he was so dang grouchy all the time."

"And it might be a connection between him and Riley and Duncan."

"The fellas that Chase is tryin' to get the goods on, right?"

"That's them," Phyllis said. "And they were at the dance last night, too. You saw them."

"Yeah, I remember. I didn't notice 'em bein' around when you called me . . . but I wasn't lookin' for 'em, either. Anyway, with all those kids dancin' and millin' around, it was hard to keep track of who was in the cafeteria and who wasn't."

"Brooks could have tried to buy drugs from them, and the deal went bad somehow. Jason Duncan is big enough to have fought with him."

"You think they'd talk to us at this Oak Trails place?"

"Probably not," Phyllis said. "Places like that are very protective of their clients' privacy, even more so than a regular medical facility. But I don't suppose it would hurt to try."

"After we get somethin' to eat," Sam said. "It's already past lunchtime."

Phyllis smiled. "It certainly is."

They stopped at the Chinese buffet Sam had mentioned earlier, and when they came out forty-five minutes later, they were pleasantly full. Enough so that it was hard to focus on a murder investigation instead of the need for a nap.

Thinking about Ronnie was enough to renew Phyllis's sense of urgency, though. She told Sam how to find Oak Trails, which was on the old Fort Worth Highway east of town.

It was a sprawling, well-landscaped facility which could have just as easily been a retirement home or an assisted living complex. You had to look closely to see the bars on the windows along one wing. The artfully trimmed shrubbery concealed them for the most part.

"Got any idea how you're gonna get 'em to talk to you?" Sam asked as he parked the pickup.

"I suppose I'll have to lie," Phyllis said.

Sam grinned. "Sort of hard to walk the straight and narrow when you're a detective."

Unfortunately, that was true, Phyllis thought. Sometimes, discovering the truth was more important than moral considerations.

She supposed that Saturday afternoon was a popular time for visiting, because the big common room that opened off the lobby had quite a few people in it, including some children. Phyllis and Sam went to the desk on the other side of the lobby, where a pudgy, balding young man greeted them with a professional smile and asked, "Can I help you?"

Phyllis linked her arm with Sam's and said, "We'd like to talk to someone about our grandson."

"Is he one of our clients?"

"No . . . but I'm thinking that perhaps he should be."

A solemn look replaced the man's smile. He said, "That's something that has to be determined by a medical professional, ma'am. If you'd like to schedule an appointment for your grandson to be evaluated, you can do that, but you have to understand, all our clients come to us on a voluntary basis."

"Of course," Phyllis said. "I wouldn't want it to be any other way. I just thought that we could take a look around, talk to someone in charge, get an idea what your program is like . . ."

Her voice trailed off as the young man shook his head. "I can make an appointment for you to talk to one of our doctors next week, but here at Oak Trails, we pride ourselves on our discretion and consideration for your clients. I'm sure you'd want that for your grandson."

"Naturally," Phyllis said. She wasn't ready to give up, despite the front that this man was putting up. "It's just that this facility was highly recommended by a friend of ours, a man named Ray Brooks—"

He held up a hand to stop her. "I'm sorry, I really am, but that doesn't matter. We have our protocol, and it has to be followed."

Sam sighed and said, "Looks like maybe we'll have to try somewhere else, darlin'."

"No, let's not be hasty. You know what Ray said."

"Well, I don't know . . ."

The act didn't do any good. The young man behind the desk continued to look up at them with a bland expression on his face that gave absolutely nothing away.

Phyllis made one last try. "This *is* the facility that Ray recommended to us, isn't it? We're not in the wrong place."

The young man shook his head and said, "I wouldn't have any way of knowing about that, ma'am. You'll just have to go talk to your friend again. Would you like to schedule an appointment for your grandson?"

"No, not right now," Phyllis said. She and Sam turned and headed back to the glass doors at the front entrance.

There were two sets of double doors, with a tiny foyer between them, and they had just gone through the second set and let the doors swing closed when they opened again. A woman said, "Excuse me."

Phyllis and Sam stopped and looked back. The woman who had followed them out of the rehab clinic was in her thirties, Phyllis guessed, although it was difficult to be sure. Her face was thin, and she had the look of a person who had been through a lot in life, most of it unpleasant.

Her eyes were clear, though, and had a look of anger and determination in them.

"I heard you say something in there about Ray Brooks," she went on.

"That's right," Phyllis said. "He's a friend of ours—"

"No, he's not," the woman interrupted sharply. "I know all of Ray's friends. Trust me, there weren't that many. But I was one of them."

Phyllis noticed the way the woman phrased that. She said, "Then you know—"

"That he's dead?" The woman's voice caught. "Yeah, I . . . The cops talked to me . . . last night."

She lifted a hand and brushed the back of it across her mouth. She was obviously shaken. But something strengthened her resolve and she took a deep breath.

"I want to know who you people are and why you're coming around here poking into Ray's business."

"When you say Ray's business," Phyllis said, "do you mean he *owns* this facility?"

"What? No!" A harsh laugh came from the woman. "Ray was a rent-a-cop. Some big corporation owns this place."

"That's what I thought. Then he must have been a patient—"

The woman's features tightened and she took a step toward Phyllis.

"You don't know what you're talking about, lady. If you start going around and spreading lies about Ray, you'll be sorry. I'll—"

Sam lifted his hands and said, "Hold on, hold on. I think we all got off on the wrong foot here. We're not tryin' to spread lies about Ray Brooks or do anything else to hurt his reputation."

"That's good, because I won't stand for it." The woman swallowed hard. "I owe that man so much. I . . . loved him . . ."

Her voice had broken again. She turned away abruptly, and as she did, Phyllis saw the weak autumn sunlight reflecting from the tears running down her cheeks.

"I'm so sorry," Phyllis said. "We never meant to upset anyone. I can tell that Mr. Brooks was special to you."

"He was a big old jackass," the woman said. "But he was my big old jackass."

There was a small area to one side of the parking lot where some concrete benches and a round concrete table were shaded by a post oak tree. Sam pointed to it and suggested, "Why don't we go sit over there and talk? It wouldn't hurt anything to clear the air."

"Why should I talk to you?" the woman asked with a trace of defiance in her voice.

"Because I think you'd like to know who killed your friend," Phyllis said, "and so would we."

"You're not cops. What do you care?"

"I was the one who found him, right after he'd been attacked," Phyllis said.

The woman stared at her. "Really?"

"I wouldn't have any reason to lie about something like that."

"You lied inside, to Ralph. I heard you."

"Because I was trying to get information about Ray Brooks's connection to this facility. He had a card from here in his pocket when he was killed."

"How do you know—" The woman stopped and shook her head. "Never mind. You're some sort of a detective, aren't you?"

"Some sort," Phyllis agreed.

"Oddest-looking one I've ever seen." The woman sighed. "All right. Let's go sit down and talk."

A moment later they had taken seats on the benches, with Phyllis and Sam across the table from the woman, who said, "My name is Keeley Gifford."

The name meant nothing to Phyllis, but she nodded and said, "We're pleased to meet you, Ms. Gifford. You and Ray Brooks were . . . close?"

"He was my boyfriend, if that's what you mean."

"For how long?"

Keeley Gifford made a face. "Only a month or so. But that doesn't mean it didn't matter."

"No, of course not," Phyllis said quickly. "Did the two of you meet . . . here?"

"Yeah." Keeley laughed humorlessly. "But not the way you probably think. I was a patient, but Ray wasn't. He vol-unteered here."

Phyllis had to frown. The concept of Ray Brooks doing something selfless was just so strange that she couldn't help it.

Keeley saw the reaction and laughed again. This time the sound was a little more genuine.

"Yeah, I know," she said. "Ray wasn't an easy guy to get along with. Most people didn't like him. But he didn't care. He wanted it that way. He didn't want to let anybody get too close to him, because of his mother."

"What about his mother?" Sam asked.

"She was a junkie. She used pretty much all the time while he was growing up. She'd try to get clean, and she'd get off the stuff for a little while, but then she'd slip and go right back to it. Ray was fifteen years old when he came home from school one day . . . and found her dead from an over-dose."

"Good Lord," Sam muttered.

Phyllis reached across the table and clasped one of Kee-ley's thin hands. "That's terrible. Is that why he didn't use drugs?"

"He hated the damn stuff! Drugs destroyed his mother. He had to go live with a foster family, but as soon as he could, he went out on his own. He started working with different anti-drug and rehab programs, trying to make a difference so other people wouldn't have to go through the things he did."

"I had *no* idea."

"Not many people did. Like I said, Ray liked to keep peo-ple at arm's length . . . except for the ones he was trying to help. Like me." Keeley sniffled. "I don't know if I would have made it . . . if I'd be clean today . . . if not for Ray. And now he . . . he . . ."

She sobbed for a few minutes. Phyllis and Sam let her cry. There was nothing they could say to ease the pain of Keeley's loss.

But there might be something they could do, Phyllis thought. Finding Brooks's killer wouldn't bring him back, but it might help Keeley find closure and acceptance.

When the woman had gotten her composure again, she said, "The police found my number in Ray's phone and saw that he had called me a lot. So they came to see me and told me that he'd been killed and asked a lot of questions." She shrugged slightly. "They might have considered me a suspect, since Ray and I were dating, but I've moved back in with my parents and I was with them all evening. I guess the cops believed them when they said I was home. I've been volunteering as a counselor here, too, and I almost didn't come in today after finding out about Ray's death last night. But it's always better to stay busy, so I figured . . . I figured I might as well . . ."

Keeley had to take a moment again.

"How are you two involved with this?" she asked after she had drawn in several deep breaths.

Phyllis explained their connection to the case, and as she spoke, Keeley's eyes widened.

"I remember now!" the woman said. "I've read about you. You really *are* a detective."

"I try to figure things out," Phyllis said.

"And you think you can figure out who killed Ray?"

"I'm going to try."

"Good. But I don't envy you the job. Except for me and a few other people, everybody hated him. I can admit that. He was always talking about the trouble he'd had with people at school."

"Did he ever mention someone named Chase Hamilton?" Phyllis asked.

"Hamilton . . . No, I don't think so."

"Alan Riley or Jason Duncan?"

Keeley shook her head. "Ray never mentioned names much. It was always some crazy bitch or some no-good . . . Well, let's just say that Ray had a colorful vocabulary and knew how to use it. But that didn't mean he was a bad guy. His whole attitude, that was just a way of putting up a wall so people wouldn't try to get too close to him. He might not have ever let me in, if he hadn't just broken up with his last girlfriend. He didn't deserve to get killed for being like that, though. Some people in this world maybe deserve killing, I don't know about that. But I'm absolutely sure that Ray Brooks wasn't one of them."

Chapter 27

"Do you believe her?" Sam asked as they drove away from Oak Trails a short time later.

"About what?" Phyllis said. "Ray Brooks actually being a decent human being? I'm not sure. I barely knew the man, and she seemed awfully sincere about the way she felt about him." She thought for a moment and then nodded. "Yes, I'm inclined to believe her."

"Then he wouldn't have been tryin' to buy drugs from Riley and Duncan. Wouldn't have wanted anything to do with anybody who was mixed up in that business."

"That's the way it seems to me. So the motive for his murder must be something else. A disagreement with some other teacher, maybe?"

Sam frowned and said, "Not so fast. Brooks wouldn't have been buyin' drugs from those two, but maybe he caught 'em sellin' to somebody else. That makes a lot more sense than somebody gettin' mad enough to kill because Brooks yelled at 'em for parkin' in the wrong place or somethin' like that."

"You're right," Phyllis agreed. "That brings us back to something we can't really investigate, though. You and I aren't equipped to try to bring down a drug ring."

"I dunno. Jason Norris is blamed near our age, and I'll bet he probably could."

"Neither one of us is Jason Norris."

"Well, that's true. You know why he doesn't wear a watch?"

"Who, Jason Norris?"

"Yeah. It's because he tells the rest of the world what time it is."

Phyllis laughed in spite of herself and said, "Okay. Good point."

Then she went back to thinking about Ray Brooks. They had found out more about him than she had really expected to when they paid a visit to Oak Trails . . . but they still didn't seem to be any closer to finding his killer.

Nor were they by the time Monday morning rolled around and it was time to go to school again. Phyllis had spent the rest of the weekend pondering the case from every angle she could think of, but the answer still eluded her. She felt like it was out there just beyond her reach, that she ought to be able to grasp it, but whatever the theory that was trying to form in her brain might be, it kept slipping away from her.

And school, like death and taxes, waited for no one. The bell would ring when it was scheduled to ring.

Ronnie rode with Sam. They left a few minutes before Phyllis did, so by the time she reached the school and parked, she didn't see them anywhere in the parking lot and knew they had gone inside already. She knew Ronnie was disappointed that she hadn't solved the murder yet. When she and Sam got back to the house on Saturday afternoon, Ronnie had been waiting for them, and she obviously expected to hear that the real killer was in custody and Chase's name had been cleared. That hadn't happened.

Ronnie was also worried about how the other kids would treat her. She hadn't made any secret of her crush on Chase, and now he was considered the prime suspect in a bloody murder. Ronnie didn't know if that would make people ostracize her—or treat her like a celebrity. Neither possibility was all that appealing.

High school was a gauntlet that had to be run, Phyllis thought as she walked inside. Sooner or later, everyone was made fun of for *something*. It was how you dealt with such things that determined what sort of person you were.

Frances Macmillan's door was open, and Frances was at her desk when Phyllis walked by. She stood up quickly, causing Phyllis to pause.

"Have you heard anything?" Frances asked as she came over to the door. "About the murder, I mean?"

"No, there haven't been any new developments over the weekend, as far as I know."

That wasn't strictly true. Phyllis had confirmed her suspicions about Chase's real identity, and she knew more about Ray Brooks's background than she had. But she wasn't going to share those things with Frances, especially since she wasn't sure what any of it meant yet.

"I talked to Tom Shula when I came in. He's had some pressure from parents—and the school board—to ban dances and other fundraisers in the future. I think that's just crazy. The *dance* didn't have anything to do with Mr. Brooks being killed. That might have happened anyway."

Phyllis cocked her head and was about to say that she

wasn't sure about that. If not for the dance, Brooks probably wouldn't have been at the school on the evening of Friday the Thirteenth. And more than likely, his killer wouldn't have been, either.

Pointing that out to Francis wouldn't help matters, though, so Phyllis just said, "I hope Tom doesn't decide there won't be any more dances. I know the students enjoy them."

"He said he'd take it under advisement, but he hasn't made up his mind yet. I just wish this whole thing would go ahead and blow over. Maybe it will if they arrest that boy they took in for questioning and he's convicted."

"What if he's not guilty?" Phyllis asked.

Frances frowned. "Do you really think that's possible? I mean, they took him out in handcuffs. Surely they wouldn't have done that if they didn't think he killed poor Mr. Brooks."

So the security guard was "poor Mr. Brooks" now. People's perception of him would probably improve since he was murdered. No one liked to speak ill of the dead.

"I guess we'll just have to wait and see," Phyllis said, but then she noticed that Frances wasn't really paying attention to her anymore. Instead the other teacher was looking along the hall with a cool, unfriendly expression on her face.

Phyllis turned to look as well and saw Amber Trahearne coming toward them.

"I'll see you later, Phyllis," Frances said. "I have work to do."

"Of course," Phyllis murmured as Frances went back into her classroom and closed the door. She knew that Frances was leaving because she didn't want to have to speak to Amber. The murder might have distracted everyone, but nobody had forgotten the rumors about the alleged affair between Amber and Chase Hamilton. Any teacher who carried on with a student was going to be a pariah, at least among many of the faculty.

Phyllis might well have felt the same way, if she hadn't known the truth about Chase Hamilton. Amber didn't know about that, she reminded herself. As far as Amber was concerned, she had crossed a line she never should have.

Amber summoned up a smile, though, and Phyllis returned her friendly nod.

"Hi," Amber said. "I hope you're doing okay this morning, Phyllis."

"Why wouldn't I be?"

Amber looked a little surprised by the question. "Because . . . well, I mean . . . you're the one who found the . . . the body . . ."

Phyllis's answer was a little more casual than she really felt. "It's not the first time, I'm afraid. But I'm all right. I was pretty shaken up Friday night, but I kept busy over the weekend and I'm fine this morning."

Kept busy trying unsuccessfully to solve Ray Brooks's murder, she thought.

"Well . . . good. I'm glad to hear it. Because I have a favor to ask of you, and I really hate to, especially under the circumstances."

"What sort of favor?" Phyllis asked.

"You know we're having a math meet Saturday."

Phyllis nodded, even though she hadn't actually known about it.

"We always have parents and some of the other teachers volunteer to help out, and I've, uh, had quite a few of them get in touch with me the past couple of days and say that they can't come after all."

Phyllis wasn't surprised. Between the murder and the scandal involving Amber and Chase, there were bound to be people who didn't want to volunteer for another school event, especially one Amber was sponsoring.

"I'm afraid I don't know anything about helping at a math meet," Phyllis said. "My son wasn't on the math team when he was in school."

"But you *do* know about food," Amber countered, "and I really need someone to be in charge of the hospitality room. We provide breakfast and lunch for all the other coaches and the volunteers who work at the meet. I know it's a lot to ask, but if you could make something for breakfast and maybe some desserts for lunch, and kind of supervise things . . . Well, it would just be an enormous help, that's all."

Even though Phyllis wished Amber hadn't asked her, she couldn't stop her culinary instincts from kicking in. She said, "I suppose I could make some breakfast casseroles. I know Carolyn has a good recipe."

"We'll have people bring donuts, too, but not everybody wants sweet stuff for breakfast, so casseroles would be great. And maybe some cookies or something to go with lunch. We always order a giant deli sandwich for the main part of the meal."

Amber was right: it was a lot to ask. Something else occurred to Phyllis.

"I suppose you've already talked to Sam?"

"Of course." Amber smiled. "And he didn't let me down. He's going to be in charge of the proctors. I asked him if he thought you'd be willing to help out, too, but he said I'd have to ask you about that."

Sam knew better than to speak for her, but Phyllis knew that since he was volunteering, he would like it if she did, too. For a moment, she mulled it over. To be brutally honest, she didn't particularly like Amber, but she wasn't going to sit in judgment over the young woman, either.

"I know what you're thinking," Amber said into the lingering silence.

"You do?"

Amber's expression was serious now as she said, "You're trying to decide whether you want to be associated with a tramp like me."

Phyllis shook her head. "That's not at all—"

"No, it's all right, I understand. I did a really stupid thing. I was in kind of a bad place. I'd just dumped Ray—may he rest in peace—and Chase and I had become friends and . . . well, he just seems *older* than he really is, you know. When I was around him and it was just the two of us, it was easy to forget that he's a student. Too easy." She stood up straighter. "But that's over and done with, and it'll never happen again. If it winds up costing me my job in the long run, then so be it. But I don't want it hurting those kids who practice for hours and hours for a meet like this."

"I didn't say I wouldn't help," Phyllis told her. "Especially if I can get Carolyn and Eve to pitch in, too. If they're willing, we can take care of the hospitality room for you."

A hugely relieved expression appeared on Amber's face. "That's great!" she said. "I can't tell you how much I appreciate this, Phyllis. I'll be in touch with you during the week to coordinate everything."

"Have you been in touch with Chase?" Phyllis ventured to ask.

Amber drew in a sharp breath and said, "No. Absolutely not. The last I saw of him, he was being taken out of the school in handcuffs. I've heard rumors that the sheriff's department didn't hold him, though."

"That's what I heard, too," Phyllis said.

"They must not have enough evidence to charge him yet."

"Do you think he did it?"

"I don't know what to think," Amber said. "Around me, he was always so gentle and kind. But there's a dark side to him, as well. If there wasn't, he wouldn't hang around with those other kids who are his friends. They're not good kids. I hate to say it, but they're just not."

Phyllis nodded, and Amber brightened again.

"I'm going to just look ahead," she said. "There's been enough bad things. This is the first meet of the year coming up, and I want to see what our team can do."

"These math team kids . . . they really get up early on a Saturday morning and come to school to take a test?"

"Four tests," Amber said. "Number sense, calculator, general math, and science."

"They do this for fun?"

"Yeah. And some of them are really, really competitive, too. If they do well, there are some good scholarships they can get for college. It can help a lot if you're good enough to qualify for the state academic meet in the spring."

"I didn't know about any of that."

"Just wait until Saturday," Amber said. "You'll see. It'll be fun!"

Chapter 28

As far as Phyllis could tell, Chase wasn't at school that day. She didn't see him in the halls during any of the passing periods or in the cafeteria at lunch. Alan Riley and Jason Duncan were holding court at their usual table with their circle of friends, but Chase wasn't with them. Phyllis wondered if he had "dropped out", which wouldn't be difficult to do since he wasn't actually a student there to begin with.

When she got home that afternoon, she brought up the subject of volunteering at the math meet to Carolyn and Eve.

"What's a math meet?" Carolyn asked. When Phyllis explained, Carolyn shook her head and added, "We didn't have such things in elementary school."

"I remember them," Eve said. "I know there was always an academic competition in the spring. The journalism department always participated in it, and I certainly remember hearing about the math and science and computer teams. I didn't realize that the meets went on all year, though."

"Technically, they're just practice meets for the district,

region, and state meets later on, I suppose," Phyllis said, "but the students and coaches who participate seem to take them very seriously. I told Amber I'd help, and I was hoping you two wouldn't mind lending a hand as well."

"I don't know this Amber," Carolyn said with a frown, "but from what I've heard about her, I don't like her."

"And you know I'm not a cook," Eve added.

"You wouldn't have to cook anything," Phyllis told her. "You'd just have to be there to make sure everything gets put out on the tables and refill things that we run out of."

"Well, I suppose I could handle that." Eve thought for a moment, then asked, "Are any of those math team coaches single men?"

Carolyn rolled her eyes while Phyllis shook her head and said, "I don't have any idea. But I suppose they could be."

"I'll do it," Eve said.

"Oh, all right," Carolyn said. "It's something different, anyway. I love retirement, but it *can* get a little monotonous."

Sam and Ronnie came in a short time later. Ronnie immediately put her backpack down and asked Phyllis, "Did you solve the murder today?"

Sam said, "I told you, I reckon we would've heard about it if that had happened."

"I'm afraid Sam is right," Phyllis said. "It's not that easy or simple."

Eve said, "You have to admit, dear, you've made it look that way at times in the past."

"Maybe, but this one has me stumped." Phyllis didn't like to admit that, but it was true. Her thinking had hit a brick wall. "I may have to sit back and let everything percolate for a while."

"What does *that* mean?" Ronnie asked.

"It's how folks used to make coffee," Sam explained. "Sort of a slow drip, drip, drip."

Phyllis smiled. "That's the way my thoughts feel right now. A slow drip."

"Oh!" Ronnie said in exasperation. She picked up her backpack and headed for the stairs.

Once the girl had gone up to her room, Phyllis said to Sam, "I didn't want to say anything while Ronnie was here, but I thought I might go over to Chase's apartment again and tell him what we found out about Ray Brooks's background."

"Not a bad idea," Sam said. "I'll go with you."

"I was hoping you'd say that."

"I'll take care of supper," Carolyn said. "You two go on about your detecting business."

"More like shot-in-the-dark business these days," Phyllis said.

They took Sam's pickup and drove over to the apartment complex where Chase lived. Phyllis didn't know what vehicle he drove, so she couldn't tell from the ones in the parking lot whether he was home.

But as Sam turned into the lot, she suddenly said, "Park here at the far end."

He did what she told him, then said, "What's wrong?"

"Those two boys getting out of a car down at the other end of the lot . . ."

"Yeah, I see 'em now," Sam said. "Riley and Duncan. Good job of spottin' 'em."

"I suppose they want to know why Chase wasn't at school today, too," Phyllis said as she watched Alan Riley and Jason Duncan climb the stairs to the complex's second floor where Chase's apartment was located.

"What do you want to do now?"

"We'll wait until they leave and hope it's not too long."

"Yeah, because I don't want to miss out on whatever Carolyn is makin' for supper."

Riley and Duncan were at the door of Chase's apartment.

Riley knocked while Duncan brushed something off the front of the jacket he wore. The door swung open, but Phyllis couldn't see into the apartment from where she and Sam were parked. She assumed Chase had opened it, because Riley and Duncan went inside and the door closed behind them.

Sam had rolled the pickup's windows part of the way down, so a cool breeze blew through the vehicle, making it comfortable as they waited. To pass the time, Phyllis said, "I agreed to help Amber with the math meet this Saturday."

"She told me," Sam said with a nod. "I was glad to hear it, too. That way I know the food'll be good in the hospitality room."

"She said you're going to be in charge of the proctors? I'm not sure I know what that is."

"They're the ones who give out the tests and watch the kids to make sure nobody's cheatin'. She's got a sheet printed up with all the instructions, so all I have to do is go over it with the folks who have volunteered for that job. Then I sort of just wander around and make sure there aren't any problems. It doesn't sound like a very hard job, so I figured I could handle it." Sam grinned. "Best part about it, once the tests are finished, I'm done. I can go hang out with you and eat the rest of the time."

She smiled back at him. "Those are your favorite jobs, aren't they?"

"You got that right."

Phyllis sat up straighter and grew more serious as she saw Chase's door open again. The two young men came out. Jason Duncan paused and turned back to say something through the open door, then joined Riley in going down the stairs and back to the car they had come in. They got into the car and drove off.

Phyllis waited until they were completely out of sight before she opened the pickup's door and got out.

Chase looked surprised when he opened the apartment door and saw the two of them standing there.

"This is your day for company, son," Sam drawled.

"I guess you saw Alan and Jason leaving."

"That's right," Phyllis said. "We saw them come in, too. We arrived at almost the same time. That could have been awkward."

Chase grunted. "I'm glad you were discreet about it." He stepped back. "Come in."

As Phyllis stepped over the threshold, she glanced down and saw several small pieces of broken blue stone lying just in front of the door. It looked like some sort of decoration that had been stepped on and broken. She would have picked up one of the pieces to study it, but Sam was right behind her and Chase was waiting for them to come in.

"I suppose people noticed that I wasn't at school today," he said as he closed the door. "That probably created a lot of rumors, like I was in jail or something. That's why Alan and Jason came by. They wanted to know if I was still out—and if I was coming back to school."

"Are you?" Phyllis asked.

"I don't know yet. It's really too early to tell if the operation is blown or not. But Jason was pretty clear about one thing: as long as I'm under suspicion, he doesn't want me having anything to do with him and Alan. I'm bad for business. Not low-profile enough anymore."

"And Jason Duncan calls the shots for the ring selling drugs?"

Chase laughed. "No, I don't think so. He acts like he does, but he's not smart enough. He gets his orders from somebody else. I've been trying to get him to trust me enough to let me in on who that is, but so far . . ." Chase shrugged and shook his head. "As long as they keep me at arm's length because they don't want any extra attention from the cops, I won't get that information. Which is why it's tempting just to chunk the whole thing. I don't like to give up, though."

Sam said, "I can understand that. I don't like to be a quitter, either."

"The sheriff's department might get better results by pulling me out, waiting a while, and putting somebody else in. I'll give it another day or two and try to figure it out." Chase paused. "Is there anything I can do to help your investigation?"

"I don't know," Phyllis said. "We found out some things about Ray Brooks. Evidently, he wasn't exactly the sort of man that everyone at school believed him to be. Or rather, he was, but there was more to him than that."

Chase frowned and said, "Now you've really got me curious. Sit down and tell me. Can I get you something to drink?"

Phyllis and Sam passed on the drink but sat down on the same sofa where they had sat before. Sam didn't have to clean it off today, so evidently Chase had been tidying up some since they were here last. Phyllis told Chase what they had discovered about Oak Trails and how Keeley Gifford had overheard them mention Brooks's name.

"So Brooks was actually a nice guy?" Chase said when Phyllis was finished. He shook his head. "I find that hard to believe. He always acted like a complete . . . jerk . . . at school."

"Yeah, I'd be tempted to use a stronger name than that, too," Sam said.

"From what Ms. Gifford said, he kept his life at school totally separate from his efforts to help people with drug problems." Phyllis spread her hands. "Of course, we have only her word for any of this, but for what it's worth, she seemed very genuine to me. My instincts say that she was telling the truth."

"I thought the same thing," Sam said. "The lady meant what she was sayin'."

"Which kind of ruined a theory I'd been toying with," Phyllis said with a faint smile. "When we found out that Oak Trails was a drug rehab facility, I thought maybe Brooks had been buying drugs from Duncan and Riley and something went wrong."

"Doesn't sound likely," Chase agreed. "Anyway, those two might hurt somebody if they were cornered, but they don't strike me as killers. I could be wrong, of course. Do you have any other ideas?"

Phyllis shook her head. "Not at the moment. I hate to say it, but you seem to have more means, motive, and opportunity than anyone else."

"And being a cop won't get me off the hook for murder if the DA decides he's got a reasonable case. I'm new around here. Is the guy likely to do something like that?"

"He's been known to grandstand in the past," Sam said. "It usually hasn't worked out for him, but the voters don't seem to remember that. They keep electin' him anyway."

Chase laughed. "Well, then, what's the over-under? How many days will it be before I'm in jail again, for real this time?"

"I don't want that to happen," Phyllis said. "For one thing, I believe you're innocent, and for another, Ronnie would be very upset. She already thinks I should have solved this case before now."

"I know you're giving it your best effort. How is Ronnie?"

"Mopin' a lot," Sam said. "So . . . no different than a lot of other teenage girls."

"When all of this is over," Phyllis said, "you need to tell her the truth about who you really are, Chase."

"You're probably right. Do you think it'll make a difference?"

"When she finds out you're that much older than her? It might."

"I give you my word I'll do that, then, as soon as it's safe for everybody concerned."

"Thank you."

There didn't seem to be anything left to say. The investigation was stalled, and they all knew it. But none of them were going to give up, either.

Chase checked to make sure Riley and Duncan hadn't come back before Phyllis and Sam left the apartment. As she stepped out, Phyllis paused long enough to bend over and pick up one of the pieces of blue stone she had noticed earlier. Holding it on the palm of her hand, she showed it to Chase and said, "Do you know what that is?"

He frowned at it and shook his head. "I have no idea. A blue rock, that's all I can tell."

"You know what it looks like to me?" Sam said. The other two looked at him. "You know those rock kits that kids get when they're studyin' geology, the ones that have samples of a bunch of different kinds of rocks? That's what it reminds me of."

Phyllis held up the stone and squinted at it. "You could be right," she said. "I think Jason Duncan brushed this off his jacket as he was coming in. Do you know if he takes geology?"

"He does," Chase said. "You think it's important?"

"I don't see how it could be," Phyllis said.

Chapter 29

However, the broken blue stone continued to nag at her thoughts, and the next morning after she arrived at school, before classes started, she walked over to the hall where most of the science classes were located. She wasn't sure who taught geology, but she asked one of the teachers she knew and was directed to the classroom occupied by Noah Burdette, a short, stocky man in his forties with rust-colored hair and beard.

"Help you?" he asked as he looked up from his desk when Phyllis came in. No students were in the room; the bell releasing them to go to class had not rung yet.

"Hello," she said. "I don't think we've met. I'm Phyllis Newsom. I'm the long-term sub for Molly Dobson."

"Oh, yeah, I remember seeing you at convocation when the superintendent introduced all the new teachers. What can I do for you?"

It had been a long, long time since anybody had referred to her as a new teacher, Phyllis thought, but she supposed that to Burdette, that's what she was. She said, "I'm told that you teach the geology class, and I have a question about it."

Burdette sat back and laced his fingers together over his stomach. "Shoot."

"Do you use those rock collection kits that students used to buy, with samples of the different kinds of rocks?"

"I have a lot of samples I use here in class, but I don't require the kids to buy those kits, no."

"But they might?"

"Sure, I suppose so," Burdette replied with a shrug. "There are plenty of places you can order them. If somebody was really interested in the subject, they might get one." He laughed. "I've got one kid who probably has two or three of them. Walter really likes rocks."

"Walter Baxter?" Phyllis said. It was entirely possible that more than one student named Walter attended Courtland, but the Walter she knew seemed like the sort that Burdette was describing.

"Yeah, that's right. Do you know him?"

"I do, although he's not in any of my classes. I thought he was a freshman."

"Yeah, but he's got lots of advanced science credits, so he was able to take an upper level class like geology. Smart kid. Really smart."

"Yes, that's the impression I had of him. What about Jason Duncan?"

Burdette frowned and lost his casual attitude as he sat up straighter. "He's smart enough . . . when he wants to be. He's not interested in working at it, though. Why all the questions, Mrs. Newsom? I'm not in the habit of gossiping about students."

"I'm not either, and I appreciate you being honest with me." Phyllis took a breath. "The son of a friend of mine has been hanging around with Jason Duncan, and she'd heard some things that made her worried he might be a bad influence on the boy."

Burdette frowned. "It's not my place to say anything about that. But . . ." He grimaced. "Your friend is probably right to be worried. Duncan and his crew aren't the best bunch for her son to be running with. Just to be clear, though . . . this 'friend' of yours, it's not really you, is it?"

Phyllis smiled. "My son graduated from high school a long time ago, Mr. Burdette."

"Yeah, that's kind of what I thought." The bell rang, causing both of them to look up. Burdette went on, "You didn't hear anything from me, right?"

"Not a thing," Phyllis agreed. Quickly, before any students could reach the room, she gave in to a whim and asked, "Walter Baxter isn't friends with Duncan, is he?"

Burdette frowned again and said, "It's funny you should mention that. No, I wouldn't say they're friends, but they've worked together on a couple of group projects and seemed to get along all right. Of course, that's probably because Walter did all the work and let Duncan take some of the credit."

Phyllis nodded. That was usually the way it was with group projects.

Still, it was interesting that Walter at least was acquainted with Jason Duncan . . . and Walter had been there the night of the dance, too.

Now, *that* was an insane thought to have, Phyllis told herself. Walter Baxter wasn't the sort to hurt a fly . . . unless maybe he was trying to dissect it for a biology class.

But she had run into some very unlikely murderers in the past, and while she tried to be reasonable about where she directed her suspicions, she had learned not to be too quick to rule out anything.

Still . . . *Walter?*

Phyllis filed that away in the back of her mind.

She thanked Noah Burdette again and left the classroom, heading back to her own hall. By the time she reached her class, several students had come in already, and the day really began to get underway.

That afternoon, after school, she walked over to Sam's room and found that he still had students at some of his desks. Five girls and three boys sat there with calculators in front of them, apparently working problems from sheets of paper sitting next to the calculators. Their fingers flew so fast that Phyllis couldn't have hoped to follow what they were doing, even if she knew all the formulas and tricks they were using.

Sam stood up from his desk and came over to her, smiling. He held a small timer in his hand. With a nod, he indicated that they should go out into the hall.

Phyllis did, but before she stepped out of the room, she noticed that Walter Baxter was one of the boys working with the calculators.

"Math team practice," Sam said quietly once they were in the hall with the door pulled up but not completely closed behind them. "That bunch is the calculator team."

"I figured that out," Phyllis said. "You don't know anything about that, do you?"

"I can use a calculator to add, subtract, multiply, and divide," Sam said, "but I've got to think about what I'm doin' and take my time with it. That stuff they're doin'?" He shook his head. "Way beyond me. But Amber's workin' with some other kids on the team right now and she needed a place for these to take their practice tests." He held up the timer. "I can run one o' these things just fine and tell 'em when to start and stop."

"I noticed that Walter is one of them."

"Yeah, Amber says he's pretty good. Might be good enough to go to state, even though he's just a freshman."

"He's in geology class with Jason Duncan. They've even worked together on some group projects."

Sam's eyes widened. "Now hold on. You're thinkin' that little nerd might be mixed up with the bunch sellin' drugs? Or did you think . . . Oh, no. *Walter* killin' somebody, let alone a bruiser like Brooks? That's just too far out there, Phyllis."

"I agree," she said. "But he was here that night, he seems to know everyone involved, he's extremely smart . . . and let's face it, who would ever suspect him of being a drug kingpin? If you could call it that on this level. But you remember what Chase said about believing that Duncan was getting his orders from someone else."

"Yeah, but that's just crazy. I mean, no offense, but . . . *Walter?*"

Phyllis said, "You'd better keep it down or he's going to hear you. I know how far-fetched it sounds, Sam. And it's pure speculation. There's not a shred of proof so far linking him to any wrongdoing. I just thought I'd mention it so you can sort of keep an eye on him."

"Yeah, I reckon I can do that. But I figure he's got his hands full with bein' smart and havin' that crush on Ronnie."

"I hope that turns out to be true. Speaking of Ronnie, is she going home with you?"

"Yeah. She wanted to do some work in the library first, which worked out well because I told Amber the calculator team could practice in my room. She'll come over here when she's done."

"If Walter is still here, he'll like that. Ronnie may not, though."

"She can put up with it," Sam said. He looked at the timer. "They're about to run out of time to do those crunchers. I'd best get back in there."

"Crunchers?" Phyllis repeated.

"The problems that just have numbers in 'em. The actual tests have what we used to call story problems, too. But the crunchers are the ones they try to do so fast. At least, that's what Amber tells me."

Phyllis just shook her head and then started toward the front of the school.

Tom Shula was in the main office talking to the secretary. He smiled at Phyllis as she came in.

"Can I talk to you for a minute, Tom?" she asked.

"Sure, come on back." He led the way along the short hall to his office and waved Phyllis into the chair in front of the desk. "What can I do for you?"

"Have you decided what to do about Chase Hamilton?"

Shula's shoulders rose and fell. "What is there to do? I suppose I could still suspend him for that scuffle with Ray Brooks, but with Brooks being dead and all . . . To tell you the truth, I've sort of been waiting for the police to solve the problem for me. If they arrest the Hamilton kid for Brooks's murder, then I don't have to do anything about it, do I?"

"That's true enough," Phyllis agreed, not adding that she believed Chase was innocent and didn't want to see him arrested. She waited a moment to see if Shula would say anything about Chase being an undercover police officer, but the principal didn't bring it up. For all he knew, Phyllis was completely unaware of that, and she supposed he thought he was doing the right thing by keeping that knowledge to himself.

She went on, "Last Friday, when I called Sam and told him to find you and come back to the Dungeon, what were you doing?"

Shula frowned. "Wait a minute. Are you interrogating me, Phyllis?"

"Oh, no, not at all," she said quickly. "Sam mentioned he found you doing something with the sound system, and I just wondered what that was about."

"Still sounds a little like an interrogation," Shula said, "but I was trying to balance the speakers better. One channel gets out of whack pretty easily, so somebody has to monitor it. One of the kids was supposed to be doing that."

"Walter Baxter," Phyllis said.

"Yeah, that's right. He volunteered, and he's been working with the sound system for the drama department, so I thought it would be all right. From what Miss Franklin tells me, the kid's great at sound, special effects, stuff like that."

Walter seemed to be good at a lot of different things, Phyllis thought.

"But he'd gone off somewhere and disappeared," Shula went on. "The bass was too loud, so I was turning it down when Sam found me." He smiled. "I used to be in a band, you know, so I know about things like that. The Atomic Frogs."

"I beg your pardon?"

"The Atomic Frogs. That was what we were called. The band I was in at college. We even played a few gigs, you know. We weren't bad. But that was a long time ago."

"A lot of things were," Phyllis agreed. "Did you ever find out where Walter was when he was supposed to be taking care of the sound system?"

"I didn't try to," Shula said. "Didn't figure it was important. I'm sure he'd gone to the bathroom, or he was off trying to get some girl to dance with him. You know, the important things to a fourteen-year-old boy."

"Fourteen," Phyllis mused. It sounded so young. It *was* young. And yet a part of her mind was trying to cast him as a criminal mastermind.

Sam was right: the idea was insane. Phyllis put it out of her head and stood up.

"Thanks, Tom."

"That's it?"

"I was just trying to get everything about the night of the dance straight in my mind."

"Because you're trying to figure out who killed Ray Brooks." Shula nodded. "I know what you're up to. I've read about all those other cases you solved. But it seems to me you ought to just let the cops handle this one, Phyllis. We've known each other a long time, and I sure wouldn't want to see you get yourself hurt or in trouble." His voice became a bit more stern as he added, "Besides, it doesn't look good to have one of my teachers running around playing detective."

She wanted to tell him that she wasn't "playing" anything. Unwilling or not, whenever she got dragged into one of these messy situations, she took it completely seriously.

But instead she said, "Don't worry, Tom. I'm not going to get in trouble. And I won't do anything to harm the school's reputation, either."

"You know I don't care about that nearly as much as I do about you."

"Of course. I'm just a nosy old woman. I need to be careful about that."

"Nobody thinks that," he said as he got to his feet. "Just be careful, that's all."

She smiled and nodded and left the principal's office. As she walked back toward her classroom, she thought about what Shula had told her.

According to him, Walter Baxter was unaccounted for at

the time of Ray Brooks's murder. But, Phyllis reminded herself, she had only Shula's word for that. And when you got right down to it, she didn't know where Shula himself had been during that short but crucial period of time. Sam had had to look around for him. It was possible Shula had just reached the area where the sound system was located when Sam found him.

Phyllis smiled faintly to herself. She might as well just go ahead and suspect the entire school, she thought. That was what she seemed to be doing. It would help if there was some actual *evidence* . . .

Something danced past the edge of her mind, but when she turned her thoughts toward it, whatever it was had disappeared.

Chapter 30

A week had passed since the murder of Ray Brooks at the Friday the Thirteenth dance, and Phyllis was no closer to solving that murder than she had been at the moment she had seen Brooks's bloody form slump to the floor of the Dungeon, never to move again.

Ronnie had been moping around all week, sullen and resentful that Chase was still under suspicion. But he hadn't been arrested yet, so there was that for her to be thankful for. However, he hadn't returned to school, either. Phyllis had a feeling the undercover operation had been called off.

She had kept busy all week getting ready to be in charge of the hospitality room at the math meet. She and Carolyn were making three different kinds of breakfast casseroles and muffins as well as cookies and brownies for dessert at lunch. Eve had volunteered to pick up the giant deli sandwich from the store that was making it.

"I'll have them load it in my car," she told Phyllis, "and

then you can send some of those high school boys out to fetch it in when I get here with it."

At times in the past, when she'd been plagued by a particularly difficult problem, Phyllis had turned her attention to other things like this, clearing her mind, as it were, in the hope that the answers to her questions would drift to the forefront of her thoughts. The tactic had worked more than once.

But not this time. Whatever it was nagging at her brain, it consistently eluded her. Something she had seen . . . something she had heard . . . maybe both . . .

She had everything ready to load into the car early Saturday morning so she could head to the high school and get the hospitality room set up by the time the coaches and volunteers began to arrive. She had just put the last of the casseroles in the refrigerator when the cell phone in her pocket rang. She took it out and saw Jimmy D'Angelo's name and number on the display. The lawyer was calling her on his cell phone.

"Hello?"

"I just got some news," D'Angelo said without preamble. "Appleton, that sheriff's department investigator, just picked up the Hamilton kid and brought him in to book him for murder. A contact of mine in the department tipped me off. He remembered I'd been there last week asking about the kid."

Phyllis had caught her breath as soon as D'Angelo told her what was going on. She said, "Why now? Why wait a week? Do you think they have some new evidence?"

"No idea at this point. I'm on my way there now to see if Chase will let me represent him. Could be the DA has been feeling some pressure and decided to go ahead with the case he's got, which is pretty circumstantial. But a murder inside a school, folks want that solved and an arrest made."

"Yes, I'm sure they do," Phyllis said. She hesitated. She hadn't told D'Angelo what she and Sam had discovered about Chase Hamilton. If he was going to represent the young man, he would need to know that. "Jimmy . . . there's something I should tell you about Chase."

D'Angelo's voice was sharp with suspicion as he asked, "What's that?"

"He's actually an undercover police officer."

"What! Geez Louise, Phyllis, I almost ran off the road there. How long have you known this?"

Phyllis spent the next couple of minutes giving him the details, with D'Angelo interrupting now and then to ask a question in a clearly irritated tone. By the time she finished, though, he seemed somewhat mollified.

"So the cops already know about this?" he asked.

"Well, Victor Appleton does, anyway. And I'm sure Sheriff Haney does. Probably a few other people in the department. I should have told you sooner—"

"No, no, you gave the kid your word that you'd keep quiet about it. I understand that. And since he hadn't actually been arrested yet, there was really no need to spill it to me. You told me now, and that's what matters." D'Angelo paused, then said, "Listen, you know that Hamilton being a cop isn't a get out of jail free card, right? Undercover cops have been busted plenty of times in the past, especially when they were mixed up in something that wasn't directly related to their assignment. Some of them do such a good job of pretending to be bad guys that they actually turn out that way."

"I don't believe that's true of Chase. I still think he didn't kill Ray Brooks."

"Well . . . now would be a good time to prove it."

Phyllis knew that, and the fact that she hadn't left her feel-

ing that she had let the young man down, even though it
wasn't really her responsibility.

"Look, I'm here at the detention center," D'Angelo went
on. "I'll be in touch when I know anything, okay?"

"All right. Thank you, Jimmy."

"Don't thank me yet. I haven't done anything. And with a
murder charge, it'll be hard to get the kid out on bail, even,
until Monday. But I'll try. So long."

The lawyer broke the connection. Phyllis slipped her
phone back into her pocket as Sam came into the kitchen. He
said, "I heard you talkin' to somebody and figured Carolyn or
Eve was in here."

Phyllis shook her head. "No, I was on the phone with
Jimmy. He'd heard that Chase has been arrested, and that this
time they're actually going to charge him with murder."

"Dadgummit." Sam looked around. "Ronnie doesn't
know?"

"She's upstairs, I think."

"You reckon we can keep it from her?"

"I don't see where telling her would do any good," Phyllis
said, "although she's bound to find out sooner or later, and
then she'll be angry with us for keeping it from her."

"More than likely. But I'd like to keep things on an even
keel for as long as we can. I even got her to agree to come to
the meet with us tomorrow and work as a runner, pickin' up
tests and takin' 'em to the gradin' room. Let's see if we can
get that behind us before all hell breaks loose."

"All right," Phyllis said. "I hate keeping secrets, though."

"We're just lettin' discretion be the better part of valor, as
the old sayin' goes."

"That's not exactly what that saying means. And wasn't it
coined to refer to battles in a war?"

"Dealin' with a lovestruck teenager sometimes *is* a war,"
Sam said.

Instead of calling her, D'Angelo sent Phyllis a series of text messages later that evening. Chase Hamilton was still in custody but had not been charged officially yet. D'Angelo's theory was that the authorities were dragging their feet and wouldn't charge him until Saturday because that would insure it would be Monday morning before a bail hearing could be held.

The only bit of good news was that D'Angelo had been permitted to talk to Chase, and the young man had agreed to let him act as his attorney. According to D'Angelo, it was his association with Phyllis that had led Chase to agree. Chase seemed to trust her, and Phyllis wondered if that was because she instinctively trusted him.

D'Angelo promised to be at the jail bright and early the next morning to make sure that Chase was treated fairly and according to the law.

Phyllis was in her bedroom but hadn't turned in yet when she got the messages. She went to Sam's room, knocked softly, and when he told her to come in, she opened the door and found him sitting up in bed reading a paperback.

Phyllis went and sat on the foot of the bed as she told him what D'Angelo had said. Sam nodded. "I wonder if they're stallin' because they hope they'll find some more evidence over the weekend."

"I don't know what evidence there could be to find at this late date," Phyllis said. "Surely they've gone over all the physical and forensics evidence by now."

"I don't know. Sometimes that forensics stuff takes a lot longer in real life than it does on TV."

"True. Maybe they think Chase will break down and confess. They could threaten to put him in with the other prisoners and let it leak that he's really an officer."

"Somethin' like that might occur to the DA, but I don't figure Ross Haney would go along with it."

"You're probably right about that," Phyllis said. She and the sheriff had clashed on occasion in the past, but she had never doubted his fundamental honesty and dedication to doing his job the right way . . . unlike her feelings about the district attorney.

"I don't know of anything we can do for Chase right now," Sam said, "so let's just go to the math meet and trust Jimmy to look out for his interests."

Phyllis stood up and nodded. "I agree." She went to the head of the bed, leaned over, and kissed Sam on the forehead. "Good night. We both need to get a good night's sleep . . . although I'm not sure how well I'll do that with so many things going around and around inside my head."

"Maybe instead of countin' sheep, you should count murderers. You've rounded up enough of 'em."

"That's not funny. I never expected things like this to happen. This . . . this whole business of solving crimes seemed to come out of nowhere, and now it just won't stop!"

Despite what she had said to Sam, Phyllis did sleep fairly well. Well enough that it took the alarm to get her out of bed the next morning. A lot of mornings, she woke up before it ever went off.

She was the first one in the kitchen, so she got the coffee going. The previous evening, she had set aside some of the muffins for them to eat this morning, so she got them out. Carolyn and Eve came in, both yawning, followed a few minutes later by Sam and Ronnie, who appeared to be equally sleepy.

"I just don't understand this," Ronnie said as she sat down

at the table with a cup of coffee.

"What?" Sam asked her.

"Getting up this early on a Saturday morning to take tests! What kind of kid *does* that?"

Sam chuckled. "Math team kids are a special breed. I've just started bein' around 'em, but I can tell that already. You know what? They're a lot like the band kids, and the ball players. They all get up early to practice, too. I reckon when you find somethin' you really enjoy, somethin' that you're driven to be good at, you don't mind as much losin' a little sleep."

"Well, I sure wouldn't want to do it all the time."

Eve said, "What *do* you want to do, dear? I don't think I've ever heard you talk about what your plans are for when you grow up."

"Do you have to make plans this early? I mean, when you're sixteen?"

Carolyn said, "Good grief, parents these days start thinking about their children's careers when they're in pre-school. Most of them have the future all mapped out by the time they're in junior high, let alone high school."

"Well," Ronnie mused, "I think I might like to be a doctor. Not a cut-people-open kind of doctor, but maybe a psychiatrist. Something like that."

Sam said, "Wantin' to help people is a noble ambition."

Ronnie grinned. "Maybe I just think it'd be fun to mess with people's heads. What better way to do it?"

Carolyn said, "That . . . that's terrible!"

Ronnie shrugged, stood up with her coffee, and grabbed one of the muffins. "I'm gonna go get dressed. Time and nerds wait for no man."

"A literary reference," Eve said when Ronnie had left the kitchen. "Maybe she should be an English teacher . . . or a writer."

Carolyn had stood up and moved over to the counter, where she muttered something. Phyllis couldn't make it out, but she didn't ask her friend to repeat it.

Less than an hour later, they were all ready to go. Phyllis and Sam loaded all the food for the hospitality room into her Lincoln. Sam and Ronnie would take the pickup, Carolyn and Eve would go in Carolyn's car. The sun hadn't quite peeked over the eastern horizon when the little convoy headed toward J.C. Courtland High School. Buses and SUVs from the other school districts competing in this meet would be on their way there, as well, carrying the teams vying for trophies and ribbons and bragging rights. Phyllis found herself looking forward to it. This would be something new in her experience, and at her age she was always glad to encounter something fresh and exciting.

Early it might be, she thought, but this was going to be a good day.

Like Amber had said a few days earlier, it would be fun.

Chapter 31

There was only one car parked at the school when Phyllis got there, a sporty little two-door. She wasn't surprised to discover that it belonged to Amber, since the vehicle fit the young teacher's personality.

Amber must have seen her coming, because she was at the main entrance holding one of the doors open when Phyllis walked up carrying several casserole containers. She was dressed stylishly and expensively, as usual, wearing the gem-stone-decorated jacket that Phyllis had seen her wearing several times in the past.

"Hospitality's going to be the first classroom on the left down the second hall," Amber said, pointing across the mall, "right across from the library. That'll be the grading room, so everything is handy to each other. I guess there's more stuff in your car? Can I help you?"

"No, Sam should be here any minute, he can help me with everything else," Phyllis said. "You won't need him for a while, will you?"

"No, the proctors' meeting isn't until eight-thirty," Amber said as they walked across the mall. "Thanks again for doing this, Phyllis."

"I'm happy to."

"You don't know how happy *I* am that this day is finally here. Maybe now things can start getting back to normal."

"I hope so," Phyllis said as they reached the corner where the second hall extended to the right.

"I have to go put up signs on the testing rooms, but I'll be around. Holler if you need me."

"Of course." Phyllis turned and headed for the hospitality room while Amber walked on the way they had been going, her high heels clicking rapidly against the tile floor.

Phyllis found that some folding tables had been set up in the hospitality room. She placed the containers on one of them but didn't uncover the casseroles just yet. They would stay warmer if she left them covered until people began arriving to eat breakfast.

She had just done that when Sam and Ronnie walked in, carrying some of the other containers from the car. Sam had a key to Phyllis's Lincoln, so she wasn't surprised that they had brought in more of the food.

"We'll get the rest of it," Sam said. "You can go ahead and start settin' things up in here."

Ronnie said, "That little pest Walter is outside. His dad dropped him off just as we got here. He wanted to help us and come in, too, but I told him he had to stay outside."

"That boy likes you, you know," Sam said.

"He's two years younger than me!"

"There'll come a time when that won't be important. Two years is nothin'."

"Well, it's something now," Ronnie said. "Anyway, we don't have a thing in common. And I'm nowhere near as smart as he is."

"You don't know that. Shoot, y'all are at an age when you're just startin' to figure things out. Everything will look a lot different five years from now, ten years from now."

"Maybe, but I have to live today, not five or ten years from now. Anyway, nobody's guaranteed that, are they?"

That was true, Phyllis thought . . . but it was a shame that someone as young as Ronnie already felt that way.

They left to fetch the rest of the food while Phyllis got out paper plates, plasticware, and napkins from a big plastic tub where all those things were stored. There were ice chests for drinks, too, and she took them down to the ice machine next to the band hall and filled them. She was starting to realize that putting on one of these meets was probably a lot of work. It was barely eight o'clock in the morning, and she was already getting tired.

Sam and Ronnie returned, followed by parent volunteers bringing boxes of donuts, packs of canned drinks, bags of chips and candy, and other things they were donating for the meet. Phyllis saw students out in the hall, too, including Walter, and knew that the members of the math team were being allowed in now.

Carolyn and Eve arrived, ready to help any way they could. People began getting plates and plasticware and lining up for breakfast. The noise level in the school rose as more students came in. Phyllis felt more excitement in the air than she would have expected from an academic competition. It really did have a little of the same feel as a football game, she realized as she uncovered the casseroles and put out big plastic spoons so the volunteers and coaches could help themselves.

Even though the cookies she had brought were intended primarily for dessert at lunchtime, she put them out as well.

She left the brownies covered, though, so they wouldn't dry out. She had baked sugar cookies again, this time with the white icing. She left off the splatters of red icing, so they weren't exactly what she had dubbed killer sugar cookies, but they weren't plain, either.

Amber passed by in the hall, hurrying here and there to make sure everything was going according to schedule. After a while, she poked her head through the open door of the hospitality room and said, "Sam, you need to get to the proctors' meeting."

"On my way," he said. "Ronnie, you come along, too, since you're gonna be a runner. We'll gather them up on the way." On his way out, he paused at the end of the table where the cookies were and picked up one of them.

"Ooohh," Amber said with a smile when she saw it in his hand. "Are those Phyllis's sugar cookies?"

"Yep."

"They're so good! I got the last ones at the dance and wished I had tried them earlier." She stepped into the room, picked up two of the cookies from the plate, and smiled at Phyllis. "These'll keep me going. No time to stop and eat!"

She hurried out after Sam and Ronnie. Phyllis watched her go. Then Carolyn said, "Do we have more donuts? One of the boxes is empty."

Phyllis bent and retrieved another cardboard box of the donated pastries from where she had placed them under the table.

They were very busy for a while, with a steady stream of coaches and volunteers coming through the hospitality room for breakfast before the competition got underway. After a while, Carolyn said, "That's it. We've run out of the casseroles. People will just have to make do with muffins and donuts now."

"And from the looks of the muffins, they won't last much longer," Eve added. "But we have cookies, too, of course. Everybody likes cookies."

Phyllis nodded slowly and said, "Yes, they do." She stood for a moment, staring out into the hallway, but she wasn't really seeing the people going by.

Then a booming voice distracted her as one of the visiting coaches, a man with a large stomach under a sweatshirt with his school's mascot on it, asked, "Are all the casseroles gone? I was looking forward to that!"

"I'm sorry, dear," Eve said. "Perhaps you'd care for a donut?"

"Well, yeah, if that's all that's left," the visitor said ungraciously.

Then another voice came over the loudspeaker. This one belonged to Sam. He said, "Students, if you're taking the number sense test, please report to the testing rooms now. The number sense test will begin in five minutes."

"Goodness, he sounds different, doesn't he?" Eve said.

Phyllis said, "He's reading from a script. I didn't know he was supposed to announce the contests, too."

"That Amber talked him into it, I'll bet," Carolyn said.

"Well, somebody has to do the announcing, I suppose."

Sam read the instructions for the test over the PA system, emphasizing that the students taking the number sense test weren't supposed to turn their tests over and start until he said, "Begin." When he finally intoned the command solemnly, Phyllis could almost see all the kids eagerly flipping over their tests and plunging into them.

With the competition officially underway, there was another small boom in the hospitality room as coaches who'd been giving their team some last-minute instructions or pep talks came in to get something to eat. The contest was out of the adults' hands now, and everything depended on the students and how well they did.

Sam wandered in, carrying a timer like the one he'd been using in his room during math team practice. "I'm free," he said, "but not for long. The number sense test only lasts ten minutes. Thought I'd grab a couple more cookies and head back to the office." He picked up two of the sugar cookies and asked, "How'd I sound? Do I have a face made for radio, or what?"

"You sounded fine," Phyllis assured him. She stepped away from the table and inclined her head to indicate that she wanted him to follow her. They drifted over to the other side of the room, where she asked him quietly, "Sam, you remember looking at Ray Brooks's body that night?"

He frowned. "I don't reckon I'm likely to forget it any time soon."

"You said he had something around his mouth, something that might have been cookie crumbs."

"Yeah, I recall that. Nobody ever seemed to think anything about it, though. You had a bunch of cookies on the snack table. He could've got some any time."

"But he didn't," Phyllis said. "He never came over to the table. I'm certain of that. And if those *were* cookie crumbs, he must have eaten them pretty soon before he was killed, or else they would have gotten brushed off by then."

"Yeah, I guess," Sam said, still frowning. He glanced at the timer in his hand and went on, "Shoot. I've gotta get back. But once I get the next contest started, I'll come back over here and we can talk about it some more. You're on the trail of somethin', aren't you?"

Instead of answering, Phyllis gave him a little push toward the door. "Go on and stop the contest on time. Amber won't like it if things get off schedule."

"No, I guess not." He frowned at her, but he went on out of the hospitality room.

"What was that confab about?" Carolyn asked when Phyllis came back to the table. "You and Sam looked awfully serious."

"Just trying to get a few things straight in my head," Phyllis said.

A moment later, Sam's voice came over the speakers again, throughout the school. "Stop. Put your pencils down. Do not make any more marks on your answer sheet. Turn in your answer sheets now. You may leave the testing rooms. The calculator contest will begin in ten minutes."

"He sounds like a robot, doesn't he?" Eve said. "Or one of those talking elevators that announces what floor you're on."

"I hate reading from a script," Carolyn said.

The noise level in the mall rose again as students released from the testing rooms poured into it. Some of them would go back almost right away for the calculator contest, but Sam had told Phyllis that not all the kids took all the tests. It was a slightly different group each time.

When Sam gave the instructions for the next contest, she heard him say that it would last for thirty minutes. That might give her time to do what she wanted to do. She waited until it was underway, then let the little rush play out before she told Carolyn and Eve, "I'll be back in a few minutes."

"All right, we'll hold down the fort," Carolyn said.

Phyllis left the hospitality room, skirted the mall, and looked toward the office, thinking that she might see Sam coming her way. There was no sign of him, though, so she supposed he was busy with something else. Even with some of the students taking the calculator test, the mall was still crowded and loud because all the kids who weren't taking it had gathered here. Phyllis walked toward the cafeteria and along the hall beside it as well, heading into the rear part of the school where it was quieter.

She took out her cell phone and then reached into her purse for the business card she had been carrying around for more than a week, ever since Victor Appleton had given it to her. She didn't really expect to get him when she called and assumed she would have to leave a message, but he answered almost right away.

"Detective Appleton?" she said. "This is Phyllis Newsom."

"Mrs. Newsom?" He sounded surprised to hear her. "What can I do for you? Did you think of something else about the Brooks case?"

"I thought of a lot of things. I know you arrested Chase Hamilton, and I know he didn't kill Ray Brooks."

"And how do you know that?" Appleton asked.

Phyllis turned a corner. Her steps echoed in the empty halls back here. She could still hear a little noise from the front of the school, but it had faded away for the most part.

"Before I answer that, can I ask you a question, Detective?"

"I suppose so," Appleton said warily. "But I can't promise that I'll answer it."

"I just need you to confirm that cookie crumbs were found around Ray Brooks's mouth on the night of his murder."

"How the—" Appleton paused. "I can't go into the evidence pertaining to the case, you should know that."

"That's all right," Phyllis said. "I was pretty sure anyway. Just like I'm sure you don't see any way that some cookie crumbs could possibly have anything to do with the murder. But they do, and you should come out to the high school right now, Detective."

"What are you talk—"

Phyllis lowered the cell phone and slipped it back into her pocket. She had reached the isolated corner where the stairs leading down to the Dungeon were, and as she stopped, she heard the distinctive footsteps behind her. They came to a stop. She turned and saw Amber standing there.

"What are you doing back here, Phyllis?" the young teacher asked with a puzzled frown on her face. "You're supposed to be working in the hospitality room."

"I know, but this seemed more important."

Amber shook her head in apparent confusion. "I don't understand."

"I was just talking to Victor Appleton. He used to be a student of mine, you know, a long time ago. Now he's an investigator for the sheriff's department."

"I know who he is," Amber snapped. "What's that got to do with anything?"

"I asked him to come out here so I can explain to him how I know that you murdered Ray Brooks."

Chapter 32

Amber stared at her for a long time without speaking, then finally said, "Oookay, I think you've read too many stories about what a great detective you are, Phyllis, because that's just about the craziest thing I've ever heard. I admit I wasn't very fond of the guy. That's why I dumped him a while back."

"You didn't dump him," Phyllis said. "It was the other way around."

"Where'd you hear that?"

"From someone who had reason to know." Phyllis didn't mention Keeley Gifford's name.

"Somebody who'd been listening to Ray's bull, I'll bet. Of course he claimed that he dumped me. He was trying to salvage his wounded pride, that's all."

"Maybe. But what about the cookie crumbs?"

Amber came closer. "Now I'm starting to think you really have lost your mind. What cookie crumbs?"

"The ones around Ray Brooks's mouth. He'd been eating

cookies just before he was killed. Did you use them to distract him? I know you took the last two sugar cookies from the snack table just a few minutes earlier. You told me that yourself."

"So he was eating cookies," Amber said. "He could have gotten those himself."

Phyllis shook her head. "He didn't. He didn't come over to the table all evening during the dance."

"Then somebody else gave them to him."

"That's possible," Phyllis said, nodding. "Just like it's possible he could have been lying about who dumped who. But that doesn't explain the broken heel on your shoe."

"The what?" Amber's frown deepened. She glanced down at her feet. "My shoe? You mean the one I was wearing at the dance? I told you how that happened."

"You did," Phyllis said, "but did anyone actually *see* that happen? The heel could have just as easily snapped off while you were struggling with Brooks. Maybe he shoved you after you stabbed him, or tried to grab you by the throat. You see, Amber, I heard you running away down that other hall. I thought whoever it was was stumbling along because they were upset at what had just happened. But running with a broken heel would have thrown off your gait, too."

"There's no way you can prove something like that."

Phyllis nodded. "Probably not. But there's still the matter of your jacket."

"My jacket?" Amber repeated.

"And the missing blue stone." Phyllis pointed. "The one that's supposed to go right there." She reached in her other pocket, felt around, and pulled out the piece she had found in front of Chase's door, which she had been carrying around ever since, instinctively knowing somehow that it might be important. "Witnesses saw me pick this up. There might even be some pieces of it left there, if the police want to go and look. I saw it fall off of Jason Duncan's coat. How did it get from your jacket onto Duncan's coat? I suspect it was while the two of you were . . . romantically involved. That is how you've been keeping Duncan in line and getting him to do everything you want, isn't it? By sleeping with him?"

"You crazy, perverted old bitch. I'm not going to listen to any more of this."

Amber started to turn away, but Phyllis stopped her by saying, "All of that fits together, but it doesn't explain why. If you wanted to kill Ray Brooks because he broke up with you, why would you wait until the night of the dance to do it? Anyway, I can't imagine you feeling strongly enough about that to murder him."

"I don't know why not," Amber said. "You've imagined plenty of other crazy stuff!"

"But, if we take into account that you're involved somehow with Jason Duncan . . . and we know that Duncan is one of the people selling drugs here at Courtland . . . then it's not much of a stretch to think that maybe the person at the top of the pyramid . . . the person giving Duncan his orders . . . is you, Amber. And if Ray Brooks found out about that, he *would* dump you, no doubt about that. Brooks hated drugs and drug dealers. But he still had feelings for you, so he dragged his feet about turning you in. Until he couldn't stand it anymore and gave you an ultimatum: get out of it, or he would tell the authorities about you. You told him you would . . . you asked him to meet you back here to talk about it . . . you even gave him a couple of cookies as a peace offering . . . and then you killed him."

Amber stared at Phyllis for a long moment again, and Phyllis saw the truth in the young woman's eyes. She knew she was right about Amber.

But then Amber said, "There's absolutely no proof of any of that. You don't really think the cops will believe you, do you? My God, they'll chalk it all up to dementia!"

"Do *you* believe that Jason Duncan and Alan Riley will keep their mouths shut once the district attorney starts offering them deals? And you know he will. Sending a beautiful young teacher to prison for sleeping with students, masterminding a drug ring, and murdering a man right here in the school? What headlines that will make!"

"It'll never get that far," Amber said, but she didn't sound so convinced now.

"No?" Phyllis reached into her pocket and took out her cell phone. "Let's ask Detective Appleton. He's been listening the whole time."

Amber's face twisted. She let out a low, articulate cry of rage and stalked forward. Phyllis knew what had to be flashing through her mind. Amber was young and in great shape. She could snap Phyllis's neck and throw her down the stairs into the Dungeon. It would look like Phyllis had broken her neck in a terrible accident . . .

"Stop," Sam's voice boomed over the loudspeakers.

Amber froze.

Then Sam said, "Do no more calculations."

Amber's eyes widened in insane rage.

Before she could start toward Phyllis again, two figures leaped on her from behind, knocking her to the floor. Ronnie wrapped her arms around Amber's neck and locked her legs around the teacher's waist. Walter had hold of Amber's legs, pinning her down. Ronnie looked up and yelled, "Run, Phyllis! We'll hold her!"

"No!" Phyllis cried. "I can't let the two of you get hurt!"

"Nobody's getting hurt!" a man's voice said. Heavy footsteps slapped the floor. Victor Appleton, followed by his partner and two uniformed deputies, came around the corner and took over. Ronnie and Walter scrambled up, and the deputies grabbed hold of Amber's arms and hauled her to her feet. They didn't let go.

Appleton said to Phyllis, "Are you all right?"

She swallowed and nodded. "I'm fine."

"No offense, Mrs. Newsom, but you're crazy, you know? How could you be sure I'd actually come out here?"

"I remembered you, Victor," Phyllis said. "You were a very conscientious student. You may not have made top grades, but you always did your work."

"Yeah, that's me, dumb but determined." He looked over at Amber, who was glaring at Phyllis. "She's right, you know. Everything I heard was circumstantial evidence."

"But she didn't deny it," Walter said. "And we saw her try to kill Mrs. Newsom."

"We did!" Ronnie said. "If we hadn't stopped her, she would have!"

Appleton frowned at them and said, "Who are you two kids? No, wait, we'll hash it all out later. Right now I'm taking Ms. Trahearne in for questioning." He jerked his head at the men with him, and they all started back toward the front of the school, escorting a defiant Amber with them.

Phyllis looked at Ronnie and Walter and said, "Walter, you're supposed to be taking the calculator test. You missed it."

"I know. I had to go to the bathroom." He lowered his voice to a conspiratorial tone and held a hand up beside his mouth. "I have a nervous bladder." In a more normal tone, he went on, "But this is just the first meet, and anyway, I always score higher than anybody else on the practice tests. I'll have plenty of other chances. But since I'd already had to forfeit this one, I thought I might as well help Ronnie run papers."

"I didn't ask him for help," Ronnie said. "Then we saw you come back here, and Miss Trahearne looked like she was following you, and that seemed odd, so Walter said we should see what was going on . . ." She shrugged. "He's pretty smart for a freshman."

Walter positively beamed.

"Don't get any ideas," Ronnie told him, but it didn't do much to lessen the brilliance of his smile.

"Students, report to the testing rooms for the mathematics contest," Sam said over the PA system.

Walter looked up at the speaker in the ceiling. "I guess this means Coach Fletcher is the math team coach now."

"No way," Sam said a couple of hours later when Phyllis told him what Walter had said. "Not just no, but heck no. I don't know anywhere near enough to do that. I can help, like today, but they'll have to find somebody else to coach the team."

They were sitting in the hospitality room. The meet was over, and Tom Shula, summoned from home, was running the awards ceremony in the gym. The table that had been piled with food earlier was almost empty now, as if a pack of locusts had descended upon it.

Sam frowned at Phyllis and went on, "I'm not too happy about you goin' off and solvin' that murder while I was stuck in the office like that."

"And we were stuck here," Eve said. "None of us got to gasp and say, 'You've solved the murder, haven't you, Phyllis?'"

"It's more a matter of bein' worried that Amber could've hurt you," Sam drawled.

"Well, that wasn't really my intent," Phyllis said. "I was still putting everything together in my mind, and I wanted to talk to Detective Appleton, and it just seemed like that would be a quiet place to do both of those things. I guess when Amber saw me heading toward the scene of the crime, she got worried."

"A guilty conscience will do that to you," Carolyn said. She turned to Sam. "Are you upset that your little girlfriend turned out to be a killer?"

Sam raised a hand and said, "Now hold on. Nobody ever said Amber was my little girlfriend."

"I believe I just did."

"It's true that I was fond of her," Sam said, a bleak look crossing his face for a moment. "I was really lost when I started tryin' to teach math, and she helped me a lot. She didn't have anything to gain by it, either. She was just bein' nice."

"Nice?" Carolyn said. "She's a drug dealer and a murderer!"

"Yeah, that's what it looks like, all right. But that doesn't change the fact that she was nice to me." Sam shrugged. "Humans are complicated, messy creatures. Most folks have some good, and some bad in 'em. And in some of 'em the balance gets out of whack. I reckon that's what happened with Amber."

Earlier, Jimmy D'Angelo had called Phyllis to let her know that Chase had been released. Jason Duncan and Alan Riley were both in custody, along with Amber, and from what D'Angelo had heard, they were competing to see who could incriminate the others the fastest.

Because of that, Phyllis wasn't surprised when she looked up to see Chase in the doorway of the hospitality room. As he came in, he smiled and said, "Do you mind if I give you a hug, Mrs. Newsom?"

"I suppose that would be all right," Phyllis said as she got to her feet. Chase embraced her, then turned to shake hands with Sam. "Thank you both so much for everything you did to help me."

"I didn't do much this time," Sam said. "It was all Phyllis."

"Well, I appreciate it," Chase said. "You not only cleared my name, you got the ringleader I'd been after, too. That settles the question of whether my assignment here is over." He looked around. "I still need to tell Ronnie the truth, though. Where is she?"

"She and Walter went down to the gym to watch 'em give out the awards." Sam grinned. "When they were walkin' off, the boy reached over and took hold of her hand. I expected her to haul off and wallop him one. I think she thought about it . . . but the last I saw of 'em, they were still holdin' hands. I've got a hunch she may have gotten over that crush on you, Chase."

"Oh, good," Phyllis said. "I like Walter. Especially since he turned out not to be a fourteen-year-old criminal mastermind after all."

Author's Note

There is no J.C. Courtland High School in Weatherford, Texas, or anywhere else that I'm aware of. As of this writing, Weatherford has only one high school. Which means, more than ever, that all the places, characters, and events in this novel are fictitious and entirely the product of the author's imagination. Not the cookies, though. The cookies are there, and I've baked them, and they're good.

Recipes

Gluten-Free Banana Nut Oat Pancakes

INGREDIENTS
1 cup oat flour*
1/2 teaspoon baking soda
1/2 teaspoon salt
1 1/4 cup mashed bananas (about 3 small bananas)
1/2 cup crunchy nut butter (almond, peanut, or cashew)
2 tablespoons coconut oil
1 tablespoon milk (nut milk can be used)
1 teaspoon honey
2 eggs

DIRECTIONS
In a medium bowl, blend the oat flour, baking soda, salt.
In a small mixing bowl, stir together the mashed bananas, nut butter, coconut, and honey. Beat in the eggs.
Add wet ingredients to the dry ingredients. Stir until just mixed.

Let the batter sit for 5 minutes.

Spray a large nonstick skillet or griddle with oil and heat over medium-low heat. Add 1/4 cupfuls of batter and cook until bubbly on top and golden on the bottom, about 3 minutes. Flip and cook until golden on the bottom, about 2 more minutes.

Makes 10-12 pancakes.

*HOW TO MAKE YOUR OWN OAT FLOUR: To make oat flour out of old-fashioned oats, simply pour one cup of oats into a blender or food processor and process until it is equivalent to flour.

Chocolate Mint Cat Brownies

INGREDIENTS
3/4 cup baking cocoa
1/2 teaspoon baking soda
2/3 cup butter, melted, and divided
1/2 cup boiling water
2 cups sugar
2 eggs
1 1/3 cups all-purpose flour
1 teaspoon vanilla extract
1/4 teaspoon salt
16 miniature peppermint patties (like York)
32 semi-sweet chocolate chips (for decorating)
Candy eyes and icing pens, for decorating

DIRECTIONS
Preheat oven to 350°F.

In a large bowl, combine cocoa and baking soda. Blend in 1/3 cup melted butter. Add boiling water, stir until well blended.

Stir in sugar, eggs, and remaining butter.

Add flour, vanilla, and salt and stir until well blended.

Pour into a greased 13x9x2-inch pan and bake for 35-40 minutes or until brownie starts to pull away from sides of pan.

While still warm place 16 peppermint patties evenly on brownies so they'll be centered on each brownie square when cut. Lay 2 chocolate chips next to peppermint patty for cat ears. Allow to slightly melt on warm brownies.

Cool, cut into squares, Pipe a cat face on each peppermint patty with white icing pen, and add candy eyes, or use a green icing pen for the eyes.

Makes 16 servings

Killer Sugar Cookies

INGREDIENTS
2 3/4 cups all-purpose flour
1/2 teaspoon baking powder
1 teaspoon baking soda
1 cup butter, softened
1 1/2 cups white sugar
1 egg
2 teaspoons vanilla extract

DIRECTIONS
Preheat oven to 375°F.

In a medium bowl, stir together baking soda, flour, and baking powder until blended.

In a large bowl, cream together the butter and sugar until smooth. Butter must be soft for batter to work right. Beat in egg and vanilla. Gradually blend in the dry ingredients. Scoop tablespoonfuls of dough with cookie scooper, and drop into a bowl of white (or colored) sugar. Roll around and then place onto ungreased cookie sheets, flatten with bottom of cup or glass.

Bake 8 to 10 minutes in the preheated oven, or until lightly golden. Do not overcook. Let stand on cookie sheet two minutes before removing to cool on wire racks.

Makes 4 dozen

Ranch Cheez-Its

INGREDIENTS

One 12.4 OZ box of Cheez-It crackers
One packet of Ranch Dressing mix
2 tablespoons of fresh minced Dill
2 tablespoons canola oil

DIRECTIONS

Combine all ingredients in a large bowl, then scatter out onto a baking sheet. Bake at 350°F for about 10 minutes, stirring after 5 minutes. Remove from oven and let cool.

Makes 12 servings

Lit'l Mummy Dogs

INGREDIENTS
32 Lit'l Smokies Sausages
1 (8 ounce) can refrigerated crescent dough rolls
Mustard or ketchup, if desired

DIRECTIONS
Preheat oven to 375°F.

Carefully unroll dough, you want to end up with 4 rectangles, so separate at right angle perforations, creating 4 rectangles. Press diagonal perforations to seal.

With a knife or pizza cutter cut each rectangle lengthwise into 8 strips. So, cut the rectangle in half, cut those halfs in half, and then the quarters in half. Do this with each rectangle, and you'll have a total of 32 strips. Wrap one strip of dough around each sausage stretching dough slightly to look like bandages, leaving a small area exposed to create face. Place on ungreased cookie sheet.

Bake 12 to 14 minutes or until golden brown.

Draw in the open area to create face using ketchup or mustard. Serve with mustard or ketchup, if desired.

Makes 32

Chocolate Mummy Cupcakes

INGREDIENTS
3/4 cup all-purpose white flour
3/4 cup white sugar
1/2 teaspoon baking soda
1/2 cup salted butter, cut into 1" slices
2 ounces dark chocolate, chopped
1/2 cup cocoa powder
1/2 cup milk
1/4 cup coconut oil
2 eggs
1 teaspoon vanilla extract
1 1/2 teaspoons white vinegar

INSTRUCTIONS
Preheat oven 350°F.

Place 12 cupcake liners in a cupcake pan.

Mix flour, sugar, and baking soda in a large bowl.

Place butter and chopped chocolate in a separate, large microwavable bowl. Microwave for 30 seconds, mix, then microwave for another 30 seconds. Mix until chocolate is melted and smooth (keep microwaving in 30 second bursts and mixing until chocolate is melted).

Add cocoa powder to melted chocolate and mix.

Add milk and oil, mix, then eggs, vanilla and vinegar to chocolate. Whisk until smooth.

Add flour mixture and whisk until completely blended.

Pour into cupcake liners. I use an ice cream scoop for this. They should be just over 3/4 full.

Bake for 18–20 minutes, or until toothpick inserted comes out clean.

Cool on rack.

Once cool, spread with white frosting using a flat tip to make it look like bandages.

Frosting:

INGREDIENTS
1/2 cup butter, room temperature
1 teaspoon vanilla extract
1/2 cup marshmallow crème
2 cups powdered sugar, sifted
1-3 tablespoons cream
24 candy eyes or M&M's

DIRECTIONS
Put butter in a medium bowl, and using mixer beat at medium speed until smooth. Beat in the vanilla extract and marshmallow crème. With the mixer on low speed, beat in the powdered sugar. Add 1 tablespoon of the cream and beat to combine. Then, on high speed, beat frosting until it is light and fluffy (about 3 minutes). Add more cream or powdered sugar if necessary to get the right piping consistency. Pipe onto cupcakes and add candy eyes.

Makes 12 cupcakes.

Slow Cooker Texas Chicken and Dumplings

INGREDIENTS
1 1/2 lbs of skinless, boneless chicken breast halves, cut into 1-inch pieces
2 medium potatoes diced
1 large carrot sliced
2 large celery stalks sliced
4 cloves of garlic finely minced
3/4 cup milk
1 cup of heavy cream
1 chicken bouillon cube
3 cups of chicken broth
1/2 teaspoon salt
1/4 teaspoon ground black pepper

DIRECTIONS
Put the chicken, potatoes, carrots, celery, and garlic in a 6-quart slow cooker.

Stir the milk, cream, bouillon, chicken broth, salt and black pepper in a medium bowl. Pour the soup mixture over the chicken and vegetables.

Cover and cook on low for 7 to 8 hours or until the chicken is cooked tender.

DUMPLINGS INGREDIENTS

2 cups of all-purpose flour
1/4 cup white cornmeal
1 tablespoon baking powder
1/4 teaspoon baking soda
1 teaspoon salt
1 egg
1 cups milk

DUMPLINGS DIRECTIONS

Mix dry ingredients in a medium bowl and make a well in the center. Add one well beaten egg into the well, add milk slowly and stir until dough is stiff enough to knead. If dough is too thin add flour.

Place dough on a well-floured surface, sprinkle extra flour onto dough and knead it several times.

Using well-floured rolling pin roll out dough until it is 1/2 inch thick, sprinkling more flour as needed.

Cut dough into 1 inch by 1 1/2 inch strips

Add dumplings to crockpot on top of chicken and vegetables. Increase the heat to high. Vent the lid and cook for 30 minutes or until the dumplings are cooked in the center. To check for doneness, insert toothpick and it should come out clean. Take one dumpling out and cut in half to make sure. This is also a great time to taste.

Serves 8

Spinach, Mushroom, And Egg Casserole

INGREDIENTS

1/2 pound fresh mushrooms, sliced
1 tablespoon butter
11 large eggs
3/4 cup milk
2 cups shredded sharp Cheddar cheese
1 (10 ounce) package frozen chopped spinach, thawed and drained
1 teaspoon dried oregano

DIRECTIONS

Preheat oven to 350°F. Grease a 9x13-inch baking dish.

Heat a large skillet over medium-high heat. Melt butter in skillet, and cook and stir the mushrooms until tender.

Beat eggs and milk together in a large bowl. Stir sausage, Cheddar cheese, spinach, and oregano into egg mixture; pour into prepared baking dish.

Bake in the preheated oven until a knife inserted into the center of the casserole comes out clean, 30 to 40 minutes.

Sausage Egg Casserole

INGREDIENTS

3/4 pound ground pork sausage
1 tablespoon butter
4 green onions, chopped
1/2 pound fresh mushrooms, sliced
10 eggs, beaten
1 (16 ounce) container low-fat cottage cheese
1 pound Monterey Jack cheese, shredded
1 (4 ounce) can diced green chile peppers, drained
1 cup all-purpose flour
1 teaspoon baking powder
1/2 teaspoon salt
1/3 cup butter, melted

DIRECTIONS

Preheat oven to 350°F.

Lightly grease a 9x13 inch baking dish.

Place sausage in a large, deep skillet. Cook over medium-high heat until evenly brown. Drain, and set aside. Melt butter in skillet, and cook and stir the green onions and mushrooms until tender.

In a large bowl, mix the eggs, cottage cheese, Monterey Jack cheese, and chiles. Stir in the sausage, green onions, and mushrooms.

In a bowl, sift together the flour, baking powder, and salt. Blend in the melted butter. Stir the flour mixture into the egg mixture. Pour into the prepared baking dish.

Bake 40 to 50 minutes in the preheated oven, or until lightly brown. Let stand 10 minutes before serving.

Cheesy Bacon And Egg Brunch Casserole

INGREDIENTS

8 slices bacon
1 medium onion, chopped
1 loaf Italian bread, cut into 1-inch cubes
2 cups shredded Cheddar cheese
1 cup shredded mozzarella cheese
1 cup cottage cheese
8 eggs
1 1/2 cups milk
1/2 teaspoon McCormick(R) Ground Mustard
1/4 teaspoon McCormick(R) Black Pepper, Ground

DIRECTIONS

Preheat oven to 350°F. Cook bacon in large skillet until crisp. Reserve 2 tablespoons of the drippings. Drain bacon on paper towels; crumble and set aside. Add onion to drippings in skillet; cook and stir 3 minutes or until softened.

Spread 1/2 of the bread cubes in 13x9-inch baking dish. Layer with 1/2 each of the onion, bacon, Cheddar cheese and mozzarella cheese. Spread evenly with cottage cheese. Top with remaining bread cubes, onion, bacon, Cheddar cheese and mozzarella cheese.

Beat eggs in medium bowl until foamy. Add milk, mustard, and pepper; beat until well blended. Pour evenly over top. Press bread cubes lightly into egg mixture until completely covered. Let stand 10 minutes.

Bake 40 to 50 minutes or until center is set and top is golden brown.

About the Author

Livia J. Washburn has been a professional writer for more than twenty years. She received the Private Eye Writers of America Award and the American Mystery Award for her first mystery, Wild Night, written under the name L. J. Washburn, and she was nominated for a Spur Award by the Western Writers of America for a novel written with her husband, James Reasoner. Her short story "Panhandle Freight" was nominated for a Peacemaker Award by the Western Fictioneers, and her story Charlie's Pie won. She lives with her husband in a small Texas town, where she is constantly experimenting with new recipes. Her two grown daughters are both teachers in her hometown, and she is very proud of them.

NINE DEADLY LIVES An Anthology of Feline Fiction

Livia J. Washburn, Deborah Macgillivray,
Cheryl Pierson Mollie Hunt, Isabella Norse,
Rochelle Spencer, Clay More, C. A. Jamison,
Mariah Lynne, Faye Rapoport DesPres, Brandy Herr,
Angela Crider Neary, Bill Crider

From magic to murder, from felines to faeries, the authors of NINE DEADLY LIVES spin thirteen tales featuring those sometimes aloof and occasionally dangerous but always adorable creatures we know and love as cats! Whether it's mystery, fantasy, historical, or romance, these cat tales provide plenty of entertainment and thrills!

CPSIA information can be obtained
at www.ICGtesting.com
Printed in the USA
LVOW11s0110281017
554097LV00001B/76/P